D0013048

With Wings As Eagles

CALIFORNIA PIONEER SERIES

With Wings As Eagles

ELAINE SCHULTE

LIFEJOURNEY
BOOKS

DAVID C. COOK PUBLISHING CO.

LifeJourney Books is an imprint of David C. Cook Publishing Co.
David C. Cook Publishing Co., Elgin, Illinois 60120
David C. Cook Publishing Co., Weston, Ontario

WITH WINGS AS EAGLES
© 1990 by Elaine Schulte

Edited by LoraBeth Norton
Cover design by Dawn Lauck
Illustration by Kathy Kulin

First Printing, 1990
Printed in the United States of America
94 93 92 91 90 5 4 3 2 1

Schulte, Elaine L.
    With wings as eagles / Elaine Schulte.
        p.   cm. — (The California pioneer series: bk. 4)
    ISBN 1-55513-989-2
    I. Title   II. Series: Schulte, Elaine L. California pioneer series; bk. 4
PS3569.C5395W5   1990
813'.54—dc20   90-6305
                                                 CIP

THE CALIFORNIA PIONEER SERIES

*In memory of our
sisters and brothers
who brought His love
through teaching
in the pioneer schools*

Prologue

Benjamin Talbot settled back into his black horsehair chair and inhaled the pleasant grassy fragrance that wafted through the open windows of his whitewashed adobe parlor. He had just eaten a fine supper, birds twittered from the California pepper trees outside *Casa Contenta,* and his shipping and chandlery establishment in town prospered. All was well with the world.

Then he heard his daughter, Betsy, say to their guest, "It is forward of me to mention it, Mr. Wilmington, but I would so like to teach at your school in Oak Hill."

"You wish to teach at Oak Hill?!" Benjamin asked with amazement.

His nineteen-year-old daughter nodded calmly as she served a cup of coffee to Jonathan Wilmington, an old friend who was also the superintendent of the Oak Hill School Board. "I truly would, Father," she replied. "I've taught here for three years, even if it has only been my nieces and nephews and neighborhood children. I think I could teach in a regular school, and I would like to attempt it."

Benjamin tried to reign in his growing alarm. "Oak Hill is no place for a young woman. Life is far more dangerous out at the gold diggings than it is here." He forced himself to sit back as she served his coffee. The fact was, he had arranged life much as he wished: he and his adopted son, Daniel, had their Wainwright and Talbot Shipping and Chandlery office in San Francisco and their home in the countryside, where two other sons had charge of *Rancho Verde* and the women-folk were protected from the worst evils of the gold rush.

Betsy placed the pewter coffee server on the dark oak chest. Golden light streaming through the window bright-ened the auburn of her upswept hair, and, as she stood there in her dark green silk frock, Benjamin was reminded that his youngest child was no longer a spindly girl with thick red braids, but a lovely young woman.

"Father, it *is* 1854," she objected, her green eyes serious. "There's a church and a school in Oak Hill now, civilizing forces, as you call them. You tell us to be salt and light in society, but we're so sheltered here that we have no oppor-tunity to do so."

Benjamin shifted his weight in the chair. Betsy was right, he supposed. Even in his distress, he observed that she hadn't lost her temper as she might have a year or two ago, but spoke with reason and deliberation.

Jonathan Wilmington had been listening in silence, but now he spoke up. "I should have told you, Betsy, I am actually looking for a *man* to teach at our school at Oak Hill."

"Another man?" Betsy asked with a hint of dismay.

He nodded.

"But didn't you mention that every man you have hired thus far has left your school?" she returned. "Every one?"

"Unfortunately, that is the case," Wilmington replied. "With the easy pickings in Oak Hill's fields over, teachers who've come for gold head elsewhere for new diggings."

Benjamin said, "In any event, Betsy, you do not have a teaching certificate."

Betsy turned to Wilmington. "As school superintendent, are you not empowered to test and certify teaching applicants?"

"Yes, yes, I am—"

"Would you be willing to test me to see if I'd qualify?"

"I leave that to your father," Wilmington replied with an uncertain glance at his friend.

Before Benjamin could answer, Betsy was at his side, her eyes imploring. "I've studied so hard, Father. It doesn't seem fair if I can't try for a certificate. If I don't do it now, we'll never know if I qualify for a regular school."

It was true, and she was as smart as the proverbial whip, this youngest of his five living children. Benjamin wondered how her mother would have responded. Most likely Elizabeth would have reminded him that it was no longer a nine-day trip by covered wagon to Oak Hill and that their youngest must be allowed to try her wings. Nonetheless he said, "I do not think it a wise idea for you to go, Betsy."

"It's not as though I'd be alone at Oak Hill," she protested. "Half of our family is there . . . Rose and Joshua, Louisa and Jonathan . . . not to mention old friends like Tess and Hugh Fairfax. Rose, Louisa, and Tess are women—"

"All married women—under their husbands' protection," he pointed out, then felt a stab of remorse, for he feared she was beginning to consider herself a spinster. "I have your best interests at heart, Betsy. I wish to protect you."

She nodded abjectly. "I know you do, Father, but at times I feel almost—" She pressed her lips together. "If you'll both excuse me—" Shoulders stiff and taffeta frock rustling, she hurried from the parlor.

"Forgive us," Benjamin apologized to his friend, a gray-haired widower himself. "It is sometimes difficult for me to deal with a young daughter."

"As I know all too well from my own experience," Jonathan Wilmington replied.

"This takes me by surprise, though. Betsy has always been so tractable. She has a suitor here, Thad Zimmer, who grew up on a neighboring farm in Independence and came with us by covered wagon in '46. Just this week he asked me for Betsy's hand."

"Did you give your blessing?"

"I did," Benjamin admitted uneasily, "though I have reservations. He's a good man, a prosperous farmer, and, like you, he found a substantial amount of gold in '48. He bought his farm outright. But is he the right husband for Betsy? I don't know. . . ."

Jonathan's eyes filled with sympathy. "Life isn't always simple."

"No, it is not." Benjamin sipped his hot coffee, and it tasted bitter. This evening's discussion had not ended the question of Betsy's teaching at Oak Hill, of that he was certain. *Lord*, he prayed, *give us wisdom!*

1

Betsy arrived in her schoolroom the next morning, her mind brimming with consternation. Would she spend her entire life teaching here at home? Would she never marry and have children of her own? Much as she disliked admitting it, nineteen years of age was no longer young.

She sat down at her dark oak desk and looked at the schoolroom in which she'd taught for the past three years. The room was actually the ballroom-sized central hallway of their old Spanish-Mexican *hacienda,* a common feature in such houses to accommodate the previous owners' passion for dancing.

Indeed, it was said that *Californios* would scarcely stop dancing for an earthquake—an idea she usually found amusing. This morning, however, the thought of such joyful exuberance made her feel even worse.

Perhaps if she hadn't heard about the teaching position at Oak Hill . . . or if Thad Zimmer weren't coming for supper tonight again . . . or if she hadn't learned about her sixteen-year-old cousin's wedding in Missouri.

The children's voices in the courtyard brought her to her senses, and then to her feet. She opened the French doors to a sunny spring day. "Good morning, children!"

"Good morning, Miss Talbot!" "Good morning, Aunt Betsy!" the neighborhood children and Betsy's nieces and nephews responded eagerly.

The wooden floors, broken down by years of dancing, bounced and squeaked under the children's feet, and the children seemed noisier than ever as they carried the chairs and narrow tables to their places in the middle of the room.

Betsy opened her Bible at random to the Psalms and, once her students were settled, said, "We shall begin this morning with Psalm 102." It seemed, as she read, that she had not really chosen that psalm, but that it had chosen her.

*"Hear my prayer, O Lord, and let my cry come unto
Thee.*
*Hide not thy face from me in the day when I am in
trouble;*
*Incline thine ear unto me: in the day when I call answer
me speedily,*
For my days are consumed like smoke . . . .
My heart is smitten . . . ."

My heart is smitten, her mind echoed. To her amazement, a sob nearly escaped her throat.

The children stared at her, and, swallowing with difficulty, Betsy read on.

When she'd finished, she said, "We shall now have roll call," but her voice sounded strange. Had she announced roll call in that same hollow voice every day these past three years? The formality of a roll call suddenly struck her as foolish in such a small school, a room with nine nieces and nephews and eight neighborhood children, yet she and Aunt Jessica wanted them to be properly prepared if any of them ever had an opportunity to attend a regular school.

Calling out their names, she eyed the children as though for the first . . . or the last . . . time: "Little Daniel," Cousin

Abby and Daniel's son, who was six. "Little Benjamin" and his sister, Marian, who were brother Jeremy and Jenny's children. Sister Martha and Luke's two sets of twins. Including the Ryder and Sinclair children, not one of them was over ten years of age, and it occurred to her that perhaps she'd be unable to control older children.

The children gazed at her oddly again, and Betsy quickly put in her usual, "We shall all do our lessons now while those in the First Reader come forward."

The little ones rose and stepped to her desk with their McGuffey's Readers, and the morning moved forward. Her restlessness remained, however, as well as a thought: *How could she think of leaving these dear children?*

At ten o'clock, she announced recess and followed her charges out to the sunlit courtyard. Aunt Jessica and several younger Talbot children sat on the round wooden seat under the sprawling pepper tree. The sunlight dappled her elderly aunt's gray hair, which was pulled back into its usual neat knot. She was reading *Rumpelstiltskin* aloud, her face so alight with pleasure that the wrinkles lining her dear face were barely noticeable. She wore her brown poplin dress and, having regained her weight since their covered wagon trek west, resembled a plump hen surrounded by attentive chicks. As she neared the end of the story, she read with increased enthusiasm:

"Today I bake; tomorrow I brew my beer;
The next day I will bring the Queen's child here,
Ah! lucky 'tis that not a soul doth know
That Rumpelstiltskin is my name. Ho! Ho!"

Reading on about the queen thus learning his name, Aunt Jessica made the most of delivering Rumpelstiltskin's furious reply, "The devil told you that! The devil told you that!"

The older children who had joined them stood by smiling. When Aunt Jessica finished the story, eight-year-old Rena said, "Rumpelstiltskin told the queen his name himself! The devil didn't have to!"

Aunt Jessica laughed. "Yes, we often do ourselves in, don't we? So, there ends a tale about a greedy gold-seeking miller who lied so he could marry his daughter to the king. You must guard against lying and greed yourselves." She smiled, then looked up at Betsy, and her brown eyes grew serious. As the children scattered to play, her aunt asked, "Are you feeling well?"

Betsy managed a wry smile. "I daresay I must have spring fever. I feel so restless."

"Benjamin told me about your wanting a teacher's certificate," her aunt said. "You may be feeling restless, but I think he's suffering the throes of guilt for not giving in."

"As I am for forcing the issue," Betsy admitted. "I fear I took him by surprise."

"I expect you did." Her aunt gave her a long look. "I'll take your afternoon classes if you'd like to rest. And you'll have Saturday and Sunday free, too. It's a strange thing, but often rest is the best cure for restlessness."

"Thank you," Betsy replied, grateful for her aunt's thoughtfulness. "Perhaps I will go to bed."

In any case, the children would enjoy having Aunt Jessica teach them again. Her aunt had taught her and the rest of the family, not to mention hundreds of other children long before the covered wagon trek west. Yes, perhaps an afternoon's rest would be the best cure for her restlessness.

At suppertime Betsy hurried from her room, appalled at having overslept. Tonight all of the grown Talbots would come from their nearby houses for supper to visit with Mr.

Wilmington. She should be helping in the kitchen. She rushed through the hallway schoolroom in her green silk frock, glad to see that the children had placed their tables and chairs neatly alongside the walls.

In the dining room, the table was already set, and Aunt Jessica was just stepping in with the butter and relishes. "Good, you look rested," she said. "You seemed so done in."

"I hope I'm not too late to help," Betsy said, although the delectable aroma of pot roast already filled the air.

"We're nearly ready to serve, and I have plenty of help. You go on into the parlor, Betsy. Thad is already here."

At the mention of his name, their eyes met for an instant. Betsy quickly turned and said, "I—I was just thinking how lovely the room looks."

The dining room did look especially nice with the white linen tablecloth and the new tall coral and green candlesticks. It was her favorite room at *Casa Contenta* since Cousin Abby had stenciled a charming coral and green flowered ivy border at sideboard height and painted a green wash under it to the dark wooden floor. The room seemed like a garden—a relief from so many white walls in the adobe house. Perhaps someday she could have a room like it in her own home. Perhaps—

"Betsy?"

"Yes. I'm going now. Thank you for letting me rest." She moved on with reluctance.

The men were gathered in the parlor with Father and Mr. Wilmington: her brother-in-law, Luke; her redheaded brother, Jeremy; and her darkly bearded adopted brother, Daniel Wainwright. On the settee was Thad Zimmer, who was tall, dark, clean-shaven, and lanky, and looked as though he had outgrown both the sleeves and trousers of his black suit.

"Here comes our slugabed," her father said when he saw her. "Aunt Jessica tells us you are suffering from overwork."

Betsy smiled. "Not likely. I feel like a shirker."

"Not you," Daniel objected with a laugh. "I have never seen you shirk anything yet."

"Oh, Daniel—" Betsy protested. "The fact is, if Aunt Jessica hadn't sent the children to wake me, I would probably have slept right through supper!"

Thad had belatedly risen to his feet, and his Adam's apple bobbed as he asked, "Feelin' all right now?"

"Yes, thank you, Thad," she replied.

"Good," he said. "Glad to hear it."

She recalled his once saying, "It takes a strong woman to work a farm with her husband . . . a mighty strong woman." Perhaps he was assessing her strength. The place beside him on the black horsehair settee was empty, and she felt constrained to sit beside him.

Jeremy spoke next. "I understand you tried to talk our friend Wilmington out of a teacher's certificate so you can teach at Oak Hill."

"I would at least like to see if I qualify," Betsy explained quietly.

"Why'd you be wantin' that?" Thad asked, a baffled expression on his sun-weathered face.

"Why . . . to teach in a regular school."

His pale blue eyes examined her closely. "No need for that, far as I can see."

An odd silence hung between them. Most likely he meant only unmarried women needed to teach.

Now he asked, "Why'd you want to live in such a rough place?"

"I'd like to see what it's like to live in a town, in a real community instead of in such a protected one as this."

18

"You're restless for a woman," Thad said, not unkindly, "just like I was when I set out for California."

"Then perhaps you understand."

He shook his head. "Ain't the same thing, restlessness in woman as in a man."

Perhaps it wasn't. She wished she could explain her restlessness to him, but it was inexplicable. It was a sense that she was doing everything for the last time now, as though God were moving her on. She gave Thad a small smile and turned to Mr. Wilmington. "Did you hire a teacher in town?"

"Unfortunately not. It seems we're unable to pay qualified men well enough to lure them from town. And at Oak Hill, we can't keep them from the diggings." It appeared he might say more, but his eyes went from Betsy to Thad and then back to Betsy. Aunt Jessica stepped into the room and announced with a flourish, "Supper is served."

As everyone stood, Thad remarked to Betsy, "Yer wearin' the green dress you got on in the paintin'. How come I never seen it before?"

She glanced at the painting behind the settee. Abby, a fine artist, had done it last year. "It's silk, a spring and summer dress," she explained.

"Didn't know there was a difference." He flushed at his ignorance. "Comes of not havin' sisters, I reckon. I hope you won't hold that . . . my not knowin' much about females . . . against me."

"Of course not," she replied.

Whatever does he mean? she wondered as they started for the dining room. She wished she hadn't always been quite so friendly to him. She could still remember him eight years ago, working as a bull whacker when they came west. He'd been all knees, elbows, and Adam's apple at sixteen, too, and likely would always be gangly.

"What you thinkin'?" he asked.

"I was recalling our covered-wagon trek, and . . . what an effort it took you to keep the oxen moving at first."

"Did my best," he replied.

"I know you did, Thad. It's just that it seems amusing in retrospect."

"It was hard work," he assured her. "Hard, hard work."

She regretted having mentioned it. "I'm sure it was. Come now, at least we won't have to eat a supper cooked over a camp fire tonight."

"Especially a supper cooked over buffalo chips," he said.

Leave it to Thad to refer to buffalo droppings just before they ate, she thought. The only good things about the dried buffalo droppings they had gathered to fuel their cook fires was that they'd been plentiful and had burned with relative lack of smoke.

In the dining room, he accompanied her to their chairs, his pale blue eyes intent on her.

Why is he acting so peculiar tonight? she wondered.

Cousin Abby, sister Martha, and sister-in-law Jenny came from the kitchen and, as they sat down at the table, it seemed to Betsy that they eyed her and Thad with more interest than usual, too.

Discomfited, she turned to Mr. Wilmington, who stood behind the chair to her left. "It's unfortunate that you've had a fruitless journey here."

"Perhaps not," Wilmington replied. "Perhaps not."

She was about to inquire further, but from the head of the long table, Father spoke. "Shall we join hands and sing Old Hundreth?"

Betsy reached out to hold Mr. Wilmington's hand on one side and Thad's on the other, and it felt as though she were being pulled in two directions. She sang out with all of them,

"Praise God from whom all blessings flow,
Praise Him all creatures here below,
Praise Him above, ye heavenly host,
Praise Father, Son, and Holy Ghost!"

As the harmonious "Amen" sounded, Betsy prayed for the Lord to quiet her restlessness.

For supper, there was the steaming pot roast with carrots, potatoes, onions, and gravy as well as spring greens and Aunt Jessica's biscuits with butter, honey, and jellies. The lively talk at the table ranged from Spanish land grant title problems and San Francisco's building boom to the lawlessness out at the diggings. Thad, she noticed, was too occupied with eating to join in the conversation.

At length the discussion turned to gold, and Mr. Wilmington said, "The miners are beginning to see they're engaged in a science and a profession, not a mere adventure."

Thad finally spoke up, looking at Jonathan over a forkful of potatoes. "What do you mean?"

"With most gold gone from the streambeds and surface quartz, what's left is far below in the hillsides and solid rock."

Father nodded. "At the chandlery, we're receiving a good many orders for heavy mining equipment from back East and even from England."

Thad said, "In the end, the thing California's best for is farmin'."

"Perhaps it will be," Wilmington said, "but not yet, even with gold production down."

Thad swallowed a big mouthful of potatoes and gravy, and said defensively, "We've got us a State Agricultural Society now, and even a magazine, *California Farmer.*"

"All the more reason for farm boys to learn to read," Mr. Wilmington said, "though I believe gold mining will continue for a good many years to come."

"Long enough to bother about schoolin'?" Thad asked.

"*Bother*?" Betsy asked with indignation. No doubt he thought if gold mining didn't continue, the miners would pack up and move back East, making the education of their children here unnecessary . . . or perhaps that they could all remain uneducated like him.

Thad flushed again. "You know what I mean."

Mr. Wilmington said, "To answer your question, Thad, yes, I think the gold will last long enough for us to concern ourselves about educating the children. Even if it didn't, I think we should educate as many children as we are able."

Trying to hide her irritation at Thad, Betsy turned away and took up a bit of beef on her fork. She was glad to hear Mr. Wilmington say that the children of miners were not merely learning to read, but studying from the Bible and McGuffey's textbooks, thus also learning biblical principles. Why, she wondered, did Thad aggravate her so? And why was Father studying her and Thad like that?

For dessert, there was dried apple pie with warm cream and steaming coffee, and the conversation returned to Mr. Wilmington's problems in finding a teacher. It appeared he would have to return without one, which did not ease her restlessness.

When they all stood up from the table, Thad murmured to her, "I want to talk to you outside. Alone, please"

"If you like . . ."

With a sinking sensation, Betsy followed him out of the dining room.

When she stopped in the entry hallway, he took her elbow and began to steer her toward the French doors leading out to the courtyard. "It's all right," he assured her, "I talked to your pa already."

He'd talked to her father already!

Suddenly all the strange looks and comments she'd been observing all evening made sense. She knew precisely what he wished to discuss, and her heart surged with dread. Thad was a neighbor and an old friend, but as for marriage . . . she felt nothing for him. The two of them were not in the least compatible. She couldn't face this conversation.

"If you don't mind, Thad," said Betsy, "I prefer not to go out into the cool night air." She added, and it was now true, "I'm not feeling well. I—I'd better return to bed."

He gave her a long searching look. "I reckon—" he began, then clamped his mouth shut. "I'll be here Sunday then, at the church service."

"Yes," she replied. "I shall see you then. But there is no need for you to leave yet. I'll just go into the parlor for a minute to tell the others good night."

"I'll take my leave now," he said, rather grim.

He turned to Aunt Jessica, who was halfway to the parlor. "Thank you fer dinner. That Indian woman workin' fer me ain't much of a cook." He shifted his feet nervously. "Guess I told you that before. Well, I got new colts and calves to see to. A farmer's work ain't ever done."

While the others bade him good night, Betsy stood by as dispassionately as possible. Under no circumstances did she wish to encourage him.

She felt a flood of relief as the door closed behind him. Deep in her heart she still hoped that God had a special man for her to love, but she was as certain as certain could be that the man was not Thad Zimmer.

Just as she turned, her father made his way back from the parlor. "Let's have a stroll outside, Betsy," he said in an overly cautious tone.

Full of consternation, she allowed him to lead the way. What if he asked her to marry Thad? What if he insisted?

He closed the door behind them. She inhaled deeply of the warm spring air as she stared at the pink and gold sunset.

He took her arm and they walked across the courtyard. He looked out at the setting sun, the pepper trees, and a thousand other things before he said, "Betsy, I suppose you've guessed that Thad has asked for your hand in marriage."

She nodded unhappily. "I suspected as much."

"Do you care for him in that way?"

"We have so little in common—"

"I thought so myself," he replied with a frown. "Still, a good many couples marry and eventually grow to love each other."

Panic rose in her throat. "And you think Thad and I—"

"I only wished to mention it. If we lived at Oak Hill or any other town by the diggings, or right in San Francisco, you would have hundreds of suitors calling. You are a pretty young woman, even if you don't think so. But, as you pointed out last night, you are stuck here in the countryside and—" He hesitated. "I only want your happiness."

"Father, if you care for my happiness, what I really want is a chance to teach somewhere like Oak Hill!"

His face fell slightly, but understanding filled his eyes. "If you are certain you do not wish to marry Thad, my dear, then I must tell you that Jonathan Wilmington would like to test you for a teacher's certificate. He thinks you would be a suitable teacher if you don't plan to marry for some time—"

"A suitable teacher!" she repeated with astonishment.

"You mustn't get overly excited. I can't allow you to live there alone, nor to impose on any of our young married couples by your moving in with them. The district is providing a log cabin for the teacher, but I would be an irresponsible father if I allowed you to live there by yourself."

"But I may take the test . . . and pray about going?"

He smiled. "Yes, that much has my blessing."

She threw her arms around him. "Thank you . . . oh, Father, thank you!"

"Just don't let Wilmington see you so exuberant," he said, not quite hiding his amusement. "He was impressed with your calm manner when you asked to be tested. I didn't let on that you are not usually such a restrained young lady."

"Oh, Father . . . !"

He chuckled. "I suggest you go to bed and bear down on your prayers."

"I'd like to tell Aunt Jessica, but that would mean telling everyone, and . . . now I'd rather they didn't know until we see the results of the test."

"I'll tell her and make your excuses to the others—and tell Wilmington to be ready tomorrow morning to administer the test. Now to bed. Likely I should pray against your wishes, but I will only pray that God's will be done."

"Thank you, Father," she replied. "That's what I shall pray as well."

At noon the next day, Betsy's heart thundered with wonder and gratitude. How was it that the answers to Mr. Wilmington's examination questions had come to her with such complete assurance? Surely God would not have given her such calm and clarity of thought if He did not mean for her to teach at Oak Hill! She had spelled; she had answered questions in geography; she had given a review of history. She had diagramed sentences and quickly parsed them, she had recited Marc Antony's oration on the death of Caesar.

When the test was over, Mr. Wilmington said, "We shall expect you to teach the three R's—reading, writing, and religion."

She'd passed! She had earned the certificate!

Trying to conceal her excitement, Betsy forced herself to listen carefully to his words.

"The three R's are the three-legged foundation upon which our educational system was built. When the Pilgrims came on the *Mayflower*, they created schools so that children might be taught to read the Bible. We must never forget that this was their purpose."

"I won't. I promise."

He eyed her carefully. "You doubtless know about the Philadelphia school that made the unprecedented request to teach morality but not Christianity. That was ten years ago."

She nodded. "Father has spoken of it."

"Then you know how the court ruled?"

"That public schools must include the Bible and Christianity in their instruction."

"Yes," he replied.

"I agree entirely," she assured him. "Without the Bible we would have no absolutes upon which to base morality."

He smiled. "Then on behalf of the Oak Hill School Board, I would like to offer you employment for the summer term. But first we must speak with your father to see if he will allow it."

He will, Betsy thought. *He must!* Now she read her beautifully inscribed certificate again on the way to the kitchen.

DEPARTMENT OF EDUCATION
Oak Hill, California
Teacher's Certificate

This is to certify that Miss Elizabeth Anna Talbot has been examined by me and found competent to give instruction in Reading, Writing, Arithmetic, Geography, English, Grammar, and History, and, having

*exhibited satisfactory testimonials of Good Moral
Character, is authorized by this certificate to teach
those branches in any school in the Oak Hill District
for the term of twelve months.*

> *Dated this 4th day of April, 1854*
> *Jonathan E. Wilmington*
> *School Board Superintendent*

She had a certificate! Really and truly! But now came the more difficult test. *Lord, I do so wish to go!* she prayed as she hurried through the dining room and into the big white-washed kitchen.

Aunt Jessica looked up from stirring a pot of stew on the black stove. Seeing the certificate, she beamed. "You have it, Betsy! Congratulations!"

"Thanks to your fine teaching."

"And to your fine mind and perseverance," her aunt said.

Betsy responded with all sincerity, "For which I praise God, to whom I turn now for another miracle. It goes without saying that Father does not wish me to live there alone!"

"You prayed, didn't you?" her aunt asked.

Betsy nodded. "With all of my heart!"

"As did I after Benjamin told me about it last night," Aunt Jessica said, turning to stir the stew again. She cast a playful glance at Betsy. "I received an answer. Have you?"

"No . . . only that I passed the test," Betsy said. Quite suddenly excitement mounted even more in her chest. "What is your answer, Aunt Jessica?"

"Your father doesn't yet know it, but it seems I am to accompany you to Oak Hill."

"That *you* are to accompany me?!" Betsy exclaimed.

"God often sends His people out in pairs," her aunt reminded her.

"Yes, but—" She had entertained a fleeting wish to go on her own, but now she realized it was entirely impossible. It was enough of a miracle that Aunt Jessica would come.

"Surely you didn't expect me to be stuck out here in the countryside forever, too!" her aunt said with a laugh. "Or that you'd be salt and light out in Oak Hill by yourself!"

Dozens of reasons why her aunt should not go flew to mind: she was needed here by Father and the family; she played the pump organ for the worship services; she was sixty-nine years old. . . . Yet squelching each and every one of the reasons was the amazing answer God had given to her prayers: *He was sending Aunt Jessica with her to Oak Hill!*

2

The birds sang their first sweet notes while the earth hung between darkness and rosy dawn, and Betsy stood gazing out of her bedroom window at what might have been a pastoral painting. In the background were green hillsides that grew greener by the moment; hundreds of cattle grazed in the middle distance; nearer in, California pepper trees fluttered. In the foreground, a hummingbird whirred over the crimson blossoms by her window as though to bid her farewell.

Despite her excitement about teaching at Oak Hill, a bittersweetness began to creep into her heart. True, she had been offered the position for only three months, but if she did well, Mr. Wilmington had said it might be far longer. She was leaving this wondrous place where she'd lived since her family's arrival in what was then known as the California Territory. She'd been eleven, wide-eyed at the sight of the vast ranch and the adobe *Californio* house Father had purchased. Even now, she knew God had had a hand in it, for there had been few houses to buy in '46, and *Casa Contenta* was an exceedingly lovely place.

She tried to imagine the teacher's log cabin at Oak Hill. Most likely it would not resemble the commodious Missouri log house that had been home to their large family on the outskirts of Independence before the trek west.

"Betsy? Are you awake?" Aunt Jessica asked as she knocked at the bedroom door.

Betsy hurried to open it, still in her yellow cotton nightgown. "I was just looking out the window and—" She hesitated.

"And feeling sad about leaving?"

Betsy nodded.

Aunt Jessica was already dressed in her brown poplin frock and looked as though she had few compunctions about their departure. "It seems there is never any going forward in life without some misgivings over what one leaves behind. Nonetheless, we are going forward."

"In any case, I can't change my mind now," Betsy said, "not with Mr. Wilmington under way to inform our relatives and the school board at Oak Hill. And not after the announcement at church—"

Yesterday the new pastor had informed the small congregation that Betsy and Jessica would be leaving. Everyone had been genuinely saddened to hear of it, but had wished them well—with the exception of Thad Zimmer. Betsy could still recall his pinched words: "It's foolhardy to move to such a dangerous place when we might have had . . . a—a good life and—"

"Thad, please—" she'd interrupted as quickly as possible. "Please wish me well."

Now as Aunt Jessica stood in Betsy's bedroom she asked, "What's that new American proverb? . . . 'Hats off to the past; coats off to the future!'"

Betsy gave her a smile. "Yes, hats off to the past. Coats off to the future!"

Her aunt's lively brown eyes went to the leather valise

Betsy would carry with her and then to the trunks, which were to be sent to Oak Hill with a freight consignment. "Are you packed?"

Betsy looked around the familiar room. "Everything except this nightgown and my slippers. I'm unsure about taking some mementos . . . my sketchbook from the trip west and such."

"Best to take it now," her aunt advised. "You might like to show it to your students to discuss the trip west. You could use it to show them how Abby taught you to draw, too." She drew a quiet breath. "I've found it best to take everything one holds dear. One knows not what the future holds."

Aunt Jessica's thoughtful expression brought to Betsy's mind another quote: Age and sorrow have the gift of reading the future by their past. She suddenly felt compelled to ask, "Aunt Jessica, are you going to Oak Hill only so I might teach?"

"Not at all. You mustn't trouble yourself with that," her aunt said. "You know I've lived in Boston and in several small towns, though most often in the countryside. The fact is I like a small town best. Raucous or not, Oak Hill seems a fitting place for me to go now."

How old her aunt looked now, Betsy thought. Even her hair, knotted back as usual, was no longer entirely gray, but was beginning to turn white.

Her aunt shook her head at herself and smiled. "You are not the only one who feels called to be salt and light in the world."

"But everyone here will miss you so terribly. . . ."

"Perhaps," her aunt said, "but there's nothing like necessity to force them into action. Martha, for example, can play the organ for Sunday services far better than I, and now she will be forced to practice. As for our school, Abby and Jenny are perfectly able to take over for us. And the others are more than happy to tend to your father's needs. Much as I dislike admitting it, they will manage well enough without us, whether it is three months or longer."

"I expect they will," Betsy responded, heartened to see the matter in that light. "I'm grateful you're not just going so I might try a new life."

"I had mixed sentiments about it in the beginning," her aunt admitted, "but I prayed, and the Lord filled my heart with a great eagerness to go. So, no recriminations. We are off on an adventure! Perhaps the greatest of our lives!"

At eight o'clock Betsy and Aunt Jessica were helped up into the new black carriage while Father climbed up front with Daniel, who was taking them to their Sacramento riverboat on his way to the Wainwright and Talbot office in town. Father would accompany them to Sacramento, where he had business to attend to, then go on with them by stagecoach to Oak Hill.

The others stood outside to bid them farewell. Abby, Martha, and Jenny had cooked a special breakfast—eggs, steaks, hotcakes, nut and raisin bread—and it had taken all of Father's considerable power of persuasion to prevent them from packing a hamper of chicken for the first day's journey. They'd all eaten breakfast together in the dining room, even the babes, as though it were a state occasion, and then in the midst of the bustle of leaving, there had been tearful embraces as though they would never see each other again.

Now the grown-ups stood by the hitching post and called, "Farewell!" and "Write as soon as you arrive!" And the children called out in their sweet voices, "'Bye, Aunt Jessica! 'Bye, Aunt Betsy! Keep away from the desperadoes!"

"Farewell! We shall!" Betsy replied with Aunt Jessica, who sat beside her in the carriage.

Grieved at leaving and reminded of the dangers ahead, Betsy remembered the painting Abby had made of their departure from Independence by covered wagon. *The Ache of Leaving* was the title of the poignant scene sketched in 1846, when Betsy had been too young and excited to feel the sorrow of their exodus.

"Ho!" Daniel shouted to the horses from up front, and they started forward, their hoofs clopping against the dusty lane to the opened gates.

As the carriage bumped along, Betsy returned the others' waves and watched them grow smaller in the distance. Before long, some of the dearest people of her life were only small figures waving, then turning back to *Casa Contenta*—the men to the fields, the women to clean up the kitchen.

Aunt Jessica blew her nose and announced with determination, "A new adventure begins." She sat back in the seat and straightened the skirt of her brown frock with her age-freckled hands. She wore a matching brown cabriolet bonnet with a grosgrain ribbon around the brim, and she looked like a sensible countrywoman who did not wish to draw undue attention to herself in the streets of San Francisco.

Not that Betsy was flamboyantly arrayed. She smoothed the skirt of her ecru-colored cotton frock, a color that struck her as bright enough for an auburn-haired young woman, and hoped that it and the matching bonnet would still be clean when they arrived in Sacramento City and later at Oak Hill. As for her hands, in comparison to her aunt's, they were unwrinkled and young.

She looked out the carriage windows at the sunlit pastures and hillsides of *Rancho Verde*. The countryside, dotted here and there with California oak, was beautiful in its spring greenery, and it seemed a day of heaven's own choosing. She could not resist a last look back, and she saw the shining white adobe walls of *Casa Contenta* far in the distance. "I didn't know leaving would be so difficult."

Her aunt nodded. "It always is."

"You've left so many places," Betsy said, realizing at last the pain it must have cost.

Aunt Jessica glanced out the window. "Yes, that I have."

"I do hope you've brought the roots from the Boston lilacs and the red rosebush!"

Her aunt smiled at her. "I did not forget."

Betsy recalled her aunt's oft-told tale of her moves farther and farther west, each time carrying along the rose and lilac roots her mother had given her in Boston. After marrying, Aunt Jessica and Uncle Noah had moved to a farm in Pennsylvania, then to Ohio by covered wagon when Uncle Noah felt there were too many people moving in. Next, they'd moved to Kentucky with an ox cart. There Uncle Noah overcame his restlessness, and they'd remained in one place until his death. Shortly thereafter, Father had invited Aunt Jessica to move to Missouri to join them, and then, of course, came the wagon trek to California.

"Surely if you and the rose and lilac roots have endured so many uprootings, this move to Oak Hill will not be too unsettling," Betsy said, half to reassure herself.

"Yes, that's what I always tell myself," her aunt admitted.

The one aspect of the account that had always dismayed Betsy was Aunt Jessica's coming to Missouri nineteen years ago. It was her own birth that had caused her mother's death and had brought her aunt to help Father raise the family. It was an unhappy fact Betsy had finally accepted, for she like everyone else knew the dangers of childbirth and also that God numbered one's days on earth as clearly as He numbered the hairs on one's head. Nonetheless, her birth had caused the death of a mother everyone had loved.

At length Betsy said, "If only we might know the future."

Her aunt gave a little laugh. "Augustine believed that God keeps us from a knowledge of the future, for if we knew of coming prosperity, we would be careless, and if we had a foreknowledge of troubles, we would despair and act senselessly."

"Perhaps," Betsy replied, hopeful that she would always take the way of carefulness. Yet look at her now—en route to a gold town! Was that carefulness?

As they rode on, wisps of fog hung in the air and, at the edge of San Francisco, the morning sunshine was almost swallowed by clouds of white. One could still see the town below the fog, though, and Betsy's excitement mounted at the sight.

San Francisco was no longer a canvas town with candles and oil lamps in the tents, turning the hills into a golden magic-lantern show at night. One conflagration after another had burned down the tents and old shanties, which were replaced by buildings of brick and stone.

San Francisco was called the busiest town west of the Mississippi, and now that the U. S. mint had opened and streets held three- and four-story buildings, not to mention gas lamps, many went so far as to call it a city. Others found the elegant appellation of "city" too refined for such a roisterous place.

As they drove through, a school bell rang out, and groups of bright and smiling children made their way to one of the seven public schools already established.

"It does look as if San Francisco is settling down to more sedate living," Aunt Jessica remarked as she glanced out the carriage window.

Betsy nodded in agreement. "A sight I'd much rather see than one of their vigilante parades . . . or a public hanging!"

Ahead, San Francisco's waterfront still presented a colorful sight. Over five hundred ships stood in the bay abandoned, some with cargos still moldering in their holds. Nearby, hulks of ships had been dragged ashore to serve as warehouses, and the brig *Euphemia* was anchored off the Sacramento Street wharf, at the corner of Battery, as a prison ship. Yet, for all of California's riotousness, the decent citizens were making headway with civilizing the place. Why, out in Oakland a group of Presbyterians and New England Congregationalists spoke of chartering what they called the College of California.

Daniel stopped the carriage at the Sacramento riverboat dock, and they all climbed down into the wharfside tumult. Young runners called out, "Finest steamer on the river!" "Famous cuisine!" "Just overhauled and entirely safe!" "Fastest ship afloat!" Father brushed off their "Fastest ship afloat!" with a laughing, "We are taking the *Sacramento Queen*. No wild steamboat racing and boiler explosions for us!" With that, the young runners backed off slightly, and the Talbots pressed through the crowd.

Numerous craft lined the wharf, but Betsy thought the *Sacramento Queen* a finer steamboat than any of them; certainly it was far superior to the ramshackle boats that had been pressed into service at the beginning of the gold rush. Even the stevedores loading cargo into her black hull appeared proud of the graceful white craft.

Betsy hurried along the gangway with her family and passengers of all types: gold seekers, Chinamen, gunmen, tinhorns, painted women, Kanakas from the Islands, merchants, bankers, and Filipino farmhands. It was a colorful crowd, and she flushed at the curious gaze of the men.

"Ain't she a pert beauty?" a fiercely bearded one asked his cohorts. "Looks like jest the gal fer me!"

"Pretend you don't hear, Betsy," her aunt whispered. "Don't look at them."

"I won't!" She was reminded of the time she was fourteen and had come to town to visit their pastor's wife. Several drunken miners had grabbed her and, if it had not been for Aunt Jessica—and Father's early arrival, who knows what might have happened. Thereafter, Father had truly joined the battle against lawlessness and pressed for statehood. Unfortunately, he'd rarely allowed her to come into town at all after that, and then only if accompanied by him or other men in the family. As for sailing, her greatest excursion to date had been on a San Francisco ferry.

Once they were all aboard, Betsy's father explained the steamship to them. On the forward hull was the "China hold" for Oriental passengers; above that was the machinery space. The main deck held cargo as well as offices and a few staterooms. Topside was another deckhouse or cabin which held the "social hall," and above that the weather deck, marked by the roof of the main cabin. Last came the topmost deck, where the officers and more expensive cabins, like theirs, were located.

"Time to sail," Daniel said sadly.

Such a sadness swept through Betsy that she could scarcely bid him farewell. "Thank you for bringing us, Daniel," she said, embracing her dear adopted brother. "I shall miss you."

His white smile split his dark beard, and his blue eyes held hers. "And I shall miss you. Be careful, little sister."

"I shall. I promise, I shall."

"And see if you can't sketch some new scenes for Abby."

"I'll try," Betsy replied, "though they will never equal hers."

For an instant she wished she weren't leaving, but only

for an instant, for her heart thundered with excitement over the upcoming adventure.

Daniel embraced Aunt Jessica, then started for the gangway and sent them a final wave.

The sailors shouted rapid orders, and in no time the *Sacramento Queen* gave a great warning blast and moved away from the dock, black smoke puffing from its stack. "We're under way!" Father announced.

Betsy and the others waved at Daniel, who waggled his arm at them as he headed for the carriage. He grew smaller and smaller in the dockside crowd as the ship steamed away, leaving a wake behind them in the fog-shrouded water.

The broad expanse of San Francisco Bay was beautiful, but once it was behind them, Betsy watched the scenery with heightened interest, for she had only heard of places like San Pablo Bay and Benica, where they stopped to take on passengers and cargo. When they steamed on from Benica, one of the state's four recent capitals, it seemed the entire world lay before her. The exhilarating sensation brought to mind moments during their covered-wagon trek, although steaming along like this in a riverboat was not in the least arduous.

At length sunshine burned off the fog and beamed down on the forested islands in the delta; beyond the islands were pastoral lands where prudent miners who had prospered had turned to farming the rich delta soil.

Father remarked, "California now raises the best potatoes and other vegetables in the world near here."

"Just seeing these places makes it seem like a new life has begun!" Betsy said with excitement.

Uncertain as he was whether he approved of this new life for Betsy, Benjamin couldn't help but be caught up by her enthusiasm. "Look at this magnificent place!" he said. "To think that our orators in Congress wanted to know why anybody would want California with what they called its 'endless mountains, vast and worthless deserts, and cheerless coast.' Why, Daniel Webster himself declared that only San Francisco Bay had any value and the rest of California was not worth a dollar."

"They hadn't seen it as we have," Jessica remarked.

Benjamin nodded. "I recall when we came through the Sierra passes and looked down on this vast central valley. I knew then it was true about growing almost anything on earth here."

"I remember how excited we were," Betsy put in. "I'll never forget that moment."

As excited as she looks now, Benjamin thought, realizing it made her all the more fetching.

Nearby, two miners who had been eyeing her sidled over to him. "Ve couldn't help overhear you say you'd come by covered vagon," the blond, bearded one said. "Ve did ourselves in '50. If ve might introduce ourselves—"

"Of course," Benjamin said, eager as always to meet strangers, yet suspicious because of Betsy's presence. "I'm Benjamin Talbot, and this is my sister, Mrs. Alcott, and my daughter, Miss Talbot."

"I am Sven Lindborg," the blond fellow said with a Swedish accent, "and this is my friend Ralston Stone from Ohio."

Benjamin shook hands with Lindborg, then with the dark-haired, clean-shaven giant named Ralston.

"What takes you to Sacramento City?" Ralston asked.

Benjamin gave a nod toward Betsy. "My daughter has accepted a contract to teach school at Oak Hill."

"A teacher! Ve are both university graduates ourselves," Sven said.

As they watched the countryside pass, Ralston said rather grandly, "I remember coming to the Rocky Mountains foothills. For as far as we could see behind us, an animated mass of human beings came into view. Endless trains of white-covered wagons moved along, a multitude of horsemen pranced on the road, many wagons displayed banners. It looked like a mighty army on its march."

"A colorful way to describe the sights," Benjamin said dryly, sure that Ralston was speaking so impressively for Betsy's benefit. With half of the miners between the ages of twenty and thirty, and a population of only one-twelfth women, she was bound to attract undue attention.

"But there vas tragic sights for some," Sven added. "Imagine the Donner party . . . the cannibalism to stay alive."

Benjamin nodded, appalled as always at the thought. "We went through there before the snows hit. For us, it was a place of a wedding and happiness."

The young men were engineers, hired by a large company to start a hard-rock mine that would be tunneled through the Sierra Nevada. "Someday soon, ve vill have hydraulic mining vashing down the gold-bearing dirt from the hills," Sven said.

Benjamin noticed Betsy's interest as they told about the new mining methods. She had never even seen anyone panning for gold. It would not do for her to show such great interest in men's conversation, but she had always been curious about everything.

Finally they came to the mouth of the muddy Sacramento River, and Benjamin said to the young men, "If you will excuse us, we shall take a rest in our cabin before dinner."

"Yes, of course," Sven said, "I hope ve did not intrude vith your family." His blue eyes went to Betsy, who smiled all too kindly at him as far as Benjamin was concerned.

"It was a pleasure to meet both of you," he said with a note of finality.

At noontime, they came down to the dining room and, much to Benjamin's pleasure, were invited to sit at the ship master's table. They had no more than been seated, however, than Sven and Ralston came to the table, doubtless having finagled invitations to sit there, too.

"Betsy will sit between her aunt and me," Benjamin said.

She darted a rueful glance at him, but sat down with grace and dignity.

Despite Benjamin's misgivings over the young men's presence, the dinner was a sumptuous feast: fresh fish and venison, oversized oysters, beef roasts, spring peas and potatoes, preserves, and hot biscuits.

Captain Keller, aware of the family business, turned the conversation to shipping needs in California. "The headlong boom of the gold rush can only be kept up if people, things, and money are moved around fast enough to match the fevered pitch of her inhabitants," he said with conviction.

"Our centers of commerce are in easy reach of the inland waterways," Benjamin assured him. "Look at the amount of passengers, produce, machinery, lumber, and gold dust already going between Red Bluff, Marysville, Sacramento, Stockton, and San Francisco, not to mention a hundred brush-and-board riverbank stops along the way. It's shipping that ties California together, from the gold camps of the Mother Lode to the wharfs of San Francisco."

"The question is whether such prosperity can be maintained," Captain Keller replied with concern.

Benjamin noticed that the young men were far more interested in Betsy than in the state of shipping or the precariousness of the economy. Indeed, they had already announced their plans to visit her at Oak Hill!

When they finished off their dessert of fine pastries, Aunt Jessica with her usual good humor pronounced their dinner the height of gluttony. She added, "We surely will not need an evening meal in Sacramento."

Benjamin sincerely hoped they would not. He did not wish to face supper in their hotel with young men chasing after his daughter. Now that the state legislature had proclaimed Sacramento City the permanent state capital, there would not only be miners and shopkeepers, but likely politicians in pursuit of her, too.

"If you will please excuse us," he said to Sven Lindborg and Ralston Stone, "we will take our exercise around the deck." He ignored their disappointed expressions and reminded himself that soon they would travel on to the northern goldfields. As they walked around the deck, Benjamin gazed out across the winding river with Jessica and Betsy at the pastoral scenes of the Sacramento Valley. Here and there, their riverboat stopped at a brush landing to take on a passenger or farm produce. Now and then, another steamboat rounded the bend, and the boats exchanged blasts while the passengers waved at each other across the river.

"I do wish we could see a race," Betsy said, to her father's amazement.

"I've seen enough steamboat racing to last a lifetime," he replied more adamantly than he intended. "This year already, the *Ranger,* the *Helen Hensley,* and the *Secretary* have exploded . . . all in the name of racing. Let's hope the new California Steam Navigation Company will make navigation more businesslike and less bedlamic."

"I'm sure you're right, Father," Betsy said, "but I do wish I could just once see a race."

"Since when have you cared about anything so dangerous?" he asked her.

She took his hand in hers. "Forgive me, Father. I shall try not to worry you further."

"Why should you think I am worried?" he asked in protest.

She smiled up at him. "Because you seldom look so stern."

He had to smile with her. "Perhaps because I have never before allowed a daughter to work away from home."

"I won't let you down, Father."

"It's not so much you, but the miners who worry me."

Jessica smiled at him. "Oh, if our father could hear you now, Benjamin. You are the very fellow who chased after the girls with such enthusiasm in Boston! Now the shoe is on the other foot!"

Benjamin flushed. "Times were different then. Now everything is so unsettled."

Jessica gave such a laugh that he couldn't help grinning himself.

It was early evening when Sacramento City came impressively into view. Its high levee ran all along the river, with steamboats and tall-masted sailing ships tied to it. The wide streets were lined with wooden buildings and houses, many painted white and trimmed with green. There were also several blocks of brick buildings, and throngs of people everywhere.

"How different from San Francisco," Betsy said as the *Sacramento Queen* tied up in the long line of ships at the riverfront. "I surely didn't expect trees among the buildings and houses. They give it a more settled look."

"Sacramento's citizens made a good job of rebuilding since their great flood," Benjamin replied.

He glanced in the direction of Mark Hopkins's hardware business and wondered why the shrewd shopkeeper wished to see him. No doubt about the Sacramento Valley Railroad notion everyone was discussing. He was unsure whether he wished to invest with Huntington and Crocker, however, if they were to be the main backers. Hopkins, at least, was the quietest and least aggressive member of the financial group. "I have to conduct my business immediately," he said. "I trust you ladies will not go around town on your own."

"Oh, Benjamin!" Jessica protested, "you know we won't get into too much mischief, though I do hear there are elderly gentlemen looking for wives with my qualifications . . . mature, good cooks and housekeepers . . . ."

"And I thought I had only to be concerned about Betsy!" Benjamin returned with amusement.

A moment later, however, he sobered, for here came Sven Lindborg and Ralston Stone with their valises, both of the men eyeing Betsy again.

"You vill be a velcome sight to all of the men in Oak Hill," Sven told Betsy. "You must be careful."

Lord, give me peace about these women! Benjamin prayed, very nearly aloud so Sven and Ralston could hear him.

The next morning in front of the Sacramento City Hotel, Betsy felt she might burst with excitement as she waited near the dusty black stagecoach. Their baggage had already been weighed and was being packed on top of the coach and tied to the iron railing.

The ticket agent opened the coach door, and Father helped them in. "Up you go, ladies!" he said, then climbed in himself. The three of them took the backseat, a pile of trunks and mail sacks near their feet.

Two bewhiskered men sat down opposite them, one at each window; they looked none too clean and somewhat under the weather. Betsy took them for miners, for they wore the usual miner outfits: rough trousers and knee-high black boots, battered wide-brimmed black hats, and flannel shirts. They also wore huge guns in their belts.

Catching her eye, they nodded, put their feet up on a trunk, and, without further ado, tipped their hats halfway over their faces so they might slumber.

Betsy settled back and took a last look at Sacramento City. Everywhere men were hammering together buildings and houses, and the riverfront was still crowded with ships. It would be the nearest city to Oak Hill, and it seemed to be thriving. Last evening, she and Aunt Jessica had taken a short stroll outside before dark, then had bowls of soup sent up to their room. With the exception of seeing so many saloons, it had been a pleasant visit.

The stagecoach driver, a rangy, gray-bearded fellow named Yank Stevens, pulled on his high-cuffed yellow gauntlets and climbed up to the driver's box.

"Brace your feet against that trunk in the middle," Father warned the women.

Suddenly the ticket agent ran out and opened the door again. "One more passenger!"

"Beggin' your pardon," the elderly man said, climbing in. "Just barely made it." As he sat down opposite them between the two miners, he added, out of breath, "The name is Lucius Alden, and I hie from Maryland, near Baltimore." He tipped his hat and nodded politely as the door was shut. He was short and wiry, his merry face as weathered and wrinkled as old leather. Despite his courtly manner, he seemed a rustic in his rumpled brown suit, a kindly leprechaun sort of fellow.

Father introduced them, to which Lucius Alden replied with great courtesy, "My pleasure to meet all o' ye, I'm sure."

Outside, the driver cracked the whip over the six-horse team and yelled, "Git along, boys! Git along!" The stagecoach jerked forward, and before long it bowled through town so fast that they clung desperately to their seats.

Once the city was left behind in a cloud of dust, the horses ran even faster, and Father quoted with amusement, " . . . and the driving is like the driving of Jehu the son of Mimshi; for he driveth furiously!" which made everyone except the two bewhiskered miners laugh.

Outside, the countryside through which they rushed and rattled was pleasant: flowers in bloom and cultivation going forward with great activity.

"The soil looks more fertile here than at *Rancho Verde*," Betsy called out, and her father nodded.

After a while she settled back between Aunt Jessica and Father, and inspected the men before her. The bewhiskered miners appeared to be sleeping, though with so much bumping and jolting it was beyond her how they stayed in their seats. Between them, Lucius Alden smiled. "I hear ye be the new schoolmarm fer Oak Hill," he said over the clatter.

"How did you know that?" she asked.

"Ticket agent said so. I expect anytime a pretty young lady, who's prim and proper to boot, comes through town, there's a good bit o' interest."

Prim and proper! Betsy marveled, containing her amusement. As for being pretty, she didn't quite believe it. From what she'd seen in the mirror, her nose was a trifle too pointy and her cheeks a bit prominent, though she did have good white teeth, clear green eyes, and an ample head of auburn hair that she, like all decent women, had worn swept up since her sixteenth birthday.

"I always say ye can tell a great deal about folks by their occupations," Lucius Alden said as they jolted along.

"What sort of work do you do, Mr. Alden?" Aunt Jessica asked, hanging on to her seat.

"A peddler is what I was and always will be. It's a common name and a common trade, but wouldn't o' done anythin' else for the world. Peddlin's the best way to make a livin' while ye be seein' the land . . . and to meet people while ye be at it. Drove a peddlin' wagon on the National Road between Baltimore and Vandalia, Illinois, for a good many years."

"I've ridden on the National Road for some distance near Columbus, Ohio," Aunt Jessica said, and they were soon discussing the road's stately stone bridges, iron mileposts, and other features.

Lucius said, "Always sorry they didn't finish the road to St. Louis like they planned. Politics be in it, I suppose."

"What will you do here?" Aunt Jessica asked.

"Much o' the same, soon as I get situated. First, I aim to look o'er the country, get a lay o' the land, so to speak."

"A worthy plan," Father remarked.

Lucius Alden appeared to be Aunt Jessica's age, Betsy observed. Somewhat old to find work.

Lucius asked her father, "If I may inquire, sir, what is yer trade?"

"Shipping and chandlery," Father replied.

"A good bit like mine, but yers is on a far wider and loftier plane," Lucius said.

Father chuckled. "I am not so certain about the loftier aspect. What made you leave your old route?"

"My old horse, Traveler, gave out, so I gave up the work. But I got plain worn out with sittin' around, and I started thinkin' o' California . . . new places to see, new customers."

Betsy decided she liked Lucius Alden, but she was unsure about the bewhiskered miners who slept all too quietly across from her. For one thing, she was almost certain that the red-shirted one stole glances at her and the rest of them. For another, they were too quiet and seemed the sort who would snore.

By midday, she was hungry and glad for the stage stop, though the place was a filthy hovel, and the beans and coarse bread unappetizing. Before long, they were on the stage again, bouncing through the countryside, and the hills became higher and the gulches deeper. Alongside the road now and then were streamside settlements with towering trees and small log cabins, and in the distance, a few miners panned, picked holes, or washed out dirt in a wooden contraption that Father explained was called a miner's rocker or cradle.

"Behold the miner at work," he said. "The sun pours its scorching rays on his devoted head. He works day after day and week after week in a stooping posture, at as severe toil and great exposure as man ever felt or knew, and scarcely gets a return for his labor now."

"But who has ever been prudent in the pursuit of gold?" Aunt Jessica asked with a shake of her head.

It did seem a sorry sight, Betsy mused as they drove on.

At length they rode on through a wooded, desolate section. "Half an hour to Oak Hill," Father said.

Betsy's excitement mounted, but her father's words were suddenly followed by a burst of gunfire in front of the stagecoach.

"Road agents! Get down!" the blue-shirted miner yelled as he pulled his gun and glanced out the window. "Get down! Get down!"

"Lord, help us!" Aunt Jessica called out as the red-shirted miner began to shoot out the other window.

Betsy glimpsed a bearded gunman riding toward them from the woods, kerchief over his face, a terrible scar on his forehead.

"Down, teacher!" yelled one of her bewhiskered coach-mates and tore her from the window. The stage bumped and swayed wildly, throwing her onto the floor with Aunt Jessica.

"They got Yank Stevens!" the blue-shirted miner called out as the coach swayed and slowed.

"Three of 'em!" the red-shirted one shouted between shots.

"Looks like Yank's got to stop—"

Lord, don't let them kill Aunt Jessica or Father, Betsy prayed. *Please, Lord*— It took no special courage to shoot a man in the dark, but to ride boldly forth from a roadside thicket to halt and rob an oncoming stagecoach took nerves of iron! These men must be monsters!

The stage jolted to a stop, and Betsy expected a great shootout. Instead, shots burst from behind them, accompanied by shouting and the drumming of hooves.

"They're leaving!" one of the gunmen in the stagecoach yelled, still shooting at the assailants. "Who's that coming up behind us?"

The other glanced back. "Why, it's the doc and his darkie, Rufus. If that don't beat all!"

Finally the shooting stopped, and Betsy peered out with the rest of them. Riding up from behind them on a big bay gelding was a darkly bearded young man and, on an old gray, an elderly black man. The two bewhiskered miners leapt from the stagecoach, looked over the scene, and helped Yank Stevens down from the driver's box.

"Doc Buchanan!" Yank called out. "Last man I expected to see in a gunfight."

The doctor's white teeth flashed through his short beard as he dismounted. "I am the last man to have expected it myself, but we happened to be in the right place at precisely the right time. Are you hurt, Yank?"

"Ain't much. They shot my gun to smithereens, though. Dadburned Southerner got me."

The blue-shirted miner asked Yank, "You see his face?"

"Can't say I did, not with neckerchiefs up over their noses. But I know southern talk when I hear it."

The red-shirted one frowned, then turned to the rescuers. "Mighty grateful, Doc and Rufus. We nicked two of 'em. Expect that'll keep 'em honest fer a spell."

Rufus grinned, and the doctor said, "We assumed you must be bringing gold coin from the mint and needed help."

"That we did," the red-shirted man said. He added another, "Mighty grateful."

The doctor nodded and turned to Yank Stevens. "Let's have a look at that hand."

After a moment's inspection, he went for the black medical bag on his saddle pack. As he returned to Yank Stevens, he glanced into the stagecoach. "Anyone else hurt?"

"No, we seem to be fine," Betsy's father replied as he helped Aunt Jessica to regain her seat. "Are you, Jessica?"

She sat back and, blinking, assessed her condition. "I seem none the worse for wear, thank you."

Benjamin added, "We are most thankful for your assistance."

"My pleasure," the young man said. "Well! I am glad to see you are bringing in more ladies." His hazel eyes stopped on Betsy with interest. "You must be our new teacher."

"Yes, I am," Betsy replied, still shaken. She felt as if she must look pale.

"Jonathan Wilmington told us you'd arrive shortly. I'm sorry for such an unsettling welcome."

"Thank you for stepping in to rescue us," Betsy said.

He nodded and went to work on Yank Stevens's bloody hand.

What gentle and solicitous eyes this young doctor had, Betsy thought. He didn't appear in the least like a man who was handy with guns. It seemed that God had sent him to save them.

As for Father, there was no question in her mind that he was more uncertain than ever about leaving Aunt Jessica and her in this place. In any event, if God meant her to be here, she must trust Him no matter what the adversity. And with this in mind, she fixed her mind on staying in Oak Hill.

3

The late spring scenery became ever more beautiful as they neared the river. Snow melting in the higher elevations of the Sierra Nevada caused the river, in its steep drops, to splash exuberantly against granite and to rush through the canyons. Its beauty lifted Betsy's spirits and renewed her hope, and she began to feel more peaceful . . . until they rode into the mining settlement of Oak Flats.

There, one of the mud-spattered miners panning in a shallow side stream gazed up at them from under his battered hat and shouted with wild abandon, "Ye brought women!"

She affected a pleasant expression, but shuddered inwardly at him and the befouled surroundings. Stained tents, shanties, and shed-sized cabins stood near the hillsides, and weeds sprouted among the discarded cans and bottles strewn all around. The sight, coming just after the recent holdup attempt, was all the more disheartening.

Another miner shouted something unintelligible at them, and another something about Yank Stevens's bandaged hand.

"Mind yer manners!" Yank Stevens called out to the miners. "We're bringin' in decent folks."

Lucius Alden shook his head. "California's got more than its share o' roughnecks and ne'er-do-wells."

"Indeed," her father said, "though it's not nearly as bad in Oak Flats as it was several years back. Still, I often think we've collected most of the world's rebels. On the other hand, it also seems we've collected the world's greatest opportunity to spread the good news of Christ's redemption."

"An interestin' notion," Lucius replied.

Aunt Jessica cast a curious glance at him and said in her usual kindly tone, "There's no happier believer than one who's had much forgiven."

"Expect so," Lucius replied. "I do expect so."

As they bounced along, they saw miners working near the road, and Betsy watched with interest through the stagecoach windows. A few swirled gravel in the stream, but most used the rockers or cradles, which her father explained allowed groups of men to work the piles of gravel much more quickly.

"It's dirty work," Aunt Jessica remarked.

"Ye wonder why they keep it up now that minin' like this hardly buys grub and clothes anymore," Lucius said.

Father said, "Men often lose all reason over gold."

As her brother Joshua had once done, Betsy thought. And Joshua, who'd been so successful as a supercargo for the Wainwright and Talbot ships, had been the last man one would think likely to fall prey to such a temptation.

"Mankind's never been known for common sense or wisdom," Aunt Jessica remarked as she watched the miners.

"Nor womankind," Betsy's father returned with amusement.

Aunt Jessica laughed. "Now, Benjamin!"

As the stagecoach jolted on through Oak Flats, Betsy found the miners a muddy and tattered lot. Their red or blue flannel shirts and rough trousers were in far worse condition than any she'd seen them wear during her infrequent visits to San Francisco—though there it was commonly known that they bought new clothing and tossed out their old shirts and trousers on the streets.

Beyond Oak Flats, the stream rejoined the river, the water making a wide bend and the land rising so steeply that the mining operations were left behind. Blackberry and huckleberry vines tangled the underbrush on either side of the dirt road, and Betsy was glad to see that once again nature prevailed.

Her father pointed to a partially cleared hillside in the distance. "There's Oak Hill."

"What a majestic setting," Betsy said with pleasure as she caught a glimpse of it. Around and above Oak Hill stood foothills forested with oak, cedar, and pine, and occasionally there were views of distant cloud-crowned mountain peaks.

"The sight seems so familiar after seeing Abby's pictures," Aunt Jessica decided. "It will be interesting to see if man has brought Oak Hill to ruin, too."

Betsy braced her feet against the trunk and her mind against disappointment, for so much of California had been beautiful before man had made his imprint. She reminded herself that Joshua and his wife, Rose, liked Oak Hill. So did Cousin Louisa, whose husband pastored the church. But people often ignored the defects of their surroundings or put a good face on them.

All she knew about the place was that Mr. Wilmington had purchased the original three log cabins and farm outbuildings from settlers who'd come before the gold discovery. Of course, there were now more cabins, not to mention a church, a school, and a growing town on the other side of the wooded settlement.

At last the stagecoach bowled up the steep hill and into a clearing where a cluster of neat log cabins stood in the shade of feathery pines, fringed cedars, and acorn-bearing oaks. Behind them were log outbuildings and a corral that held burros and horses. Beyond was a pasture with grazing cattle.

"That must be the church," Betsy said, nodding toward a larger log building that overlooked the river. "Yes, see, it has a wooden cross over the doorway! Why, Oak Hill is charming!"

"It is beautiful," Aunt Jessica agreed, "far more beautiful than I'd expected."

Betsy's father smiled. "I knew you'd both like it, but I had no wish to encourage you. I've often thought I should like to live here myself, if we didn't have our livelihood in town and at *Rancho Verde*."

Lucius Alden peered out the window and asked, impressed, "Is there a town to it?"

"Yes, indeed," Father replied, "a town with shops, restaurants, a new hotel, a bank, and my son Joshua's Mercantile. Town's a bit farther on, but within walking distance. The stage stops near the hotel, too."

"Think I'll look at prospects here myself," Lucius decided. "Always did like a mountain town."

As the stagecoach drew to a halt, making a special stop for them, Betsy could scarcely believe she had arrived at the scene of her new life. Still, it was true: she was the schoolteacher and she was in Oak Hill!

"Here come Rose and Joshua!" Aunt Jessica called out.

The next thing Betsy knew she was out of the stagecoach and into the arms of her dear sister-in-law. "Oh, Rose!" she said, suddenly as tremulous as when the stagecoach holdup attempt had taken place.

"Welcome, Betsy, welcome!" Rose replied, her brown eyes bright with joy. Her lovely black hair was swept up into a chignon, and she wore a pink cotton frock that accented the circles of pink on her cheeks. "We could scarcely believe it when Father said you were coming!"

"Welcome, Miss Betsy . . . schoolmarm," her big auburn-haired brother, Joshua, teased. He gathered her into his arms for a warm brotherly embrace, his luxuriant red mustache tickling as he kissed her cheek.

Aunt Jessica had gotten down from the stagecoach, and he gave her a fond kiss, too. "I'd better help Father with the valises," he said. "Yank Stevens keeps that stagecoach on schedule no matter what."

As she stood back, Dr. Buchanan and Rufus galloped up behind the stagecoach. Betsy thought they must have stopped for a while below at Oak Flats.

The doctor slowed his bay gelding to a canter as they rode by, and she called out, "Thank you again for coming to our rescue!"

"My pleasure, Miss Talbot," he replied, tipping his wide-brimmed black hat gallantly.

He rode on, calling back to Yank Stevens to favor his wounded hand, but the driver had already cracked the whip, presumably with his other hand, and started the stagecoach forward.

Lucius Alden waved from the coach window and shouted back, "I might be seein' ye folks again soon."

"Be sure you do, Mr. Alden!" Aunt Jessica replied. "Come to church next Sunday, and I'll give you dinner!"

As the stagecoach raced forward on the dusty road, Rose asked, "What happened that you were in need of rescue?"

"Desperadoes!" Aunt Jessica said. "Road agents!"

"A holdup?" Joshua asked with alarm.

"Indeed it was!" Aunt Jessica said. "Three of them, nervy as can be, tried to hold up the stagecoach half an hour ago.

The doctor and his man, Rufus, rode in and saved us—and a trunkful of gold coin from the mint, as well."

"Adam Buchanan did that?" Joshua asked, amazed.

"He did," Father replied. "He seems a fine young man."

"He is," Joshua said, "as fine a man as can be found, albeit a most unfortunate one."

Rose warned softly, "Now, Joshua—"

"That's all I intended to say, my dear," he protested. "Not another word. I'm just grateful that he came along."

Betsy wondered in what way Adam Buchanan might be unfortunate, but her thought was interrupted by a red-haired little boy running toward them from the cabin. "Charles? Yes, you must be! You look like a miniature of your father . . . without the mustache, of course!"

Rose laughed as her three-year-old son hid behind her pink skirts. "He has decided to be called Charlie now. He's a good bit shyer than his father thus far," she said, "but he's the finest boy born since our Lord's birth!"

Father said with amusement, "There are several parents back at *Rancho Verde* who might take exception to that!"

Betsy asked, "Where's little Rosie?"

"Having her afternoon nap," Rose replied.

"Well then, I shall have to become acquainted with you, Charlie," Betsy teased. She peered at him behind Rose's skirts, making him giggle, then coaxed him into her arms.

"I want a big red mustache, too," he said, his brown eyes wide with seriousness, causing all of them to laugh again.

When Betsy thought to look, the stagecoach was well out of sight, as was the handsome and apparently unfortunate Dr. Adam Buchanan, to whom she still felt most grateful.

When they stepped into Rose and Joshua's log cabin, Betsy was glad to see it was comfortably furnished. She recalled Rose writing with dry wit about the bent-branch furniture whose pokes and scratches they had endured when she first came to Oak Hill. Some new furniture, like the black stove in the kitchen, had come around Cape Horn by clipper ship. The rest had been made in San Francisco at one of its new furniture establishments. Rose's dear old black housekeeper Maddy, who lived in a cabin nearer the outbuildings with her husband Moses, had helped Rose sew the curtains.

So as not to disturb little Rosie's nap, they sat outside on the sunlit gray slate veranda for their afternoon refreshments.

After drinking tea and eating little hazelnut cakes at the plank table with them, Joshua said, "I regret that I must ride back to the Mercantile for an hour or so. Father, would you like to accompany me?"

"Indeed I would," Betsy's father replied. "One of the best ways to gauge the condition of a community is to see what its people are buying, or not buying. If you ladies don't mind my going—"

"Of course not, Benjamin," Aunt Jessica responded with a wry smile. "You know we are eager to discuss far more important matters . . . like children."

The men chuckled and, excusing themselves, headed for the barn to saddle up another horse for Father.

When they rode away down the river road, leaving behind a trail of dust, Rose took Betsy and Aunt Jessica out back behind the cabin to see her vegetable and herb gardens. Strolling through the main path, Rose said, "What a joy it is to have you two here. I feel you are both such kindred spirits. And what a surprise! A week ago, I should not have thought such a blessing possible."

"The blessing is mutual," Aunt Jessica said. "It is somewhat of a surprise to us, too. A week ago, it seemed I would spend the rest of my days at *Rancho Verde*."

"It did to me as well," Betsy added, then had to brush off their protests. "It truly did."

Rose said, "We could not have been more amazed when Father came home and told us he'd hired a woman teacher instead of a man . . . and then to find it was you, Betsy . . . and that you were coming, too, Aunt Jessica! My heart has scarcely stopped pounding with excitement ever since."

"Nor mine!" Betsy confessed. She took little Charlie's proffered hand and dropped a kiss on the top of his head. "I only hope Father recovers from his nervousness about leaving us here. It was difficult enough for him to deal with it before the stagecoach holdup!"

"He'll recover eventually," Aunt Jessica said. "I can understand how hard it must be on parents when one of the chicks flies the nest. And then to have his youngest be a school-marm out at the goldfields! Benjamin will have to entrust us entirely to the Lord now."

Rose smiled, then inclined her head toward the cabin to listen. "I hear Rosie. Would you like to see your cabin as soon as I have her up?"

"We can scarcely wait to see both of them—Rosie and our cabin!" Betsy declared. Half an hour later, she found herself carrying one-year-old Rosie, a cuddly brown-eyed little babe, along the sunlit path that fronted the cabins.

Having braced herself for the worst, the settlement presented a wonderful sight, edged as it was on one side by woods and, on the other, by the river far below. The tang of leaves from the forest floor filled the air, and sunshine beamed into the clearing, filtering here and there through solitary oak, cedar, and pine trees. From below in the valley came the rushing sound of the river like a hushed symphony.

"We'll not be living in town at all, but almost in the forest," Aunt Jessica remarked.

"Town is nearer than one thinks," Rose replied. "Just a fifteen-minute walk and growing closer every year, it seems. We deliberated greatly about putting the school here or in town, but it seemed best by the church. I do wish we'd had more notice of your coming, though, for the cabin was always lived in by men, and we didn't have time to make it as nice as we wished."

She pointed out the log cabin ahead, the sixth from hers and Joshua's, and Betsy brightened at the sight. A magnificent cedar provided the cabin with afternoon shade.

"It's lovely," Betsy said.

"I'm glad you think so," Rose replied, pleased.

The log exterior of the cabin had darkened, and the windows sparkled as though they had recently been washed. A step led up from the gray river slate veranda to the heavy plank door, which creaked when Rose opened it.

"Oh, dear, we meant to oil the door," she apologized. "I fear the windows also lack curtains."

"We shall soon put everything to rights," Aunt Jessica replied. "I have fabric in one of our trunks that is to arrive with the Mercantile's freight shipment."

"You should probably close the shutters at night until then," Rose suggested, "and always lock the doors."

Betsy asked, "Are there still bears about?"

Rose smiled. "Not often, but we sometimes get drunken miners from Oak Flats. It's not as bad as it was several years ago, but it behooves us to be cautious. As for the bears, most have fled deep into the wilderness. There are many, we hear, in the Yosemite Valley where John and Jessie Fremont have their property."

Betsy said, "We hear there are wonderful waterfalls there, too. I should like to see it one day."

"I should like to myself, but it's said to be a difficult

journey, particularly with children," Rose said, then beamed at a thought. "Ah, I have it! You can go there on your wedding trip!"

"Oh, Rose! None of that!" Betsy protested. "I'm here to teach and nothing else. Now, let's see this cabin."

Inside, the cabin had a parlor-dining room, a bedroom with two rustic bedsteads, and a kitchen with a new black stove. The floors, like the veranda, were made of gray river slate.

"I put my spare bedding on the beds," Rose said, "but I fear there are no extra blankets to be had in town now. Joshua has been out of them all month at the Mercantile."

Betsy took note of the beautiful roseate and green quilts covering their beds and suspected that Rose had lent them her very best. Aunt Jessica must have taken notice of it, too, for she said, "Not only do we have a trunkful of bedding and curtain fabric coming, but we each brought a sheet with us. Your father only knew there was a teacher's cabin for us. He could recall no other furnishings than a new stove and two beds."

"Ah, men—" Rose said with an amused shake of her head. "I should have remembered, though, it's not the first time you've moved, Aunt Jessica."

"She has not only brought some of her lilac and rose roots," Betsy said, "but when the freight shipment arrives we shall have, among other things, our very own pots and pans."

"As it is, you have done wonders to the cabin on such short notice," her aunt said. "Even a washboard and a washtub."

"The truth is," Rose confessed, "we had only two days to get ready for our new schoolmarm and her aunt, so we all contributed our spare household effects."

Betsy eyed the jars of dried rice and beans and the new black teakettle on the stove. "Joshua contributed from his Mercantile, I would guess."

Rose nodded, pleased. "Just a bit."

"Oh, Rose, we do appreciate it," Betsy said, "but we don't wish to impose. On the other hand, I only have a three-month contract, and it seems foolhardy to invest too much work or money in the cabin."

Aunt Jessica said, "We can improvise and still make it lovely. When our freight shipment arrives, we shall return everyone's belongings, and if there are those who don't want them back, we might start an emergency household supply at the church for new residents. What would the pastor think of that?"

"Very likely, he'd say it's inspired," Rose replied. "I might have guessed you'd think of something like that. And now I'd better let you two settle in for a rest. We're having supper for you tonight at our cabin." She raised her hands to fend off their protests and said with a laugh, "Louisa and Tess are doing all of the cooking, so I have no say in it."

Late in the afternoon, Benjamin and Joshua Talbot mounted their horses and headed home toward the settlement. Benjamin cantered his chestnut gelding through the growing town of Oak Hill, pleased with his visit. The small town was still thriving despite the downturn in gold production, and it appeared that Joshua, Jonathan Wilmington, and the other early settlers had planned the place well, even planting trees in front of the Oak Hill Bank, the Mercantile, and the two-story City Hotel. Fortunately, there were plenty of saloons and gambling houses down at Oak Flats, thus keeping the number of saloons here to a minimum.

Benjamin glanced again at the people out on the boardwalks fronting the shops. Miners in black hip-length boots, aproned shopkeepers, a Chinaman with a pigtail trailing down his back, and even women and children.

Despite this morning's attempted holdup of the stage-coach, the goldfields were changing for the better, he reminded himself. Why, not far away, the place known as "Old Dry Diggins," and later as "Hangtown," was being incorporated to respectability with a name like Placerville. As for Oak Hill, it was becoming a decent mountain town that served the growing number of families moving in, most of them coming as he had, by covered wagon.

They headed their horses home down the river road, and Benjamin nudged his chestnut gelding gently as they cantered past the blacksmith's and livery stable, the last vestiges of the town before the woods began.

"It's turning into a fine place," he said to Joshua.

"I think so myself. It's not Boston or San Francisco, but I'm growing more and more fond of it." He cocked an eye at the sun. "Expect we'd better hurry. The ladies will have supper waiting. I saw Tess and Hugh Fairfax ride out in their buggy before we left."

"I shall be glad to see them again. I'll never forget four years ago when Jonathan Wilmington and the miners talked me into preaching at your church," Benjamin said. "I agreed with such reluctance, and then after I preached, Tess and Hugh came forward. To think I was barely obedient—"

"And to recall how long I rebelled," Joshua replied with a shake of his head. "When I think of not having Rose and the children, I can't imagine how blinded I was."

"I was not too different myself until I met your mother," Benjamin told his son. "She made as much of an impact for good in my life as Rose has in yours."

The father and son grinned and urged their horses on.

From all accounts, Tess and Hugh Fairfax, who'd come through Panama in '49, had done well, Benjamin thought as they galloped along the trail between the woods and the river valley. Not that he'd ever doubted Tess, who'd bustled with ambition and had even run a large tent restaurant in San Francisco. It was Hugh who had worried him. He'd been the spoiled son of an Eastern banker and was still suffering the effects of Panama fever when they'd sailed into California. Apparently his renewed faith, the responsibilities of marriage, and his knowledge of banking had turned him into an asset for Oak Hill. No doubt this invigorating mountain air had helped his health, as well.

"How is Hugh's bank doing?" Benjamin asked his son.

"Prospering, for which I'm most grateful. One of the blessings of having a real bank is my no longer having to hide the miners' pouches of gold dust in the coffee barrels."

Benjamin laughed. "We've given up banking their gold dust at the chandlery, too. Never in known history were coffee barrels so valuable as they were for a while here!"

They rode past the log schoolhouse where Betsy would teach, then the log church, which Jonathan Wilmington and Rose had begun shortly after their arrival. Sunlight filtered through the trees as they galloped to Rose and Joshua's log cabin, where Tess and Hugh Fairfax's horses and buggy already stood at the hitching post.

"Mr. Talbot!" a young man called out as he hurried toward them on foot from the direction of the church.

Benjamin slowed his horse. "Jonathan! I am so pleased to see you!" he replied to his niece Louisa's husband. "Are you still working at the church at this late hour?"

"You sound like Louisa!" Chambers laughed. "Actually, I've just returned from preaching at the northerly diggings. I travel a small circuit during the week."

"I'm eager to talk with you," Benjamin said, then rode on to the hitching post and dismounted.

Joshua said, "I'll take the horses back to the barn so you can visit with Chambers."

Benjamin almost withheld his words, then decided to speak them. "You're a fine and thoughtful son."

Joshua's eyes shone with love and gratitude, then he smiled and nodded. "I have a fine father," he said most sincerely and went off rather abruptly with the horses, as though to hide his emotion.

Jonathan Chambers hurried to him, and Benjamin shook hands with the young pastor. "How are you, my friend?"

Chambers beamed. "How could any man feel better than to see you? I've been looking forward to this moment all day."

As they stood back, Benjamin pressed his lips together to hide his sentiments himself. Finally he said, "The truth is, I could not be fonder of you if you were my own son. I am so grateful for your taking the pastorate here."

"Thank you, sir. This is where the Lord wants me," Chambers said, the cleft in his chin deepening. "I have no question of it."

"And what does the Lord say to you lately?"

Jonathan's hazel eyes met his. "That we are not only to preach salvation, but to lay the foundation of the church here for future generations, should He tarry. That we are to preach to the believers about their roles in God's plan, about growing in holiness, about pleasing our heavenly Father."

"Yes," Benjamin said thoughtfully, "in our zeal for converts during the beginnings of the gold rush, we so often forgot about laying the foundation for future generations. We must preach holiness in all things, not just in matters we might decide should be 'sacred'—and let the devil take the rest. Everything Christians do now in the world builds for the church's future."

"Agreed," Chambers said. " 'What is' always comes from 'what was.'"

"We see eye to eye entirely," Benjamin said, heartened. "God could not have sent a better man to serve at Oak Hill."

Betsy turned to the doorway as she heard the two men come into the cabin. "There you are, Father . . . and Jonathan!" She hurried forward to greet Jonathan Chambers, who, though tall and lean, strode toward her gracefully. He looked much as he did when he first came to California in '49. "How good to see you," she said.

He shook her hand and beamed with pleasure. "And you! I could scarcely believe it when I heard we were getting you as our schoolteacher. What good news! And Aunt Jessica in the bargain!"

"She promises not to interfere with the school," Betsy replied with a smile, "but I'm sure she won't be able to stay away from the children for long."

"And be a blessing to them."

"Yes, she always is," Betsy said with feeling. "And speaking of children, your little Alice even at two is the image of Louisa, and little William is going to look like you."

Jonathan chuckled. "We shall see. At the moment, he favors me most with a receding hairline."

"I hadn't taken notice," Betsy responded in all honesty. Now that he mentioned it, however, she noticed that Jonathan's dark hair had receded a trifle and turned gray around the edges, though he could not be more than thirty-five years old. What she'd always noticed about him first was an aura of kindness, then his bright hazel eyes and deeply cleft chin.

"The important thing now is to make you feel welcome in Oak Hill," he said.

"Oh, I do already—"

"Are you certain?" he asked, his eyes turning serious.

She gave a little shrug and answered with some hesitation. "I understand that someone preferred a man teacher. I suppose there is never any perfect call to teaching . . . as perhaps there is to the pastorate."

"The word 'perfect' causes a good many difficulties," he said warmly. "It always brings to mind the apostle Paul's words, 'My grace is sufficient for you, for my power is made perfect in weakness.'"

"Yes," she said and fixed the words in her mind: *His power is made perfect in weakness.* That's what she should have responded to Tess Fairfax when she'd reluctantly mentioned, "It's too bad that one person here in town thinks a woman can't teach the more unruly children."

His power is made perfect in weakness, Betsy repeated to herself.

She smiled at Jonathan and quoted in return, "'A word fitly spoken is like apples of gold in pictures of silver.' Thank you, Jonathan."

"That's what I am here for," he replied, returning her smile.

Just then Louisa called with joy from the kitchen, "There you are, Jonathan! I was worried you would miss this evening and seeing Uncle Benjamin."

"Excuse me, Betsy," Jonathan said, "I've been out preaching and haven't seen my dear wife and children since Monday morning."

"Of course."

Betsy turned again to setting the table and thought how wonderful it was to see all of these old friends again. She glanced up just in time to see Jonathan drop a kiss on his lovely wife's auburn hair, then embrace her warmly. Their happiness gave her pleasure . . . and a slight pang of jealousy. Best not to look at them.

She placed the last of the forks, knives, and spoons around the plain white plates on the dining room table. Now that Father, Jonathan, and Joshua had arrived, Rose and Cousin Louisa and Tess were bustling in earnest about the kitchen, and Aunt Jessica was out back feeding the children, a job she especially enjoyed.

Betsy cast an appraising glance at the table, centered with a bouquet of colorful wildflowers. Everything seemed ready. As she stood there it suddenly occurred to her that most of the Oak Hill School Board was present: Mr. Wilmington, Joshua, Hugh Fairfax, and Jonathan Chambers. The only one absent was Dr. Adam Buchanan—the one objecting to a woman teacher.

She was still staring at the wildflowers when Rose came in with the roast beef and vegetables and called out, "Won't you all please come to the table?"

"I'm starved," Hugh Fairfax said, coming over, "but not so hungry that I cannot speak with our new schoolteacher. Betsy, may I sit between you and my good wife?"

"Of course, Mr. Fairfax," she replied.

"*Hugh*," he said, his blue eyes sparkling.

"Then Hugh it shall be," Betsy answered, allowing him to seat her at the table. He had what Tess called an Adonis smile and, with his blue eyes and blond hair, was as handsome a man as might be found in Oak Hill, but Betsy suspected that his appearance was not of great import to him since his near death while crossing the jungle through Panama.

He seated his wife, Tess, on his other side with special care.

Tess said to him with her soft southern drawl, "I fear that I misspoke, that I said the wrong thing to Betsy, Hugh . . . about some thinkin' a woman cannot control the bigger boys at school."

Hugh raised his blond brows in regret. "The truth always comes out eventually, but perhaps it might have been better for Betsy not to hear that particular opinion so soon."

Tess leaned forward between them with some difficulty, for she was expecting their first babe in August. Her soft green eyes and heart-shaped face were lovely, overshadowing her plain brown upswept hair, and she looked quite contrite. "I sincerely hope you will forgive me, Betsy."

"How could I not?" Betsy answered. "You are most certainly forgiven." She smiled, and Tess looked greatly relieved.

It was over, forgiven, and hopefully forgotten, Betsy told herself. Yet the thought of not being entirely wanted—albeit by Dr. Buchanan, whom Tess had claimed held a poor opinion of most women—remained.

Across the table, Mr. Wilmington said, "When all is said and done, I am the one who tested you and gave you the teaching position. You have my deepest confidence."

"Thank you," she answered with a nod of appreciation that did not begin to express her gratitude.

Her father, whom Joshua had asked to say grace and was apparently unaware of the problem, asked, "Shall we bow our heads and pray?"

After his prayer and their firm "Amen," Betsy was glad that the talk at the table turned to the latest news in California: the founding of Butte, Amador, Plumas, and Stanislaus counties . . . the discovery of giant red-wooded trees south of Yosemite . . . the instituting of a state fair. Surely if such great strides were made elsewhere, she could manage such a small matter as teaching the school at Oak Hill.

The next morning after breakfast, Benjamin Talbot mounted the chestnut gelding, ready to ride for the stagecoach office in town. He took a long look at his youngest child. He had already made his farewells to her and the rest of them, so now he only added, "God willing, I shall see all of you in July after our camp meeting at *Rancho Verde*."

"Which we shall uphold in prayer," Aunt Jessica replied, and the others promised to do so as well.

"Time to go, Father," Joshua warned from astride his bay.

Wilmington added with wry humor, "The stagecoach awaits neither man nor beast. The drivers' honor seems dependent upon speed, derring-do, and punctuality, if nothing else."

Benjamin smiled and nodded, then nudged his horse forward. Riding along behind Joshua and Wilmington, Benjamin turned again and waved to all of them. His family made a beautiful picture as they stood waving in front of the cabin in the wooded setting.

Jessica was right as usual, he decided as he faced ahead. He must entrust them entirely now to the heavenly Father, not to the care of this earthly vessel. He wondered whether his dear wife, Elizabeth, somehow knew in Glory that their youngest was trying her wings and, if she did, what she might say.

Bits of Scripture flashed through his mind: "Happy is the man that findeth wisdom . . . she is more precious than rubies: and all the things thou canst desire are not to be compared unto her." It was not meant to apply to a wife, for he knew the proverb about a virtuous woman and rubies too, but it seemed at this moment that both applied to Elizabeth, for she'd truly been more precious than rubies in both wisdom and virtue.

Not for the first time, he wondered whether Betsy

blamed herself for her mother's death. He had always tried to make it clear that it was in nowise her fault, but one never knew whether, deep inside, she blamed herself. She wasn't the first babe, nor would she be the last whose birth brought on a dear wife's death. Ah, but if only it hadn't been Elizabeth. . . .

As they galloped around the bend in the trail, he turned and waved back one last time. Betsy, wearing her yellow calico dress, stood out among the rest of them, waving her hand widely in farewell.

He wished Wilmington hadn't mentioned Buchanan's objection to a young woman as a teacher. Unfortunately, the doctor's low view of women was, under the sad circumstances Wilmington had relayed to him, almost understandable. Buchanan might be surprised, however, by a teacher like Betsy, who was determined not only to do her work well, but to do it as unto the Lord.

"I should like to see the school this morning if I may," Betsy said as her father rode away around the bend in the trail.

"I thought you might," Aunt Jessica responded. "I'll help Rose with the dishes and the children, and you go on. You've waited long enough."

"Only if you're certain—"

"I'm certain," Aunt Jessica insisted. "I remember how eager I was to see my first school!"

Rose put in, "Father left me the schoolhouse key since he expects to be in town most of the day. I'll get it now."

Minutes later Betsy set off, the key cool and smooth in her hand. The key to her school, her very first real school, she marveled. Most fittingly, birds sang from the trees as she made her way across the settlement by the dusty path that ran alongside the river valley. It would be no more than a five-minute walk from her cabin to the schoolhouse, she guessed.

Sun filtered through the feathery pine trees and, on the other side of the river, the steep slope of oak, cedar, and pine shimmered in the morning sunshine. Oak Hill was a beautiful place, she thought with buoyant spirits, as beautiful a place as she had ever seen. A mountain crispness filled the air, the river sang its rushing melody down below, and a woodpecker pounded furiously at a nearby tree.

She passed by the picturesque log church, feeling as if she knew it, for Father and others had so often spoken of it. There was no time to stop now; she would be there on Sunday. The schoolhouse was only a few minutes further up the path, which seemed appropriate since the school, like most schools, was supported by the church. If it weren't for Jonathan Chambers's preaching out in the diggings, he'd likely have been called upon to teach school, too, as was common for ministers.

It was a nice log schoolhouse, about as big as she'd expected for twenty-five students. The grounds were bounded to the west by the church and the graveyard behind it, and to the east, by a wooded area. There was a good amount of land, some of it shaded by oak trees and much of it overgrown. In the back were two privies—a crescent moon cut into the door for "Girls" and a round sun cut in the one for "Boys" and, to the side, a pump for water. The first thing to do outside, she decided, was to help the children plant flower seeds. It would be an improvement, too, when the windows were washed.

Lifting the skirt of her yellow calico frock slightly, she went up the step and unlocked the door. A moment later, she walked past the cloakroom and into the chinked log classroom.

It was brighter than she'd expected, for each side wall had two windows. There were four rows of homemade box desks with pew seats, six to a row, the desks in front smaller for the little children. A black stove and wood box stood in the center of the room, and, on the front wall, there was a real slate blackboard, a small flag hanging over it, and a pull-down world map. The cloakroom enclosure was built of plank walls, onto which she could tack the students' papers. Nearby was a water crock with the common dipper and, in a cloakroom corner, a broom and shovel for ashes.

She walked up the middle aisle, examined the old stove, then continued to the high platform teacher's desk in front. This was her new classroom, her very own! The school might be out in the diggings, but the parents were determined that their children be educated and have a proper schoolroom. They had even endorsed a summer term to make up for the time lost by the men teachers who'd left prematurely.

Stepping to the high platform teacher's desk, she took note of the school bell, a quill in the inkstand, a dog-eared dictionary, and a tattered history book. Beside her, a hickory rod pointer stood impaled in the desk's platform. She opened the three drawers and found chalk, paper, a ruler, a grade record book, and other supplies.

As she sorted through them, she began to feel as though someone were watching her. She glanced nervously around at the dirty windows and was taken aback to see a small face peering in from a side window.

"Hello," she said to the child. "Would you like to come into the classroom?"

The little face smiled sweetly, but there was no reply.

Betsy smiled in return and made her way through the room to invite the child in. It was a girl, she was sure, though she must be too young to be a student.

As Betsy tugged the window open, the girl jumped down from the tree stump upon which she'd stood and continued to smile sweetly. Her long, light brown hair fell well below her shoulders, but in front a small braid curved over the top of her head to keep the hair from her face. Her hazel eyes glowed with interest, and she wiped her dusty hands on the brown gingham pinafore covering her dark flowered dress.

"Hello," Betsy said. "I'm Miss Talbot, the new teacher." When the child didn't answer, she added, "Who are you?"

"Mellie," the girl replied.

"Mellie who?"

"Mellie Bu-chanan."

"Oh!" Betsy said, surprised. "Is the doctor your father?"

Mellie nodded, then said with a southern accent, "And Se-lena is my Mama, and Dil-sey and Ru-fus are my friends. I live over yonder." She pointed toward the woods, where a shake roof was barely visible through the trees.

It seemed strange that Adam Buchanan was married, perhaps because so many men in California were not. The ageless observation about all worthwhile men already being married occurred to Betsy, but she quickly put the notion aside. "How old are you, Mellie?"

Using both hands, Mellie held up three fingers, looking exceedingly proud of her accomplishment.

"Three. You do look like you're three years old. When you're five, you can come to school here."

Suddenly Mellie looked behind the schoolhouse, and her smile faded. Her voice faltered as she said, "Hello, Mama."

Betsy stuck her head out the window and, to her astonishment, saw a young barefooted woman in white gauzy nightclothes. Shocked as she was to see someone outdoors in her nightclothes, Betsy realized this was as beautiful a woman as she'd ever seen. Her brown eyes were enormous in the perfect oval of her face, her lips were generous, and her long, dark, wavy hair, parted in the middle, trailed below the shoulders of her white nightdress.

"G—Good morning," Betsy said, "I'm Betsy Talbot, the new schoolteacher."

The woman took no notice. "Mellie," she said to the girl, "you had bettah go home now before there's trouble."

Mellie nodded, her worried eyes riveted on her mother. "Yes, ma'am."

"Miz Selena, honey—" a thin black woman called out as she ran toward them, "I come to bring you and Miz Mellie home! Come along now—"

Selena Buchanan seemed not to hear, and she turned to Betsy instead, her brown eyes growing furious. "As for you, Miss Schoolteacher, don't you evah go neah my husband again!"

Appalled, Betsy protested, "But I scarcely know him!"

"Miz Selena," the black woman interrupted, out of breath, "heah I be to take you and Miz Mellie home. Come on, come along now. Mr. Adam won't like heahin' you out wanderin' in yo' nightclothes again. And, Mellie, you run on home."

"Yes, Dil-sey," Mellie said and started toward the woods.

The black woman said, "Now, Miz Selena, honey—" and started toward her cautiously.

Selena shot the black woman a crafty glance, then tore off like a barefooted sprite toward the woods.

Running wildly, she shrieked back at Betsy, "Don't you evah go neah my husband again!"

4

Betsy stood at the schoolhouse window and gazed dumb-founded at the scene before her. Selena Buchanan ran wildly for the woods, and gray-haired Dilsey chased after her as fast as her bony old body could go. In the meanwhile Mellie, her small shoulders slumped, trudged toward the house in the woods.

"Miz Selena!" Dilsey called out. "Miz Selena, you knows you gittin' me in big trouble, too!"

Selena shrieked something unintelligible and ran all the faster for the woods.

As if that were not sufficiently distressing, Adam Buchanan rode up on his big bay gelding and joined in the chase on horseback, finally dismounting and catching his wife, who struggled wildly with him. The scene seemed stranger yet to Betsy because the doctor, as befitted his profession, was respectfully attired in a black suit. Even when he seemed to have her subdued, Selena managed to tear the wide-brimmed hat from his head and toss it into a thicket.

Betsy heard Dilsey shout, "I be gittin' yer hat, Dr. Buchanan . . . doan you worry 'bout it none!"

Betsy suddenly realized she was staring, and, embarrassed, she turned and hurried from the window. One heard of deranged people, but she had never before seen one. The young doctor was indeed a most unfortunate man.

Betsy stood at the front of the schoolroom, still shaken. As if yesterday's attempted holdup hadn't been enough to unnerve one, now there was an insane woman next door to the schoolhouse! A good thing Father had not witnessed this, too, or he would never have allowed her to remain at Oak Hill.

Staring at her classroom, she reminded herself that no matter what had happened today, she must be ready to teach school tomorrow. She took a calming breath and tried to concentrate on what she should do. The blackboard . . . yes, the children would notice that first, or at least they would after they noticed her.

She found a piece of chalk and carefully printed the alphabet in capital and then in small letters across the top of the board; below, in another row, she wrote the capitals and small letters in her best script. Next she printed the common pledge they had used in the *Rancho Verde* schoolroom:

> *I give my head,*
> *I give my hand,*
> *I give my heart,*
> *To my country.*
> *One God, one country, one flag.*

That completed to her satisfaction, she wrote out the school chores she and Aunt Jessica had discussed:

Morning Chores
> *1) Fill crock with fresh water.*
> *2) Fetch wood for stove and start fire.*
> *3) Open windows to change air.*
> *4) Water school-yard plants*

After-School Chores
> *1) Clap erasers.*

2) Wash blackboard.
3) Carry out ashes from stove.
4) Sweep floor.

Finishing that, she glanced out the window and was grateful to see no further sign of the drama that had unfolded next door. Adam Buchanan's big bay gelding, however, still grazed at the edge of the school yard. Most likely, the doctor had taken his wife into the house. Betsy hoped he did not have to keep her locked up.

She returned to her desk and the nearby shelves to sort through the supplies and the books. They had a good quantity of readers and spellers, and probably sufficient arithmetic books. She must make school as interesting as possible using only these books and her ingenuity, she told herself, and began to make notes.

A *school project* . . . . Yes, that would draw the entire class together, particularly in a classroom with a great range of ages. Perhaps they could do a musicale or a pageant for the end of the summer term.

Engrossed, she scarcely heard the classroom door open. A deep male voice broke her concentration. "Excuse me, Miss Talbot."

Adam Buchanan walked around the desks toward her, his black suit slightly dusty, his wide-brimmed hat in hand.

"Hello . . . I—I didn't realize—" Flustered at seeing him so soon after the great drama with his wife that had taken place outdoors, Betsy stopped.

He nodded politely, then turned to study what she'd written on the blackboard. "I see you have already put up the chores for the children," he said rather stiffly.

"Yes. I hope you approve of them."

"I do," he said, nodding as he read. He turned to her, his hazel eyes serious. "And I have brought you the school

79

board's rules for teachers. Did you have teacher's rules at your home school?"

"No, we did not—"

"As I suspected. That's precisely why we want you to have them before school starts here. We've learned through hard experience that it's best for the teacher to know our rules from the beginning. If you'll read them now and sign this receipt saying you agree to them, I shall be on my way to town."

"Yes, of course." She accepted the sheet from him and was surprised to find her hand trembling slightly. She read:

RULES FOR TEACHERS

1) The teacher will fill lamps and clean chimneys each day.

2) The teacher will bring in a bucket of water for each day's session.

3) The teacher will make pens carefully. You may whittle nibs to the individual taste of the pupils.

4) After the school day, the teacher may spend the remaining time reading the Bible or other good books.

5) A woman teacher who marries or engages in unseemly conduct will be dismissed.

6) A teacher who performs the work faithfully and without fault for five years will be given an increase of pay, providing the Board of Education approves.

Five years! she thought. Did she wish still to be teaching in five years? Mr. Wilmington had been glad enough to have a teacher and had mentioned little about work beyond her three-month probationary contract, other than if it went well, the board would undoubtedly ask her to stay.

"Any questions?" Adam Buchanan asked.

"Yes," she replied, then decided to evade the matter of five years. Instead, she said distractedly, "With regard to number four, 'After the school day, the teacher may spend the remaining time reading the Bible or other good books.'"

"That causes a difficulty?"

"A slight one. I shall return home from school and, after I have corrected the children's lessons, I shall help my aunt with the cooking and housekeeping. I do read the Bible daily and shall teach it, but I do not know how much time there will be each evening to read additional books."

His hazel eyes sized her up again, then relented slightly. "We adapted the rules for you from those made for the previous teachers, who were men and sometimes inclined to spend their evenings in dissipation with the other miners. Nonetheless, I should like to keep it in as a reminder that you must continue to stay ahead of the best scholars."

"Of course," she replied. "And are there true scholars?"

His lips turned up only slightly between his dark mustache and short beard. "We feel several are very hopeful. We would like our students to be qualified for acceptance at the Eastern preparatory schools or at the college at Oakland that is now under discussion."

"I should hope so, too," she replied. Fortunately the Eastern preparatory schools would teach scholars to understand the classical Latin authors and to speak true Latin in verse and prose, and, of course, to decline the paradigms of nouns and verbs in the Greek tongue.

"So, will you sign this receipt?" he asked with a trace of impatience.

"Yes, of course. I do hope, however, that our definitions of 'seemly conduct' for the teacher coincide." Not daring to look at him after that remark, she accepted the sheet of paper. He had a fresh cut on his wrist, she noted. Most likely his wife had scratched him during their tussle, for it was a single mark, not as though he had been scratched by brambles.

She took the paper to her desk and found a well-cut quill and ink. While he watched, she signed in her neatest penmanship, *Elizabeth Anna Talbot*.

Handing it over to him, she said, "I understood that Mr. Wilmington was the superintendent of the Oak Hill Board of Education."

"He is," Adam Buchanan replied. "But I am in charge of teacher rules, regulations, and conduct."

"I see."

She wondered whether he'd acquired that particular position at the forming of the Oak Hill School or whether he'd demanded it upon learning that a woman had been hired. She was almost tempted to say he was not so successful with the conduct of his own wife, but that would be cruel. Instead she said, "I shall endeavor never to give you grounds for complaint."

"I am glad to hear it, Miss Talbot."

He struck her as a hard man, not at all the same man who had so gently cared for Yank Stevens's wounded hand.

"Are you matrimonially inclined?" he asked.

Matrimonially inclined? her mind echoed. The silence between them lengthened. She managed at last, "I am not contemplating marriage, if that is what you mean."

His hazel eyes studied her. "Never?"

She resented his scrutiny, and she answered as evenly as possible, "'Never' is an exceedingly long time, Dr. Buchanan."

"As is 'forever,'" he said both harshly and reflectively, and she wondered if he referred to his own wedding vows. Doubtless he was no longer "matrimonially inclined" himself, and perhaps did not care for women at all. Why, oh why, did she have to get such a man on the school board?

Seeing that he still expected an answer, she repeated, "I shall endeavor never to give you grounds for complaint."

"I hope so, Miss Talbot. I most sincerely hope so." And with that, he nodded and strode from the schoolroom.

Through the window she saw him mount his horse, wheel away, and ride off toward town. She was unsure whom she pitied most—Selena, Mellie, or Adam Buchanan.

At noontime, as she walked back to her cabin, Betsy glanced toward the woods that surrounded the Buchanan house, but there was no sign of anyone about, and she wondered whether poor little Mellie was usually confined to the house.

Minutes later, Betsy stepped into her own log cabin and called, "Aunt Jessica, I'm here!"—for it did not yet seem like home. The faint smell of fried chicken, however, was inviting, and in the chinked log parlor, their half-empty trunks and familiar belongings were scattered around the room.

"Everything arrived by freight wagon right after you left, so I set to work," her aunt replied from their bedroom. "A good thing we shipped extra household belongings. Look at the progress I've made."

Joining her in their bedroom, Betsy marveled at the sight of lengths of pale green fabric already cut and lying over their beds, ready to be stitched together for coverlets. Matching fabric was set out by the windows for making curtains. "You surely have made progress, but you mustn't wear yourself out with the work here. I want to do my share."

Her aunt protested. "I would be lost without something to do."

"Aunt Jessica—"

Undaunted, her aunt replied, "I would like to look back

at my life as a good day's work to the glory of God. You know what Luther said, 'A dairymaid can milk cows to the glory of God.'"

"But you are not a dairymaid," Betsy pointed out.

"I could still milk a cow if need be," Aunt Jessica replied with a smile that made the wrinkles at the corners of her eyes move up for an instant. As usual, she wore her gray-white hair in a knot at the nape of her neck, but shorter hairs had escaped and curled above her head like a fuzzy halo. "In any case, you know what Luther meant. Anyone can do his work to the glory of God, and thus find fulfillment and joy in it. And then there's the old proverb, 'Work won't kill, but worry will.' "

"You do have a great deal of strength," Betsy agreed, then added wryly, "and a wealth of philosophical backing for your views."

Aunt Jessica gave a laugh. "I am praying for strength right up to the day I depart for Glory! Now, do you think this will be too much green in the room?"

Betsy eyed the cloth set out in the small log bedroom. "No. It's soft, a lovely subdued shade. I do believe it's my favorite of all greens."

"It goes well with log walls and country views. I couldn't abide red calico curtains, not with all of California covered with it. The mill owners of New England seem to believe Californians will use nothing but red calico. One wonders what they must think of us, though I'm not sure I care to know!"

Betsy laughed. It was said that all of the windows and walls of California's saloons and gambling establishments were covered with red calico, not to mention the windows and walls of private houses.

As they stepped into the parlor, the smells from the cookstove grew stronger.

"Did you fry chicken, too?"

"No. Rose invited us over, but I couldn't wait to unpack the trunks, so she and Louisa insisted on sending us some of their dinner."

Betsy peered into the bowls. Fried chicken, potato salad, warm biscuits, a jar of pickles, and another of honey. "A good way to begin our cooking here," Betsy remarked appreciatively. "I'm famished. I'll set the table."

"Rose and Louisa offered to help with the sewing," Aunt Jessica said. "We'll soon have everything in order."

Betsy set out their borrowed white plates on the table. "We'll have to buy dishes and glasses at Joshua's Mercantile."

"You will eventually want to have your own things anyhow," her aunt replied, busying herself with the food.

Betsy decided not to reply, for her aunt's remark was fraught with implications it seemed better not to discuss. "I fear that by coming here, you will simply have transferred the responsibilities of one household for those of another."

"Perhaps. But I enjoy it," her aunt admitted. "I enjoyed teaching in that season of my life, and I've enjoyed raising children and keeping house. In retrospect, I see that the Lord has given me the desires of my heart. I pray He will give you yours."

"I surely do, too," Betsy agreed. She was uncertain, however, whether her desires included teaching for five years or more. Perhaps she would dislike teaching in a real school.

Their rustic plank table and benches were from Louisa and Jonathan Chambers's veranda, but they served well in the parlor for now. "We shall have to get our own furniture," Betsy said.

"All in good time," Aunt Jessica replied. "I do believe we have more than enough of the green fabric for some matching tablecloths and cushions for the benches."

Betsy shook her head at her aunt. "And I do believe you could transform a livery stable into a charming house if you had enough cloth."

After they'd sat down to lunch and said grace, Aunt Jessica said, "Tell me about your morning."

Betsy began with the school, then found herself telling about the Buchanans.

"That poor woman . . . and child . . . and man," Aunt Jessica said, "not to mention the serving woman who takes care of them. I wonder if there isn't something we can do."

"I don't know . . . . I don't think we should intrude."

"Let's pray about it . . . and pray about God using us here in Oak Hill."

That night Betsy rolled from side to side in bed, thinking what she might tell the children at school the next morning. She could quote from the great thinkers. Aristotle had said, "The roots of education are bitter, but the fruit is sweet," which could be applied to the monotony of memorization or to conjugating verbs. Francis Bacon wrote, "Reading maketh a full man, conference a ready man, and writing an exact man," but the younger children would not understand that. Galileo had said, "You cannot teach a man anything; you can only help him to find it within himself."

For her own teaching purposes, she thought of Augustine's "A free curiosity is more effective in learning than a rigid discipline." On the other hand, Aunt Jessica advised, "Never let much time pass between catching a culprit and administering the proper punishment."

She must find the perfect method to suit these children.

Betsy awakened the next morning so disquieted that she nearly sprang from the bed. *Lord, help me through this day,* she prayed as she hurried to wash and dress. Fortunately, she had laid out her rose sprig muslin dress the night before, so at least there was no decision to make about what to wear.

On the way to the schoolhouse, she felt all aflutter and took scant notice of the birds twittering in the trees. As she unlocked the door, however, she looked up and saw a great eagle flying high above, circling over the forest and the river, then wheeling around again. At the sight of it, she began to feel reassured, and she remembered the verse from Scripture: "They that wait upon the Lord shall renew their strength; they shall mount up with wings as eagles." She would stand on that promise.

Before going into the classroom, she glanced at the woods toward the Buchanan house, but there was no sign of anyone. It seemed to her that she was the only one outdoors in all of Oak Hill.

By eight o'clock, however, she was no longer alone. Children filled the school yard, and a few peeked into the classroom at her, then quickly closed the door. She glanced around the chinked log classroom. Everything was as ready as it would ever be. At eight-twenty, she took the school bell from her desk and went out to ring it.

"A lady teacher!" one of the girls exclaimed.

"Ain't that what I told ye?" another replied. "Guess they're givin' up on miners like them others teachin'."

"She don't look too strict," one of the boys said. "Not like Mr. Baehr or Mr. Volk."

"Guess we'll see, won't we?" another remarked.

"Guess we will at that."

Betsy rang the bell, watching their reactions. The smaller children turned from their play and started for the schoolhouse immediately. The middle-sized ones were not quite as prompt. The older children reacted with even less alacrity, as though eagerness might be seen as a sign of childishness.

"Come along now, students!" she called out. "It's our first day of school. Let's get off to a good start." She fervently hoped that discipline would not be a problem, particularly on this first day.

The children trooped through the door, putting their tinware dinner boxes in the cloakroom. As they started into the classroom she said, "You may take your old seats. Girls on this side of the middle aisle, boys on the other. If there are new students, please sit near others your age for now."

She counted noses. Twenty-one students, all in varied stages of cleanliness. Four of them wore no shoes.

Once she had them settled, she strode to the front of the room and led the Pledge of Allegiance. As soon as the children sat down, she knew she couldn't say a single one of the impressive things she'd thought of last night in bed. She stood before them with her very first case of stage fright. For what seemed a full minute the whole class stared at her silently, and she stared back at them. The only sounds in the log classroom were the squeakings of the desk seats.

"Well," she finally said, "let us begin with names. Mine is Miss Talbot. And now if each of you will stand and tell us your name—"

"Where do we start, Miss Talbot?" a girl in the front row asked earnestly. She had the look of a sensible little woman already, perhaps because her light brown braids were wound up on top of her head.

"Why not with you, in the front row? And please tell me which reader you are in as well."

The girl stood up like a brave soldier. "Tilda Stoddard. I can't read yet."

"Perhaps you will soon, Tilda," Betsy said, then nodded at the curly-headed blond twins who sat together at the next desk. "Next, please."

The twins stood up from either side of the desk, dimples dancing in their cheeks. "Rachel Jurgen . . . and I can't read yet, either."

"Kendall Jurgen," the boy said, scratching hard under his curly locks. "I can't read."

"Well, won't we have a lot of new readers among us!" Betsy told them. "Just wait until you see how wonderful it is to read."

"Ha!" one of the older boys shot at her from the back of the room.

She glanced up quickly, but the older boys' faces were pictures of innocence. She turned to the next child, who was already standing—a dark blond girl with trusting eyes.

"My name is Lucinda Webster," she said. "I can read Mama's Primer."

"Good," Betsy replied, knowing that would be *The Mother's Primer*, a point-to-the-picture and sing-the-word booklet for teaching little ones. "It will help you a great deal with reading."

A black-haired, blue-eyed girl stood up next. "I'm Mary O'Connor. I'm in the First Reader."

Lord, help me to remember all of their names! Betsy prayed, then went to her desk and jotted the names down with accompanying notes about each child's appearance and reading level. Best not to ask ages, since it would make matters all the more embarrassing for older children who were in the lower readers.

There were four children in the second reader, and she guessed their ages as seven to eleven: Claudia Orr, Ruby Jurgen, Hans Schmidt, and Susanna Webster. And there were seven middle-grade children: Susanna Tucker, Garnett Jurgen, Farrell Williamson, Ada and Hiram Fletcher, and Alberta and Emory Orr. Three of the older children were absent, and someone piped up with amusement, "They want us to try you out first!"

Betsy gave them a small smile and continued with the others. The older children present included Spencer Tucker, Philip Pierson, Wilma and Wanda Stoddard, and George Jurgen.

To everyone's amusement, George pronounced, "I'm named fer George Washington, our first president, who cut down a cherry tree and never lied and was first in peace and first in war and first in the hearts of his countrymen—"

"A fine godly man," Betsy interrupted, and then, to quiet the others' giggles, added, "I hope you will be as fine a man as the father of our country." She saw that George was about to put in another humorous remark, so she quickly said, "Did you know that George Washington rose at five every morning because he had a seven-mile walk to school? Instead of complaining, he made a game of surveying the route. His first drawn plans as a student surveyor were the various trails to school."

She smiled at George Jurgen, then at the rest of them. "George Washington was a fine example of all things coming together for good to those who love the Lord and are called according to His purpose."

She stepped to her desk for her Bible. "And now that we have met each other, let us turn to the Scriptures. Who will ask God to illumine our reading of His book today?"

Wilma Stoddard raised her hand, and Betsy was glad to remember her name. "Yes, Wilma, will you pray, please?"

Both Wilma and her sister—yes, Wanda—were dark and thick featured, and had a stolidness about them, almost as if they were slow-witted. Yet Wilma prayed quite nicely.

"Thank you, Wilma. Now I shall read Psalm 1." She opened her Bible and read with firmness, "Blessed is the man think it is likely meant as an introduction to the whole Book of Psalms. The psalmist sharply contrasts the two ways of life, interpreting them both with his eyes on the ultimate fate of righteous and sinful man."

"Yes, very good, Spencer," Betsy said, impressed. This, perhaps, was one of the scholars to whom Adam Buchanan had alluded. A young man who analyzed as carefully as that would keep her on her toes.

She turned to the entire class. "God would have us stay on the righteous path of life, and so let us stay to it this day, for we know not what the morrow brings." She was surprised to hear herself put it so quaintly, almost as her father might. "And now we shall discuss the morning chores I have written on the blackboard, and the class rules, as well."

George Jurgen said, without so much as raising his hand or standing, "We didn't have rules with Mr. Volk."

The class murmured their agreement, and Betsy said, "It would be difficult to run a classroom or any other kind of a community without rules." She saw that Spencer Tucker had raised his hand. "Yes, Spencer?"

"We had rules, but Mr. Volk called them customs. In the end, it was the same thing," Spencer said and sat down.

"Thank you," Betsy said. "We shall have rules in my classroom, most of which are simply common courtesy. One is that you may not speak unless you raise your hand and are called upon." She eyed George Jurgen as strictly as she could and added, "Is that understood?"

He looked down, but most of the other children nodded earnestly.

When they had finished discussing the chores and the rules, she said, "And now I shall call some of you older students forward to help me pass out the readers, spellers, and other books." She put the younger ones to work printing that walketh not in the counsel of the ungodly, nor standeth in the way of sinners, nor sitteth in the seat of the scornful. But his delight is in the law of the Lord; and in his law doth he meditate day and night. And he shall be like a tree planted by the rivers of water, that bringeth forth his fruit in his season . . . ."

Lord, let me bring forth fruit from this classroom in this three-month season, she prayed as she read on. ". . . his leaf also shall not wither; and whatsoever he doeth shall prosper. The ungodly are not so: but are like the chaff which the wind driveth away . . . ."

When she came to the last verse about the Lord knowing the way of the righteous and that the way of the ungodly would perish, she was grateful that the children listened with respect.

"Do any of you have questions or wish to comment on this psalm?" she asked them when she'd finished.

From the back of the room, Philip Pierson, a big red-headed youth, said, "Mr. Volk, our last teacher, he didn't care for reading Scripture."

"I am sorry to hear that," Betsy replied. Perhaps that was why Mr. Wilmington had questioned her so thoroughly on the matter of Christianity being taught in school.

Someone whispered, "He keered more for his bottle," and the older children laughed.

"We are discussing the first psalm," Betsy pointed out firmly. She was glad to see Spencer Tucker, a freckle-faced youth with sandy hair and an intelligent mien, raise his hand. She guessed that he might be sixteen, only three years younger than she. "Yes, Spencer?"

"The first psalm tells us there are two ways one can go, one of life and one of death, and there is a great difference between the two ways," he said with quiet deliberation. "I their names and the middle students at penmanship, copy-ing alphabetized sentences from Father's old book of good sayings that she wrote on the blackboard.

> *(A) Affectation is odious.*
> *(B) Banish evil thoughts.*
> *(C) Cease to do evil.*

By mid-morning recess everything seemed well organ-ized, and it appeared that she could manage. Outside, the children played a game called "darebase," which included galloping wildly from one base to the next when the chance offered and trying not to be tagged out. In the meantime she wrote on the blackboard the subjects in order of importance: reading, arithmetic, writing, spelling, grammar, history, geography, and literature.

When she went out to ring the recess bell, a new student had arrived on the playground.

"It's that Clyde Munroe," a girl said as the children trooped back into the classroom.

"Likely drunk again," someone whispered. "Don't know why he troubles himself to come."

Dark and hulking, Clyde Munroe looked more like an Oregon lumberjack than a schoolboy, and his hooded gray eyes were full of petulance as he nodded at Betsy. He said nothing, but simply stood there in the classroom as the other students sat down at their desks.

"Good morning," Betsy said to him. "My name is Miss Talbot. Won't you please be seated?" She indicated a desk in the back of the room. He nodded again and sat down at the box desk, his knees nearly up to his chest.

"I don't believe I know your name," she said.

He grunted. "Clyde Munroe."

"It is a pleasure to meet you, Clyde. Perhaps you don't know, but school begins at eight-thirty."

"I know," he said.

"Good. Please be here promptly tomorrow." She made her way to the front of the room thinking that he did smell of spirits. What brought him to school? she wondered. She would have to find out.

She tried to sound businesslike as she said, "Every day before first recess we shall study arithmetic. From recess until noon, we shall have history and geography—history one day, geography the next. The first half of this term, we'll have history twice a week, and the last half we'll change and have geography twice. Is that clear?"

Heads nodded, but the younger students looked perplexed.

She added, "Of course, those of you who are just beginning to read will have special reading exercises at that time."

Aunt Jessica had told of old-time teachers who'd taught as many as a hundred pupils, conducting two reading classes at once while keeping an eye on another class at the board and another doing seat work. Meanwhile, those not having classes were supposed to be studying, or perhaps one of the older "star pupils" would be hearing another group over in one corner of the building. Betsy hoped, now that she had such a spread of ages, albeit only twenty-two students, she could manage the teaching as well as those old-time teachers had.

Before she felt they had made a good start, noon was upon them, and she trusted that her ineptitude was not obvious. On the other hand, she was appalled at the amount of ignorance she had already uncovered. Very few of the students could read as they really should. How could they learn if they couldn't read?

She said, "We shall all wash our hands before we eat."

Several looked at their hands and said they weren't dirty

or that they only washed when they ate at home, but she lined them all up at the pump just the same. "We shall all wash our hands," she repeated, "and then we shall sit in small groups in the shade while we eat."

Once their hands were washed, they settled in the shade of the oak trees, Betsy with a group of the youngest children. Most of them had brought beans and bread, and made fast work of eating them, scarcely talking at all.

When everyone had finished, Betsy said, "It's too hot to play running games now. Do any of you know how to play 'Give Me a Wave'? It's a form of hide-and-seek, but less strenuous."

Enough of them knew how to play to teach the others quickly. As they played, it occurred to her that Selena Buchanan or Mellie might watch them, and she glanced toward the woods by their house. There was no sign of anyone. She wondered if Dilsey had orders to keep them inside.

At length, Betsy gave Alberta Orr the privilege of ringing the five-minute school bell—a signal for everyone to get ready to go in. Alberta flipped back her dirty blond pigtails and beamed. "Thank you, Miss Talbot!"

When they returned to the classroom, Betsy asked Philip Pierson and Farrell Williamson to open the windows. "Every day after lunch," she said, "I shall read selections from the Bible. Today we will begin with 'The Garden of Eden' and tomorrow we will have 'Noah and the Flood.'"

"Mr. Volk read us *Gulliver's Travels*," George said from the back of the classroom.

Betsy had mixed feelings about *Gulliver's Travels*, since Jonathan Swift, the author, seemed to think man nothing more than an ape rather than made in the image of God. "Just because an author or anyone else has a great talent does not mean he is using it for good. It is the kind of person behind the talent that is important," she explained, hoping that they understood. "It is important for everyone to learn to be spiritually discerning. For now I shall stick with the Bible. And you must also learn to stick with our rule about not speaking until you have permission, George."

"Yes, ma'am," he mumbled without conviction.

The boys chuckled, and Betsy feared there would be trouble with George eventually. Perhaps with Clyde Munroe, too, for he sat slumped at his desk like a great resentful hulk.

The afternoon did not seem to be passing as quickly. Mr. Wilmington arrived just after the mid-afternoon recess and sat down at a desk in the back of the room with the older students.

"It is a pleasure to have you visit us today," she said, and told the children, "Mr. Wilmington is the superintendent of our school, as most of you must know." She asked him, "Is there anything you wish to say to our students?"

"Thank you, Miss Talbot," he replied, rising to his feet. "I only wish to say that I expect you students to mind our new schoolmistress. Attending school is a privilege, and I have already told Miss Talbot that she is not required to keep troublemakers here. Education is a conquest, not a bequest. It must be achieved, and I wish to sit here and see if you are trying to achieve it this afternoon."

Having said that, he sat down. Fortunately, it was during spelling and reading, and all went well during his half-hour visit.

At four o'clock, Betsy was exhausted and glad to hear the last "Good-bye, Teacher," "Good-bye, Miss Talbot." She felt as toilworn as if she had been digging up a garden all day, and wondered if she had accomplished as much. Was anyone leaving the schoolhouse any better or wiser than when he or she had arrived in the morning? She certainly hoped so.

As she straightened up her desk, she sensed the presence of someone at the window again. She glanced up and, not surprisingly, saw Mellie Buchanan peeking in over the sill.

"Hello, Mellie," Betsy said through the open window. "Won't you come in?"

Mellie's eyes widened, and she must have jumped down from the tree stump, for she disappeared from sight.

When Betsy arrived at the window, Mellie was running wildly toward the woods. It was all too reminiscent of her mother's attempted escape yesterday, only this afternoon Adam Buchanan was not present. For a moment she thought perhaps she should follow Mellie, then she saw Dilsey meet her small charge at the edge of the woods.

What a strange situation—a distraught woman like Selena Buchanan living next door to the schoolhouse. It was a worrisome state of affairs, to put it mildly.

5

Although the next day at school went well, and there were no further encounters with Mellie, Selena, or Adam Buchanan, Betsy was grateful for the weekend. Saturday morning she sat at the table, spread honey on a piece of hot corn bread, and told Aunt Jessica, "I'm eager to explore the town at last. Is there anything else for my shopping list?"

"Green thread for the bed coverlets and the curtains," her aunt replied. "Of all things for me to forget!"

"Consider it done," Betsy said and took a bite of the corn bread. It was delicious, as always.

"I suppose I forgot in my excitement about seeing the town yesterday," her aunt explained. Joshua had driven her with him in the morning to get most of their provisions, and he would take Betsy today. "As if forgetting the thread weren't bad enough, I forgot to tell you that Lucius Alden found work in town as the stagecoach agent. He's going to work a few hours each day for Joshua at the Mercantile, as well. And, best of all, he's half-accepted my invitation for Sunday dinner after church."

"Well, Aunt Jessica!" Betsy teased. "Now that is progress!"

Her aunt shook her head with amusement. "You know very well it isn't anything like you are hinting. I expect he'd like a home-cooked dinner, though, and perhaps a sense of family. His wife died young, and it's been a lonely life for him in some ways, though he does get on well with people. In any case, I'd already invited Rose and Joshua and the Chambers family for dinner."

"And, pray tell, how did you learn so much about Lucius?"

Aunt Jessica gave her a guilty smile. "He invited me to have coffee with him at the restaurant yesterday after he'd gotten the stagecoach under way."

"And you 'forgot' to tell me all of that?" Betsy returned with a laugh. "I daresay I'd better keep an eye on you two!"

"Now, Betsy, you know better than that," her aunt said, half-pleased. "On a more serious note, the Lord has led me to pray for Lucius, and I'm sure there's a reason behind it."

Hearing horses clip-clop and a buggy rattle to a stop, Betsy downed a last swallow of coffee. "That must be Joshua now." Grabbing her reticule, she started for the front door. "I'll be home at midday."

"Don't rush on my account," Aunt Jessica called after her.

Outside, morning sunlight filtered through the trees, and Betsy's big redheaded brother was just stepping down from the black buggy. A grin spread below his luxurious mustache. "Not eager to see the town, are you?"

"I am," she admitted. "We've lived out in the country so long, I can't believe we're near a town. Aunt Jessica thinks we could walk there in fifteen minutes, but I'm glad to ride in with you the first time."

"It's usually safe enough now for a woman to come to town during daylight," Joshua said, helping her into the buggy. "Last year or the year before, I don't think I'd have let you explore it alone. The more raucous element has moved on to what they hope are richer gold strikes elsewhere."

"Thank goodness for that," she replied, sitting down on the thinly padded black leather buggy seat. She glanced toward the cabin, which was beginning to seem more like home. To the left of the front door, away from the huge over-shadowing cedar tree, short stalks already protruded from the soil. "Aunt Jessica has planted her rose and lilac roots."

"They do follow us about, don't they?" Joshua laughed as he climbed up into the driver's seat.

"As has Aunt Jessica, though I sometimes feel as if we don't quite deserve her."

"My sentiments exactly," he agreed. He called out to the horses, and they started off into the morning sunshine, the fresh smells of pine and springtime all around them.

The buggy bumped along on the road, passing the church and the schoolhouse before curving through the woods near the almost hidden Buchanan house.

"Rose tells me you had an encounter with Selena Buchanan," Joshua remarked.

"Yes. I do wish I had been forewarned."

"We should have told you, but everyone was so excited about your arrival . . . and, then, Selena usually stays inside. Adam claims southern women stay out of the sun for fear of ruining their complexions, but we have our own ideas about her, poor woman."

"Have you met her?"

"Only seen her at a distance, but well enough to see she's a beauty," he replied. "She never comes into town or to church. Her maid, Dilsey, comes to the Mercantile for the family's needs, and I expect Adam or their manservant, Rufus, tends to the rest of it. I suppose Mellie's old enough now to take an interest in the schoolchildren, and that's what brought your encounter to pass. I doubt there'll be further trouble."

"I don't know," Betsy said. "The first day after school, Mellie was peering in the schoolroom window again. I invited her in, but she ran home."

"You don't say—"

"I do. She wasn't there yesterday, however. She probably creeps out when they think she's napping."

"Most likely," Joshua replied. "Now that I'm a father, I see how resourceful and fast on their feet children can be. Strange how I never took much note of that before."

Betsy had to smile. "Sometimes I can't believe you are not only settled, but the father of two children!"

He gave her a brotherly smile, then returned his attention to the horses and the wooded road. "I'm still growing accustomed to it myself. It took me longer than most to find what I was searching for, or perhaps I should say *for whom* I was searching. Nonetheless, I finally found Him . . . and contentment." He grinned. "Seek and ye shall find."

"Indeed! It *is* a promise."

Betsy recalled the years when the entire family wondered if Joshua would ever marry—and then how they all hoped he would marry Rose Wilmington, whom he had accompanied around the Horn by clipper ship. He was an unusual shopkeeper, educated at Harvard and a former supercargo for Wainwright and Talbot Shipping—a position that had made him a world traveler.

"What's the trouble with Selena?" Betsy asked.

"They lost a babe in childbirth on the covered-wagon trek to California two years ago, and she's been unwell ever since. People from their wagon train say she was standoffish from the beginning, though—considered herself better than the rest and made no friends. Of course, it wasn't unusual for people to become unbalanced during the the wagon treks."

"I remember. For a while, we were deeply concerned

about Abby and Horace Litmer, the schoolmaster from Independence."

Joshua nodded with understanding as they rode along. "Both Rose and Louisa Chambers have tried to befriend Selena, but she'll have nothing to do with them. She claims to be either too sick or too occupied with her music."

"Her music?"

"She was trained as a concert violinist," Joshua explained. "Adam said she was considered a great talent, a child prodigy, and gave concerts in Europe."

"She must feel greatly thwarted not to use such a talent here," Betsy reflected.

"I can't imagine such frustration," he replied. "Rose is so content with the cabin and the children . . . and her sewing."

"But Rose is a different person."

"Yes . . . for which I am most grateful," Joshua said.

"I expect I'd feel thwarted myself if I couldn't teach, and I can imagine Abby's unhappiness if she were deprived of her art. Still, I don't see why Selena can't play the violin for herself or her family, or for others."

Joshua shrugged. Betsy put the thought aside as they rode on, coming out of the woods alongside the river, which shimmered far below. "It's a beautiful place," she observed. "Look at the eagle circling overhead. I saw him Thursday morning on the way to school. It was somehow reassuring."

"A golden eagle," Joshua replied, looking up with her. "They live all along the Pacific Slope."

The eagle circled lower and lower over the trees. "He's dark brown, not golden," she observed.

"They're named for the golden brown feathers on the back of their heads. I see him most mornings when I ride in to town. He lives across the river. If you look carefully, you can see his nest in that lightning-struck pine on the ridge."

Betsy squinted across the river valley and saw the dead pine and the eagle's nest near the top of the tree.

Joshua said, "I often think of him looking down on us as if he sees all, as if he might somehow understand the human condition . . . a bit like God."

"I always think of that Scripture in Isaiah when I see eagles," commented Betsy. " 'They that wait upon the Lord shall renew their strength; they shall mount up with wings as eagles. . . .' "

"That hadn't occurred to me," Joshua replied.

Betsy watched the great bird circling in silent flight against the blue sky.

The scenery remained beautiful, even as the first few houses of town and the livery stable and blacksmith's came into view. Other buggies and wagons bumped along the dusty street. There were miners astride their horses and mules, and townspeople on foot. They all eyed Betsy with interest, and she nodded politely. The streets' names were printed on wooden signs—River Street and now Main Street as the horses turned left on the first intersecting dirt road.

"Aha, we live just off River Street," she remarked.

"Indeed, we do. But in the settlement everyone calls it 'the Oak Hill road.' It's only received an official appellation in our great metropolis."

She laughed. "If Oak Hill's roads are to receive official appellations, perhaps we should call our section River Road, or Wilmington Road since Rose and her father were the original settlers."

"I'll take it up with the city fathers," Joshua replied with amusement. He slowed the horses to an easy walk as they approached the business district. "And now we have before us the metropolis of Oak Hill."

Betsy took in their surroundings with growing pleasure.

She smiled at his old name for her. "You haven't called me that in years."

"We haven't lived in the same neighborhood for years either, not since Missouri when you were a little girl."

She gave a laugh. "I'm grateful you realize that I've grown up!"

Farther along Main Street, men had hammered together three new business establishments, then came a small white clapboard house bearing a doctor's shingle—*Adam Buchanan, Physician*. Beyond that were other private houses, some with signs that said *Laundry Taken In* or *Boarding*. Off on the side streets, more houses stood among the trees, and there were plenty of lines of demarcation: picket fences, hitching posts, outbuildings at rear property lines, newly planted vegetable gardens, and hedgerows of flowers.

At length, Joshua hitched the wagon in front of the Mercantile. "I'd better get to work," he said, "but I think Lucius Alden opening up for me mornings is going to make life easier. It's difficult to find permanent help here."

Betsy accompanied him into the Mercantile. It was a good-sized establishment that smelled of everything from onions to hemp and was stocked with foodstuffs, clothing, household effects, and even gold mining supplies. Behind the main wooden counter, Lucius Alden served customers.

When Lucius saw her, his face wrinkled up into a merry smile, making him look as leprechaun-like as she remembered. "Miss Talbot, ye are a ray of sunshine, if I may say so. Makes the mornin' seem brighter, jest seein' ye here."

"Thank you, Mr. Alden. The feeling is entirely mutual!"

He chuckled and returned his attention to his stout woman customer, who looked interested in Betsy. She was dark-haired, and her frown made it clear that she brooked no nonsense. "You the schoolmarm?" she asked brusquely.

There must have been twenty or thirty buildings fr
boardwalks that were old enough to have become w
but not warped. First came the stagecoach and expres
then the Oak Hill Hotel, Hugh Fairfax's bank, a restau
butcher shop, a law office, Joshua's Mercantile, a new
office, a Chinese grocery, and two saloons, both of v
were still closed.

"I like the look of it much better than I do San Frai
co," she decided.

"It's rustic, but also a good deal more manageabl
Joshua replied. "The worst of the lawlessness seems to
coming to an end."

"Only the occasional stagecoach holdup?!"

He chuckled. "It's not entirely settled yet, and the state
laws require some adjusting. For one, the death penalty for
robbery and grand larceny has caused new problems. Hanging men for stealing means there's no greater penalty for
murder, and now we have more murders committed by robbers to prevent identification or pursuit."

"Then Adam Buchanan's rescuing us is to be even more
appreciated."

"Indeed!" Joshua said. "I am most grateful to him."

"As am I. Do you have vigilantes here?"

"We did, but to a lesser extent than in San Francisco."

"And what do you think of them?"

Joshua shrugged and said, "To my chagrin, I'm agreeing
with Father more and more often lately. Vigilante commit-
tees are a lesser evil . . . the result of unrestrained lawlessness,
but they often attract men full of moral self-delusion and
righteous sadism."

"It's difficult to imagine such problems—or such
in a quiet town like this," Betsy observed.

"Unfortunately, Little Sister, they're everywh

"Yes, I am."

"I'm Clyde Munroe's mother," the woman said.

The dark-haired, hulking young man resembled his mother, Betsy thought. "It's a pleasure to meet you," she said quite truthfully, for at the very least it was interesting to meet the mother of a student. "I hope Clyde will enjoy school this term."

"Enjoyin' it ain't the question," his mother returned sharply. "I expect Clyde to learn. I ain't takin' in washin' fer 'im to jist sit there and hold air between 'is ears. Jist 'cause I married beneath meself don't mean he's got to take after his old man who's disappeared fer easier diggin's."

Amazed by the woman's forthrightness, Betsy drew a deep breath. "I hope Clyde will learn, too, Mrs. Munroe. You have my promise that I shall do my best to teach him to his full capacity."

Mrs. Munroe took up her purchases and started for the door. "Cain't ask fer more than that. I thank ye, Miz Talbot. I do thank ye. Let me know if Clyde causes ye trouble."

Betsy hesitated. It would be easiest not to say anything about Clyde, she reflected, but that would be as bad as not speaking the truth. She spoke quietly, so no one else would hear. "Perhaps I should let you know now that he arrives late and smells as if he partakes of drink."

Mrs. Munroe's eyes opened wide, then she squared her shoulders. "Thet so? Well, I'll be takin' it up with Clyde right off! I thank ye, Miss Talbot. I thank ye very much." She nodded and marched determinedly out of the Mercantile.

Betsy subdued a smile. With other customers in the store, there was little she could do except note Joshua's nod of approval. She moved on down an aisle. Most likely, it was only the beginning of the peculiar encounters a schoolteacher in a mountain gold mining town might expect.

By the time she had found the perfect shade of green thread, a roast platter, and the other items on her list, the Mercantile was crowded. "Where's Lucius?" she asked Joshua as she signed for her purchases.

"Over at his other job, selling tickets for the stagecoach. Almost time for the morning stage to come in."

"I'd like to see him in action," she decided. "And Tess made me give my word that I'd stop at her house for coffee as soon as I came to town." Leaving her packages with Joshua, she promised to return before noon.

Outside, she started up the boardwalk for the stagecoach stop on the corner of Main and River Street. Several people waited in front, including the Jurgen children from school— George, Garnett, and the twins, Rachel and Kendall.

"Good morning, Miss Talbot," they said, nearly in unison.

"Good morning," she said to all of them and to the blond-bearded man who was apparently their father. "I hope you are not leaving us."

"No, ma'am," Garnett replied, "we're waiting for some-one to come."

The children were clean and better dressed than at school, Betsy noted as she nodded and moved on to the stagecoach office. Glimpsing Lucius through the door, she saw he had a customer.

"Here comes the stage!" someone yelled.

Betsy turned to see the horse and stagecoach racing up the riverfront road, raising a great cloud of dust. As the stage approached, she recognized Yank Stevens, who wore his tall white hat and yellow gauntlets and looked all business as he drove the six lathered bays.

"Whoa, boys, whoa!" he shouted.

Lucius rushed from the office, and the coach halted

precipitously in front of him, gritty dust flying all around. Lucius opened the coach door with a fine flourish, and a pretty brown-haired woman stepped down, showing a bit more ankle from under her blue traveling frock than was seemly.

Mr. Jurgen, who wore a black suit, stepped forward, somewhat abashed, and shook her hand. "We're purely glad to see you got here fine, Zetta."

"I am, too," she replied shyly. "I see you brought the children."

"Yes," he replied and began to tell her their names as they stepped out of the way of the other disembarking passengers.

It struck Betsy as a perplexing scene until it was explained by a nearby onlooker. "Looks like he got 'em a new mother," he muttered, "though she don't look much better than she should be. Found her in San Francisco, 'n you know 'bout most of the women there."

Mr. Jurgen reddened slightly as though he had heard, but he said to the young woman, "We thought you might want to wash up at home. Then we'll go to the church, 'n we'll have dinner at the hotel."

Zetta and Mr. Jurgen! This was the widower's wedding that Louisa had mentioned would take place today! Betsy realized. She stepped away, not wishing to overhear more. It was, however, an intriguing situation—a new mother for four of her students. She hoped with all her heart that matters would turn out happily, and conveyed her wish with her brightest smile at the group of them.

Lucius had already closed the stagecoach door behind the two new passengers, and Yank cracked the whip over the six-horse team. "Git along, boys! Git along!" he yelled, and the coach jerked forward.

Betsy backed away from the new cloud of dust and turned to Lucius. "It looks as if you do a fine job wherever you work."

"I thank ye, Miss Talbot," he said, his eyes twinkling. "That's mighty high praise comin' from a schoolmarm— maybe the highest praise any schoolmarm ever in my life give me."

"Surely you're teasing, Lucius."

"Not one whit, Miss Talbot, not one whit. Teachers ne'er thought too highly o' me or thought I'd come to anythin'."

"Then they were badly mistaken," she replied. "I hope I never misjudge a student so badly."

He beamed. "Expect ye'll be encouragin' 'em. Yes, that's what I expect o' ye."

"I should hope so!" She smiled. "Farewell for now, Lucius. I am going to explore the rest of town."

"Not a whole lot to it. Not like San Francisco."

"Thank goodness," she said. "We hope to see you after church for dinner tomorrow."

"I'm still thinkin' on it," he answered. "Give Jessica my respects."

"I shall. Good day."

Betsy strolled on down the boardwalk, pleased that in the short time she'd lived in Oak Hill, she already knew a number of people.

A bird twittered from a tree in front of Hugh Fairfax's bank, making the town even more charming. Imagine, a bird's nest in front of the town bank!

That afternoon, as they went out behind the cabin to plant the vegetable garden, Betsy told Aunt Jessica about her interchange with Lucius.

"It's such a shame when teachers don't attempt to find a

child's special talent," her aunt replied. "You'd think any teacher could have seen Lucius's interest in others, despite his garrulousness."

"Perhaps they saw him as disruptive," Betsy said, remembering George Jurgen's habit of talking out of turn and how it irritated her.

"Yes, perhaps," her aunt agreed. "The trick is to channel those who are disruptive into their life's work. Let them be the ones to disrupt the fixed ideas in those areas where God wants us to learn more."

They turned to their work. The two previous teachers, despite their yen for gold, had broken up the soil for gardens during their stay. Moses, the free black who with his wife, Maddy, worked for Mr. Wilmington, had spaded and raked the garden space for their summer crops this week. Fortunately, Mr. Volk had planted a spring garden, and, despite a thick yield of weeds, the potatoes, onions, and carrots were doing well.

Betsy rolled up the sleeves of her faded tan calico dress and asked, "What kind of seeds did you buy yesterday?"

Aunt Jessica sorted through the packets. "Peas, beans, greens, corn, radishes, cucumbers, and green onions."

"That should keep us keep us occupied and well fed!"

"I thought some of your school children might need extra vegetables this summer, and perhaps some of the newcomers might, too."

"A good idea."

Betsy brought around the sticks and string for lining up the rows. "Joshua offered to donate seeds from the Mercantile for a garden behind the school, too. The men teachers were not enthusiastic about it, but since we're having a summer term, it seems right for the children to work together. Moreover, the parents will lose some of the children's working time in their own gardens, and the vegetables they bring home will compensate to a small extent."

"Another good idea," Aunt Jessica said.

"I hope you'll visit the school next week," Betsy said. "I would welcome your ideas there."

"Only if you are certain, Betsy," her aunt said. "I have no wish to intrude."

"I'm certain," Betsy replied. "You're always welcome. And I think it might be a good idea if I invited Lucius Alden to speak to the children about the National Road as well."

Her aunt darted a curious glance at her, but said nothing else.

The next morning, Betsy was eager to see the inside of the log church and to hear Jonathan Chambers preach. He'd visited *Casa Contenta* in '49 as a young Baltimore solicitor who'd also studied theology, and had come to California to make a new life for himself. Jonathan had met Cousin Louisa in Virginia and had fallen in love with her during their terrible journey West, a journey that included sailing on a decrepit gold ship, trekking through the jungle of Panama, and finally taking a steamship up the west coast to San Francisco. Like almost everyone else, he had been unaware of what Louisa was fleeing. He had only fled a heartrending jilting, not an abusive slaver husband who stooped at nothing, as had poor Louisa.

As Betsy and Aunt Jessica made their way along the dusty path from their cabin toward the church, a soft breeze rustled the oak and maple leaves overhead.

"I wonder if Lucius Alden will come this morning," Aunt Jessica said.

"And I wonder if my students and their parents will, especially the newly married Jurgens." Yesterday as she and

Aunt Jessica had worked in the garden, Louisa had stopped by and verified that the wedding taking place was indeed that of the blond-bearded Mr. Jurgen and the young woman who had arrived by stagecoach. His children were the only ones in attendance, and the arrangements had appeared rather tentative, as if he feared the bride might not come.

Betsy darted a glance down the road to be sure the stage-coach wasn't bowling along at its usual wild clip, and they crossed over toward the church. From here she could see nearly all of the log cabins in the wooded settlement: to the right, Mr. Wilmington's, which was nearest the river, then Rose and Joshua's, then Maddy and Moses' next to the road. On the other side of the road, behind them, was Louisa and Jonathan's, then two cabins of families she had not yet met, and five more hidden in the trees behind them. Then back on the front path, her own and Aunt Jessica's. The only house more distant and somewhat separate from the rest of the settlement was the Buchanans', high over the river next to the school.

"A charming sight, is it not?" Aunt Jessica asked, looking about with her.

"Yes," Betsy agreed, "I truly like it here."

Sunshine streamed through the bright green leaves of the surrounding trees and bushes, and they continued along the footpath. Horses and buggies stopped at the church hitching post, and people converged from the various paths, greeting Betsy and her aunt with interest.

Aunt Jessica had already met their neighbors in the next cabin, and she introduced the young couple to Betsy. "Mr. Franklin has started the new sawmill halfway down the road between Oak Flats and Oak Hill," her aunt explained.

"I am pleased to meet you," Betsy said. They seemed a bit shy, perhaps because young Mrs. Franklin looked as if she might be expecting a babe, but they insisted that Betsy and Aunt Jessica precede them into the log church.

"Want ye to feel welcome," the young husband said.

Inside, the chinked-log sanctuary was rustic but lovely with its simple dark wood altar and dark wooden pews. In a sense it was more beautiful than some of the new churches in San Francisco, Betsy decided, for here they had used the trees from the hills and the slate from the riverbank, and because the members had built it themselves. A bouquet of colorful wildflowers stood near the altar, and Louisa and Rose, who had clearly been watching for them, smiled with love from the second pew.

Aunt Jessica sat down in the pew behind them, and Betsy settled beside her, smoothing the soft skirt of her peach-colored delaine dress. She was surprised to find Bibles and hymnals in the pew backs, even here at a mountainside log church. As she sat back, it occurred to her that she and Aunt Jessica, with Rose and Louisa, represented the three common—and harrowing—ways of traveling to California: she and Aunt Jessica by covered wagon, Rose by clipper ship around the Horn, and Louisa by the Panama route. Surely God had preserved each of them through such hardships for special purposes, which for all they knew might have to do with this church.

After a while she looked back for Lucius, but he was not to be seen. She did see, however, that the pews in the rustic sanctuary were filling up, and many held her students and their parents. And there were the newlywed Jurgens with all four of his children, an especially heartening sight.

Jonathan Chambers stepped to the altar and greeted them joyously, then began the service with prayer. At length he suggested, "Let us now sing one of John Newton's fine hymns, 'Glorious Things of Thee Are Spoken,' and recall that

Newton was a man who repented of his life as a slave trader and turned to Christ for redemption."

Betsy paid especial attention to the ex-slave trader's words as they sang out together,

> Glorious things of thee are spoken,
> Zion, city of our God;
> He whose word cannot be broken
> Formed thee for His own abode.
> On the Rock of Ages founded,
> What can shake thy sure repose?
> With salvation's walls surrounded
> Thou may'st smile at all thy foes.

It seemed as they sang out that the sanctuary filled with God's love. It wasn't until they finished the third verse and sat down that Lucius hurried up the aisle and sat beside Aunt Jessica. He wore the brown suit and carried the same hat he had worn when they met him in the stagecoach; he appeared as spritely and genial as ever, unabashed at being late.

At the pulpit, Jonathan looked most solemn despite the deep cleft in his chin.

"Every day, my brethren, I hear inquiries as to whether the road to heaven is really so difficult, and the number of the saved is truly as few as we represent," he began.

"Christ answers that clearly. He tells us the widow of Sarepta alone was found worthy of help by the prophet Elijah . . . that the number of lepers was great in Israel in the time of Elisha, but that only Naaman was cured by the man of God.

"We know that the family of Noah alone was saved at the time of the Flood. Abraham was chosen to be the sole depository of the covenant with God. Joshua and Caleb were the only two of six hundred thousand Hebrews who saw the land of promise. Job was the only upright man in the land of Uz, as was Lot in Sodom.

"What is the cause of this small number in our morals and manner of life? As everyone flatters himself that he will *not* be excluded, it is of importance to see if his confidence be well-founded. I do not wish you to conclude that few will be saved, but to bring you to ask yourselves if, living as you live, *you* can hope to be saved.

"Among the saved we have only two descriptions of persons: those who have passed through life perfect like Christ or those, who having lost their innocence, have regained it by repentance. Heaven is open only to the innocent or to the repentant. Now, of which party are you? Are you perfect like Christ? Or are you repentant and redeemed by Christ?"

Betsy glanced at Aunt Jessica and Lucius, and saw that they, like the rest of the congregation, sat at rapt attention.

Jonathan expanded his case as though in a courtroom, as behooved a former solicitor, then pulled in the main lines of thought and narrowed them down to the conclusion.

"In the Church of Christ are two roads," he said, "one broad and open, by which almost the whole world passes to death, and the other narrow, where few indeed enter, and which leads to eternal life. 'In which of these am I?' we must ask. 'Are my morals those common to most other persons? Am I with the great number? If so, I am on the wrong path.'"

He spoke of present times in the goldfields and the need to live in the world, yet not be of it. He returned to Scripture, then again to the present. At the end of the sermon, he reminded those who did not truly know Christ that He awaited them with open and loving arms.

They sang the last verse of "Glorious Things of Thee Are Spoken," then Jonathan gave the benediction with sureness and glowing love. When the service ended, the mood of the congregation was solemn yet quietly joyful, and Lucius said to Aunt Jessica, "Gives a good sermon, don't he?"

Aunt Jessica nodded. "Yes, God has surely called him."

Betsy glanced about behind her and was surprised to see Adam Buchanan and Mellie—just the two of them. Adam was dressed in his black frock coat and trousers, and looked even more handsome than she'd remembered. He stood talking to another man in the congregation, and beside him, Mellie listened intently. Her wavy light brown hair looked newly washed, for it shone brightly and waved luxuriantly to the waist of her flowered pink dimity dress.

As Betsy approached, the other man was just making his departure. "A pleasure to have you with us this morning, Adam. We hope you will come again," he said as he left.

Betsy stepped forward. "Good morning, Dr. Buchanan. Good morning, Mellie."

They responded pleasantly, Mellie with a bright smile and Adam appearing rather nervous, as though he were un-accustomed to attending church. He said rather formally, "We're receiving favorable comments about your first two days of school, Miss Talbot."

"I am glad to hear of it," she replied.

"It must be quite different from your home school."

For an instant she suspected he was jibing at what he considered her lack of real teaching experience, but she replied, "Yes, there are differences in the schools, but there are more similarities when it comes to the children. I am impressed that so many of them would attend a summer term . . . and that several do show scholarly tendencies as you mentioned."

His eyes lit up, and she noticed how neatly his dark beard and mustache were trimmed, and that he had thicker eyebrows than she had remembered, and wavier hair. She wondered whether his wife appreciated his being such a fine-looking man.

"Yes, well—" he began, nodding and stepping back as though sensing her admiration.

Betsy quickly put in, "I understand that your wife is a fine violinist. I—I thought perhaps someday she could play for the schoolchildren."

He stood taller and his eyes hardened. "It is very kind of you to suggest it, but she is not well . . . and she is out of practice. I thank you, however, for the thought. Good day, Miss Talbot." And with that, he nodded and turned away, holding Mellie firmly by the hand.

At the last moment, Mellie waved, and Betsy returned it, wishing now that she had not broached what must be a unpleasant topic for him. Whatever had possessed her to do such a thing? Being caught at admiring him?

Lucius Alden and Aunt Jessica joined her, and her aunt asked, "Is that Adam Buchanan's daughter?"

"Yes. Yes, it is."

"A sweet little dear, isn't she?" Aunt Jessica remarked, then added kindly, "She must be a comfort to his wife."

Betsy seriously wondered about that, but said only, "Yes, Mellie is a beautiful child."

At one o'clock Betsy and Aunt Jessica brought dinner to the table, which now filled the middle of the parlor. Last night they had set the table, using a length of the soft green fabric as a tablecloth; they had also baked the strawberry pies and prepared as much of the food as was possible. This morning they'd started the roast beef cooking before church.

Now Aunt Jessica brought in the greens and the biscuits, and Betsy carried in the meat, surrounded with onions, carrots, and potatoes on the new white platter from the Mercantile. Lucius Alden, Mr. Wilmington, Rose and Joshua, and Louisa and Jonathan Chambers sat at the table, all murmuring with pleasure at the smells and the sight of the meal.

"Nothin' in this world smells as good as a roast made like that," Lucius declared, tucking his napkin in at his collar, "'specially when ye ain't put yer teeth in a real home-cooked meal in a year or two."

Aunt Jessica said, "Why, Lucius, don't tell me you haven't eaten properly in that long. It is very bad for your health."

"Been a long time," he allowed. "Mostly I eat beans and biscuits so tough you could use 'em as weapons."

They all laughed, and Rose said, "No wonder you are so thin, Mr. Alden. Next Sunday after church you must have dinner at our house."

"Thank ye," he said, beaming. "Don't mind if I do."

As Betsy and her aunt sat down, Aunt Jessica asked, "Jonathan, I know you gave your all in that fine sermon, but I hope you can summon up just enough more stamina to give thanks before we eat."

"Praise God, I can," he said with a smile and proceeded to say a grace as fine as his sermon. The children were all down for their naps, and the mood was convivial as the adults helped themselves to the food. Mr. Wilmington urged Lucius, "Tell us about yourself. Jessica said you had a sales wagon you worked from on the National Road. What of your family?"

Lucius gave him an impish glance. "Well, now, if it's genealogy ye want, we go back to a Pilgrim father, offspring of French Huguenots who hied themselves to Holland to save their necks from the gallows. Old Phillippe was reared in Leiden under the English Puritans who hid there themselves. To the family's everlastin' regret, he just missed the *Mayflower* and had to wait for the next boat over," Lucius said with a chuckle. " 'Fore him, we hied back to old Charlemagne."

"I had no idea we were in such august company," Mr. Wilmington said, amused, "though it wasn't that background about which I inquired. We must seem most plebian by comparison."

Lucius chewed on his roast, a merry twinkle in his eyes. "Why, bless my soul, I went o'er to Europe and have rubbed against royalty. I have ate with it, drank with it, slept with it, jested with it, snubbed it, and all but kicked it. My ancestors were elevated, ye may say, but some by the use of a rope."

Everyone laughed, and Aunt Jessica said, "Few members of such families will tell the bare faced truth like that."

"Bare faced it is," Lucius replied. "Bare-necked at times, too."

Jonathan Chambers said, "Then your family were some of those Puritans fleeing England so they might have their own Bibles and read Scripture. We are told that several were even martyred for having Bibles in their possession."

"So they say," Lucius returned. "Now fer me, I ne'er cared one way or t'other about goin' to meetin' back in Maryland, not 'til I got interested in girls all dressed up in their Sunday-go-to-meetin' clothes. One o' 'em noticed me as well, 'n it turned out, my trips to meetin' weren't in vain. I pulled the wool o'er her eyes and made 'er think I was a handsome young scamp, and . . . I would like to say she's the mother o' my children, but the truth is, we ne'er had any."

"So you married," Rose put in to urge him on.

"Yes, though how I ever contrived to do so, I can't see." He raised his brows and drew a regretful breath. "She died early on, though . . . died 'n then I went on the Road—a dealer in flour, silk, lard, broadcloth, coonskins, delaines, pork, satins, bank stock, butter, 'n most anythin' else."

"Well-suited to help me at the Mercantile," Joshua remarked good-naturedly.

Betsy said to Lucius, "I was sorry to hear that your teachers did not encourage you at school."

Lucius chuckled. "I wasn't what ye call a real scholar. Why, one day, the schoolmaster pinched my ear so hard the skin almost came off, 'n fer somethin' I didn't even do."

"Did you inform your parents?" Aunt Jessica inquired.

Lucius shook his head. "No, I took care o' it myself. The next day, in some strange manner, a goose found 'er way into the schoolmaster's desk, made a nest amongst 'is papers, and deposited an egg. When the desk was opened, my sentiments were expressed by the loud hissin' o' that goose."

They all laughed, and Betsy said, "Please do not give my students any such ideas! I don't know how I'd react in the morning to open my desk to such a sight."

"Then I'll suggest it for the afternoon," Lucius returned jovially.

At length they brought out the strawberry pies, warm from sitting on the stove, and smothered them with thick cream. Due in part to the good food and to Lucius's humor, the dinner was a great success. It was only after everyone had left and Betsy helped to clean up that Aunt Jessica said, "Lucius is most entertaining, but I suspect he is compelled to be so garrulous because of an inner emptiness and a lack of real peace."

At Betsy's perplexed look, her aunt added, "I doubt that Lucius has made peace with his Maker yet. One hears that a wife's severe illness or premature death ofttimes makes a man outright angry or even quietly resentful of God."

"I hadn't thought of that," Betsy replied. It occurred to her now, however, that Adam Buchanan had a severely ill wife, and today after church there seemed to have been a lack of peacefulness about him, too. Perhaps she should pray for him, she thought—and for a good week ahead at school.

6

B enjamin Talbot sat in the front pew of the new San Francisco church, his nerves on edge. It was one thing to lead a family or a wagon train, but quite another to lead a crusade against evil. Ready to rise to his feet, he listened to the minister's introduction. ". . . one of our brethren who has worked unceasingly for the Lord and to fight lawlessness, a fine Christian man who wishes all of us to pull together in San Francisco and in this raucous new state. . . ."

A fine Christian man, indeed! Benjamin's mind repeated. He was as unworthy as could be, but this is what happened when one prayed "Here am I, Lord, use me."

"The topic of his speech is 'Making a Stand in Christ Against Evil.' And now . . . Benjamin Talbot!"

Benjamin came to his feet and hurried up to the pulpit. He had never enjoyed public speaking, but Moses himself had been halt of speech. If only this would rally the others... if only someone else would take up the cause of the churches unifying to fight evil.

Standing before them, Benjamin gazed out at his Monday morning audience. Before him were the ministers and the most influential laity from churches throughout San Francisco—the people who would spread his message or let it die here today. He sent up a heartfelt prayer: *Lord, give me the wisdom to speak clearly and give them the wish to act in Thy will.*

As he grabbed hold of the wooden pulpit, the dark, weasel face of Emile Martene, a gambling establishment spokesman, swam up before him. Surely the man would not have the gall to sit here among these churchmen. Surely it was a figment of his imagination, Benjamin decided, albeit a worthy attempt by the forces of evil to stop him. No . . . he would not be thwarted!

He began with a firm voice, "Those of us here in our new state of California ofttimes see only the problems before us, and admittedly there are a plentitude of them. We may tire of the battle, but the forces of evil do not."

He remembered to pause for effect.

"This morning I would like to put our situation into an historical perspective, so we might observe our own age more clearly. Today, my fellow believers, we stand at a great crossroads of history, for the tides of empire and of Christianity, moving east and west, have circled the globe and have met right here . . . in California."

He was glad to see that to see their interest was piqued.

"Beginning in Jerusalem, one branch of Christianity made its seat on the Tiber River," he continued. "From Rome it moved over western Europe. Checked for centuries by the Atlantic Ocean, it finally crossed that barrier. Spain's century in the sun came, and with irresistible onrush she claimed most of the Americas for the Spanish crown. Their conquest, however, collapsed from within. Its last thrust was the planting of missions and presidios from San Diego to Sonoma.

"Also starting in Jerusalem, the eastern branch of Christianity made its seat by the Sea of Bosphorus. From Constantinople it moved north over eastern Europe, but it was checked for centuries by the Tartars until the empire of the czars came. Establishing itself as the Russian Orthodox church, it expanded eastward across Asia. But the driving power of czardom failed. Its last thrust crossed the Bering Strait and occupied Alaska and part of the western coast of North America. Its farthest outpost was named 'Rossiya,' shortened by us to 'Fort Ross,' in Sonoma County.

"Interestingly, the Russian Orthodox Church at Fort Ross is only forty-five miles from the Roman Catholic Mission at Sonoma. Both branches of Christianity had circled the globe and met right here in California!"

The audience, he saw, recognized the import of the matter. Drawing a breath, he plunged on. "Neither the Spanish church nor the Russian church had experienced a strong reformation movement to purify its life from medieval incrustations. They faced each other in Sonoma County in exhaustion. It seemed that the curtain of Christianity had rung down here.

"California's development, however, brought a new, vital force. It first came in 1826 in the person of Jedediah Smith, the Methodist 'Bible-toter,' in a day when no one ever thought the mountains could be penetrated from the East. He was the first to cross them, to open the door through which the United States and reformed religion entered California.

"It came in 1841 when John Bidwell entered with the first emigrant train, bringing his faith in Christ.

"It came in 1846 and 1847 in the persons of such staunch laymen as Adna Hecox, Elihu Anthony, and James F. Reed, whose religion survived the plains.

"It came in 1849 and since in the persons of such ministers as William Taylor and Seth Thompson, and it came with each of you in this audience. It comes in the persons who seek not man's gold, but God's will—whether it is to build a church or a school or a hospital. Each generation of believers is called by God to do His work in evangelizing, teaching all nations, and in other areas of society. Let us remember the church's earlier history as well."

He began with the people of Israel's instructions to tell their children the stories of the Exodus and the wilderness. He spoke of the prophets and of Christ Himself using history to identify Himself. He spoke of Paul and the Corinthian church, who needed reminding of their historical spiritual roots.

Looking at the open countenances of the men in the pews, Benjamin had a sense of being touched by destiny. "We who stand at this crossroads in Christian history must hark back to look forward. Our plight in San Francisco is not unique, no more than it was in ancient crossroads of Corinth. Indeed, the very dissolution in this city bespeaks its possibilities, and we are not alone. Last year, there were already seven Methodist, six Catholic, five Presbyterian, four Baptist, three Episcopalian, three Congregational, and four other churches in our city.

"We churchmen hear praise for our advances here. We know that the society produced by our gold rush is not the typical society of the older American agrarian frontier. We're told we have the acme of all frontiers. We're told we have a metropolitan and cosmopolitan city that has telescoped half a century's growth into a year. Amazing, is it not?"

A murmur of pleased ascent rose from his audience.

"San Francisco's per capita wealth," he continued, "though far from evenly distributed, is suddenly the highest in the nation, and we are demanding more and more material luxuries as well as cultural satisfactions for the remarkable number of educated men who were drawn here by the gold rush. We're told we will soon be a financial rival of New York and, despite our crudeness, in some respects will soon be a cultural rival of Boston.

"Lest we puff ourselves up too greatly, however, let us remember that as Christians we are not called to bring our society to a financial acme, nor to cultural competition.

"I have come here today in hopes of spreading the message to fight together against evil . . . against the evils in politics, against the evils of gambling and drinking, against the evils even in our vigilante groups, against all things that war against a Christian society. We must stand against evil, and we must stand in unity! Imperfect though we be, we, like all generations, must stand in the light of Christian history!"

Having said that, he gathered his strength. His next words rang with fervor. "Every believer has the responsibility to fight evil and to further the church! Every believer must seek God's will for himself in today's society, for our work today, whether it be prayer or politics, is of vital importance, not only for this day's raucous society, but in the light of future generations!"

In the heat of his passion, he raised his arms and proclaimed, "I pray that every believer in this city would cry out, 'Here am I, Lord, show me Thy will for my life during this crossroads in history. . . . Here am I, Lord, use me in the battle against drinking, gambling, and debauchery! Use me, Lord, to help achieve the unity to fight evil! Here am I, Lord, use me!' "

He stepped back from the pulpit, catching his breath, unsure whether he had spoken enough or with sufficient passion. The applause, however, was immediate, and it thundered across the pews to him. Startled, he nodded and smiled at the rapt faces before him again, then strode from the pulpit in utter amazement.

It wasn't until he stepped down to the pews and was

shaking hands with his fellow Christians that he saw that Emile Martene was most assuredly among them. Indeed, the advocate for the gambling establishments awaited him at the end of the line. Benjamin made an effort to concentrate on the congratulatory words of his fellow believers as Martene advanced.

At last the man stood before him, a self-possessed smile on his narrow lips. His black hair was well-barbered, and he was resplendent in the finest of dark blue suits; his cravat and shirt were the best that money could buy.

"Mr. Martene, I believe?" Benjamin said.

The man replied in an unctuous voice. "That you have correct."

"What may I do for you?" Benjamin inquired, fighting an urge to step back from him.

"I wished to hear why the churches were in league today," Martene replied. "I must say that I commend their good works in building hospitals, schools, and libraries for the benefit of all. I agree with that portion of the Christian message."

"But you do not agree with all of it?" Benjamin asked, already knowing the answer quite well.

Martene gave him a thin smile. "You will not be wise in trying to infiltrate politics, nor to make further inroads against gambling and drinking establishments."

Benjamin stood firm. "You dare come here to warn me?"

"This is not such a lion's den," the man replied, looking about unconcerned. "Indeed, I feel quite safe, only perturbed by your rallying the believers." His eyes turned back to Benjamin and filled with menace. "I warn you now to desist."

Indignation rose to Benjamin's throat. "And if I do not?"

"Desist if you value your life and the lives of those in your family," Emile replied.

"Surely you do not wish to slide that far into evil—"

"Some men—and some women—say that I already have," Emile replied, staring fixedly at him. He gave a nod and began to make his departure. "I say again, desist if you value your life and the lives of your family. Desist."

Betsy sat down at her desk in the schoolhouse and glanced at the wall clock. If nothing else, she could start a letter before the students arrived. She took up the quill and began.

May 20, 1854

Dear Father,

We have all enjoyed reading your speech in the newspaper article you sent. My faith quick-ened just reading it. I had never considered what a crossroads this time is in Christian history, and I am heartened to hear that pastors are asking you to speak to their congregations about it. May you send them all marching forward to make a unified stand against evil!

I must smile, though, for I know how you dislike public speaking. Aunt Jessica said, "Leave it to the Lord to choose such a messenger, for then your father must especially lean upon Him." I am leaning upon Him for my teaching here as well, although I must admit I do enjoy it.

Jonathan Chambers expects to share your message with our congregation and with other clergymen he encounters out at the diggings. He preaches wherever the opportunity is presented, and he always makes a firm stand in church for evangelism, good works, and fighting against evil. I think he has a great gift for preaching.

Having mentioned Aunt Jessica, I must tell you that she has already transformed our cabin into a cozy nest. She has sewn curtains and cover-lets, put down the braided rugs, put up pictures, and arranged the knickknacks from home. We employed a carpenter to make us a plain table and benches for outdoors so we might invite more people for dinner on Sundays after church. You will be pleased to know that Lucius Alden, the elderly gentleman we met on the stagecoach, has come every Sunday after church. (Last Sunday Rose and Joshua invited him, as we dined at their house.) He is fond of Aunt Jessica, but he is the first one to admit that he is also fond of home-cooked meals.

It has been such a joy to become reacquaint-ed with Rose and Joshua, and Louisa and Jona-than, and to be with their dear children. I daresay if I had no other friends here, I would be content. I have, however, met some of the children's parents and many of the young men in town who attend church. No, you must not worry yourself about it. I am not in love with any of them, nor do I expect to be, for very few of them here are well educated. Ah, such snobbishness!

It does strike me as important, though, to be able to discuss matters intelligently with one's mate, and I have no intention of falling in love with anyone who is unsuitable. As for your other concerns, there have been no more attempted holdups or other lawlessness near Oak Hill. All is peaceful. You must not worry yourself over us.

School is going well, except that some of the older boys are often troublesome. It will be time for me to go out and ring the school bell in a few minutes, and so I shall bid you farewell. Please give our love to

everyone at home and tell them we miss them. When I
begin school here every morning, I still think of the
dear children at our home school at Casa Contenta.
Please convey my love and best wishes to them. I pray
for them and shall remember to pray for your speaking.
Thank you for your prayers for us.
Your loving daughter, Betsy

Betsy blew the ink dry, folded the letter, and quickly placed it in her desk. Although it was still early, she grabbed the brass school bell and went to the schoolhouse door. As she reached the doorstep, she saw that Mellie Buchanan peered from the edge of the woods, watching the schoolchildren at play. The child stood there every day now and sometimes ventured nearer.

What a shame she had no playmates . . . and what a shame about her mother. Her father had not brought her to church again, nor come himself, or she might have made friends there. Perhaps Betsy should offer to bring Mellie to church when next she saw Adam. She hadn't seen him since last Saturday in town.

Standing outside the schoolhouse, she recalled their encounter. He had just stepped from his office, looking every inch the young doctor in his black suit, carrying his medical bag. "Good day, Miss Talbot," he had said most politely.

"Good day, Dr. Buchanan."

He'd looked preoccupied, but came to a careful halt and his hazel eyes held hers. "I trust you are enjoying your work at our school."

"Yes, I am, thank you."

She expected him to say something else about school, but he added nothing. Finally she said, "I thought perhaps we might have some kind of social functions at school on Friday evenings—perhaps a town spelling bee or musicale. I understand that many schools have such community functions . . . Friday night socials."

He had inquired archly, "A good way for you to meet young men, Miss Talbot?"

Affronted, she replied, "That is the very last matter in which I am interested, Dr. Buchanan! Nor have I given anyone reason to think such a thing!"

"I beg your pardon," he returned. "I'm glad to see I am mistaken on that count."

She nodded, still somewhat incensed.

"Unfortunately women have so often given me the impression that their life's highest aim is to find a husband."

She spoke the words evenly. "I am not one of them."

"So I see." His half-repentant smile reached to his eyes, drawing up soft smile lines under them and causing dimples to deepen in the spaces between his neatly trimmed mustache and beard. The smile transformed his face, making him appear so much younger that she wondered if he'd been more pleasant before marrying Selena. "Am I forgiven?" he asked.

Considering Selena, whom the neighbors called a spoiled southern belle, Betsy realized why he might mistrust women. "Yes, of course. You're forgiven. I shouldn't have been so affronted."

"Thank you." He smiled again. "I shall discuss your idea about Friday night socials with the other members of the school board, but I doubt very much that they will consent to it."

"Only if you wish."

The clip-clop of horses' hooves had brought their encounter to an end, for Rufus arrived on his own horse and led the doctor's big bay. "Got yo' horse, Doctah Buchanan," he announced.

"Well then, Miss Talbot. I have a patient waiting—"

Suddenly Betsy saw she was in the schoolhouse doorway and had been so caught up in the memory of last Saturday's exchange that she'd forgotten what she was supposed to do. She rang the school bell vigorously.

"Good morning, Miss Talbot!" her students called out. "Good morning, Teacher!"

"Good morning, Tilda . . . Rachel . . . Lucinda . . . Hiram . . . Spencer." At least she knew each of their names, and other matters continued to improve. Here came Clyde Munroe on time, as was now usual. He listened in class and no longer smelled of spirits—all since she'd spoken with his mother at the Mercantile. With the Lord's help, she'd be a fine teacher, Betsy told herself. She'd show Adam Buchanan that he'd been badly mistaken.

She started the day with a psalm, then led the children in rousing songs to fire them up for the day's work. As soon as they finished "Yankee Doodle," she started the middle students on long division, and the older children on their lessons.

When they were all at work and the First Readers were coming forward, she saw Mellie's face pressed against the window closest to the back of the room. She must be standing on the stump again.

"Mary, would you begin reading?" Betsy asked. "I believe I shall open a few windows for fresh air."

Betsy raised the closest window a few inches, then slowly moved along to the one where she had seen Mellie. Pretending to be engrossed with the First Readers, Betsy raised the window. From the corner of her eye she saw that Mellie crouched against the log exterior of the schoolhouse, her eyes tightly shut as though that might keep her from being discovered. Betsy subdued a smile and moved toward the front of the room again. At least now Mellie could hear the children and learn from hearing their lessons.

As the morning passed, she occasionally saw Mellie peeking in, careful not to let the children see her. Just before recess Dilsey's voice called out, "Miz Mellie! Miz Mellie!" and Mellie raced home. It could not have been more timely either, for just then George Jurgen scared Lucinda Webster and the other little girls with, "A bear's gonna get you in the outhouse!"

After lunch recess, Mellie reappeared at the same window, and Betsy was glad to be reading about Jesus' love for the little children just then, for it seemed especially applicable to Mellie, who seemed so in need of a friend.

Betsy didn't see her again until school let out, and then she was watching from the edge of the woods as the students went home. In her loneliness, the child probably didn't recall that her father often came home in the afternoon and might catch her observing the children. Best to leave that to the Buchanan family, Betsy decided. Thus far, her encounters with the parents had scarcely been encouraging.

She returned to her desk and, glancing about the deserted schoolroom, realized that it truly looked like a schoolroom now, with pictures and lesson papers tacked onto the cloakroom plank wall, a rock collection on the bench near the cloakroom, an herb garden sitting in tins on the windowsills facing the churchyard. They had even planted their vegetable garden seeds on that side. Betsy couldn't think when she had felt more fulfilled or more certain that this was her calling.

Not that they didn't have their problems. With everyone doing different things at once, there was bound to be trouble. When the beginners grew restless, they infected the entire class. And sometimes the middle children like Emory Orr bothered the older children or scared little ones like Rachel and Lucinda with tales of bears or coyotes. The girls would cry, disturbing the others so badly that Betsy would have to find artwork or something for the little ones to do, and, punishment of punishment—make Emory sit on the girls' side of the room.

Seated at her desk, Betsy realized it was one of her favorite times of day. A cooler breeze blew through the open windows as it often did at four o'clock. She was thoroughly engrossed in Spencer Tucker's excellent English composition when she realized someone had come through the door. Looking up, she was surprised to see a heavily bearded man striding into the room. He was doubtless a miner, for he wore a red flannel shirt and rough pants, both in need of washing, as were his matted dark hair and beard.

"May I help you?" she asked from her high platform desk.

He continued to clomp up the middle aisle between the desks and around the stove, staring at her.

She rose to her feet uneasily. "May I help you?" she asked more loudly.

A slow ingratiating grin split his thick beard, showing broken yellow teeth. His eyes were wild and bloodshot.

Fear shot through Betsy's veins. "What is it you want?" she asked in her most authoritative voice. As she spoke, she was suddenly aware of Mellie poking her head in the window, and she feared for the little girl's welfare.

The man apparently did not see the child and said thickly to Betsy, "Ye know what I want."

The hair rose on the back of her neck. *Talking . . . she must keep him talking.*

"Do you have a child enrolled here? I haven't met all of the parents—" She could not think of one child who vaguely resembled him, nor were her words stopping him.

"Ain't ye a purty little thing?" he asked, stepping up onto the front platform.

Despite the added height of her platform desk, he was a head taller than she, she realized. She could see a wicked scar on his forehead and the broken veins in his bulbous nose, and could smell the whiskey on his breath. She said frantically, "I must admit, I do not know which is your child—" *Lord, help me!* she thought. *Help me!*

"Talk ain't doin' no good, teacher. Come on now, give Hollis a kiss. Ain't ye hankerin' fer a big kiss?"

"I am not!" she retorted.

She had never been truly kissed, and she did not mean to begin with this man. In her anger, she grabbed the hickory rod pointer from the desk platform and raised it threateningly. "I should not like to hit you."

A deep laugh rumbled up from his broad chest as he lunged for the stick and tore it from her hands. He snapped it in half, then the halves into halves again.

"Come 'ere, teacher," the man urged. "Come 'ere now."

"Mellie!" Betsy shouted. "Get Rufus and your father! Say there's a bad man here! Run!"

The man grabbed her, but she shrieked, "Run, Mellie! Run!"

He clapped a massive, hairy hand over her mouth and, with his other arm, clamped her against him.

Despite his terrifying strength, her right hand was free, and she struggled to tear herself away as he looked around the room to see if anyone were there.

Fortunately, Mellie was gone, but for all Betsy knew, the child might be crouched down against the cabin, her eyes shut against discovery as they had been this morning.

Hollis asked angrily, "Ye think I'm thet dumb, teacher?"

Her back was against his chest, and his breath was as

awful as the stench of his clothing. She gagged, and he removed his hand from her mouth.

"I never said you were dumb!" she countered.

"Thought it, though . . . tryin' ter fool me. Ain't no one else 'round. I been watchin' from the graveyard behind the church most all afternoon. I seen ye workin' the shcool garden with 'em, 'n I seen them brats go home."

He twisted her toward him and grabbed both of her hands in one of his. His hooded gray eyes filled with pleasure as he jerked the pins from her hair and watched it tumble over her shoulders.

Betsy tried to wrestle free, but he pulled her toward him. "I do like ye redheads! I do indeed."

He was going to kiss her, she realized, and twisted her head away.

"Ain't gonna be that easy, gettin' out of a kiss," he said, and his hand forcefully turned her face up to his.

Affronted by his disgusting lips, strength surged through her, and she kicked his shin with all of her might.

"Yiii!" he yelled, loosening his grip.

Tearing free, she ran around her desk, screaming for help, but he was too fast and caught her almost immediately.

"Ye'll pay fer thet!" He slapped her face hard, knocking her against the desk. Before she found her footing, he kicked her ankle. "How'd ye like thet yerself?"

She screamed and battled on, determined not to give in even if she were killed. Blood ran down her face as he tore at her dress. "Leave me alone! Leave me alone!" she cried out.

Shots rang out near the schoolhouse, and the man froze. Glancing toward the door, he angrily loosened his grip.

Betsy caught her breath as she saw Rufus running toward the open schoolhouse door, shotgun in hand. Hollis must have seen him, too, for he rushed across the classroom.

"I'll get ye!" he yelled back at her, his face boiling with anger. "I'll get ye yet!" And with that, he jumped out the nearest window, scattering the herb garden tins from the sill.

Stunned, it was a moment before she hurried to the window. She saw him disappear into the graveyard behind the church, Rufus firing at him.

When her assailant was out of sight, Betsy tried to regain her composure. She attempted to straighten her dress, but the yellow calico was torn at her bosom, exposing her white camisole. She raised her hands to put her tumble of curls back up, but reaching up pained her ribs terribly.

"You all right, chile?" Dilsey asked as she peered into the classroom. "You all right now?"

Betsy nodded numbly, holding the scrap of her dress over her camisole. But she wasn't . . . she wasn't . . . and she wondered if she ever would be all right again. She felt as damaged as the herb garden tins that lay scattered on the floor.

"Doctah Buchanan, he due home anytime, 'n I tol' Miz Selena and Miz Mellie to send him soon as he come—"

Betsy shook her head. "I'll be all right."

"Beggin' yo' pardon, Miz Talbot, but you shore look lak you needs doctorin'," Dilsey said.

Outside, a horse clopped up, and a voice shouted, "Did you get him, Rufus?"

"No, suh. You knows my shootin'. He got plumb away. I di'n't bring no horse, jest come runnin' when Mellie tell us a bad man heah at de school."

Betsy stood numbly in the log classroom, unable to think of a word to speak in her defense as Adam Buchanan hurried in through the door.

"Well. . . ." he said, his hazel eyes taking in her appearance. She waited for him to say that a woman teacher out at the diggings should expect something like this to happen.

Instead he asked, "Where do you hurt most?"

She pressed one hand to her mouth and chin, the other to her ribs. Her foot hurt, too. It occurred to her that Aunt Jessica might tell Father, and he'd make them come home. Best not to make too much of this. She pulled the handkerchief from her pocket, hoping to clean the blood from her face.

"Here, let me do that," Adam said. "Sit down at this desk. And, Dilsey, please bring us a crock of fresh water from the well. And tell Rufus he'd better bring the buggy here."

"Yas, suh!" Dilsey replied and ran.

Betsy sat down, and suddenly the chinked log walls seemed to spin around her. Even the blackboard circled the room, and then a whirling grayness filled her head.

The next thing she knew, Adam was holding her up against the desk, and it wasn't at all frightening . . . not like that monster, Hollis. Indeed, it was rather pleasant.

"Better now?" he asked.

She nodded, suddenly embarrassed, and she noticed that he was flushed, as well.

Dilsey came running with the water crock. "She be so white behind all that blood. She gwine be all right?"

"Yes, I think she'll be fine."

"You be careful now," Dilsey warned him, "she ain't no ugly miner to jest patch up."

"So I notice," he said dryly.

Betsy kept her eyes closed and was only dimly aware of him probing carefully at her jaw and chin, then at her ribs. He touched a painful place and she cried out.

"It hurts here?" he asked, touching her ribs again.

She nodded and, opening her eyes, saw the same air of compassion about him as when he had attended Yank Stevens after the attempted stagecoach holdup. Despite her pain and weakness, she knew that Adam Buchanan was called to be a doctor as clearly as she was called to be a teacher.

"Here?" he asked, still checking her ribs. "And here?"

She nodded, refusing to cry out.

Dilsey said, "She ain't talked yet."

Adam frowned with concentration, ignoring Dilsey as he checked Betsy's ankle.

Finally he stood up and said, "Miss Talbot, it appears that you have a cut lip, a bruised mouth, a bruised foot, and one or two ribs that may be broken. I suggest we get you into the buggy and take you home, then I can bandage those ribs with your aunt in attendance."

She nodded again, her lips quivering. She was not going to cry, she told herself; she was not going to cry, no matter what.

The flesh is heir to pain, flashed through her mind, although at the moment the humiliation of the ordeal pained her most. And now Adam Buchanan, who did not want her as a teacher, had come to attend her.

"What are you thinking, Miss Talbot?" Adam asked.

How could she tell him that she was afraid he would try to nullify her teaching contract or make sure she wasn't offered one for the fall term? That she felt humiliated before him?

"What are you thinking?" he persisted.

Her assailant's wild, bloodshot eyes came to mind again, and she knew she must tell Adam. "He told me he was going to . . . that he was going to get me yet."

He stared at her. "And how do you intend to avoid that?"

"I—am going to to be more careful and to trust in the Lord."

Adam's hazel eyes filled with faint disbelief, and Betsy

added with conviction, "We are to trust God in spite of all things, even adversity."

"I see," he said, no longer meeting her gaze. "I see."

7

Aunt Jessica was sitting outside on the veranda in the shade of the cedar tree, sewing. When Adam Buchanan drove up to the log cabin with Betsy in his buggy, she looked up from her work and, alarmed, came to her feet. "Whatever's the matter?" she asked, hurrying to them.

Betsy shook her head helplessly, all too aware of the picture she presented with her auburn hair tumbling over her shoulders.

"She was badly pummeled by a man after school," Adam explained as he helped her down from the buggy.

"Oh, my dear!" her aunt said. "Oh, my poor dear!"

"It's best to get her right to bed," Adam said.

"Yes, of course," Aunt Jessica agreed. Her eyes full of concern, she assisted Betsy on one side, while Adam lent his strength on the other. "There is nothing like rest to help with anything."

"She will have to take medicine against the pain, as well," he answered. "And I would like to examine her again."

Her face and her body throbbing ever more painfully, Betsy could not have cared less that her opinion was not solicited.

Once they'd assisted her into the cabin and she was

sitting on the edge of the bed, Adam said to Aunt Jessica, "I'll wait in the parlor while you get her into bed."

"Come, Betsy, let me help you," her aunt said.

Even in her painful and unnerved state, it occurred to Betsy that, though her aunt was not her birth mother, she had always been there to help when she was needed. "What would I do without you?" she managed as Aunt Jessica pulled off her torn yellow frock. "Oh!"

"I'm so sorry, my dear—"

"And I'm sorry to complain. I know you are doing . . . your best."

Before long, Aunt Jessica had helped her into her nightgown and tucked her into bed. "Here, let me pull your hair back more modestly." Betsy forced herself to lie still on the cool pillow while her aunt arranged her hair behind her head.

"Try to rest," she said soothingly. "I'll get Dr. Buchanan now."

As soon as Betsy closed her eyes, the scene with her assailant flashed through her mind anew. She quickly opened her eyes and let them wander about the log walls of the small bedroom, vaguely aware of her aunt's and Adam's subdued voices in the parlor.

When they came into the bedroom, he probed her ribs again, this time through her white dimity nightgown, and she thought her face, by contrast, must be bright red.

"I don't believe the ribs are broken after all. Probably bruised like the rest of you."

"I'm grateful for that, at least," she said.

"I suggest you rest in bed for a few days," he said. "Your aunt has agreed to take over your classes tomorrow—"

"But what if that . . . that Hollis returns and harms Aunt Jessica?"

"Hollis—?" Adam asked.

"Yes," she replied with a shudder, "that's what he called himself." She recalled his words clearly. *Come on now, give Hollis a kiss. . . .*

She repeated, "What if he harms Aunt Jessica?"

"I'll speak with the school board about precautions," Adam replied. "I can spare Rufus to watch the school for a few days, but as I've maintained from the beginning, we need a male teacher. This is just one of the reasons—"

"A male teacher!" Betsy protested, despite her pain. She pulled the bedclothes over her chest, not caring what kind of a picture she made with her hair spilling over her shoulders. "I have a three-month contract, and no one is going to stop me from fulfilling it, Dr. Buchanan. I know you object to a woman teacher, but I intend to teach those children. Now that I've learned this lesson, I shall keep the door locked when I am in the schoolroom alone. As for sparing Rufus or anyone else, I assure you that I can take care of myself."

"As you did today?" he returned.

"And as I will hereafter!" If she were not in her nightgown and did not hurt so badly, she would have climbed right out of bed to stand up to him.

He said, exasperated, "I have never in my life seen a woman so intent upon working."

She drew a deep breath, though it hurt her ribs. "Not all women are alike!"

"So it appears. Nonetheless, Oak Hill is no place for an unmarried woman. I shall speak to the school board about canceling the contract."

She replied as evenly as she could manage, "And I shall insist upon keeping it in force!"

He stared at her for a moment, then the dimples just above his beard deepened. "It appears that you are a very determined young woman, Miss Talbot. I suspect you will recover more rapidly as a result of it."

"I shall," she replied. "And I shall teach those children to your complete satisfaction, Dr. Buchanan."

"That remains to be seen. What is most important now is that you get well." He snapped his medical bag shut.

"Thank you for your help," she said a bit too heatedly.

"That is the job of the town's doctor."

"And teaching is the job of the town's teacher!"

He shook his head as though she were hopeless. "Rest now, just rest. I shall come by again late tomorrow afternoon. As for Friday night socials, under the circumstances there is no point in the school board even considering such events."

The moment he was gone, she realized that her body ached from her feet to the top of her head, and she suddenly felt weak everywhere. *Oh, Lord, why did this have to happen to me?* she asked. *Why did this have to take place?*

Father would probably say that even the most godly people were sometimes caught in the web of sin that mankind had spun since the day of Adam and Eve's disobedience. And she was a sinner herself, with her selfish thoughts and wishes, just as bad as the rest of them.

At length she remembered that God wanted her to give thanks in spite of all things and to forgive the wretch who had assaulted her, difficult as both admonitions seemed. *Lord, as an act of my will, whether I wish to or not, I do give thanks in this,* she prayed. *And I do forgive that man Hollis. And I forgive Adam Buchanan for being so bullheaded . . . so insistent about having a man teacher for the school.*

As Betsy persevered in prayer, the aches began to fade and she drifted into the soft graying edges of sleep. The last image in her mind's eye was of Adam Buchanan's face as he tended to her and the fleeting notion that if he weren't married and so difficult, she could easily like him far more than she wished.

When Betsy awakened the next morning, Aunt Jessica, already dressed to teach school, was carrying in a breakfast tray. "I've brought soft-boiled eggs and porridge," she said. "Rose and Louisa have promised to take turns looking in on you during the day."

"Thank you, but I shall be fine," Betsy objected. "Perhaps I can take over at school this afternoon. I don't like you having to take my classroom as we did at home. . . ." She could scarcely tell her aunt it was because she was looking so much older and more tired lately. As Betsy sat up in bed, however, her throbbing body told her she was still far from well.

Aunt Jessica smiled as she put the breakfast tray on Betsy's lap. "You would scare the little ones, Betsy. Your face is quite discolored."

Betsy touched her chin, and its soreness confirmed her aunt's words. "I expect it is."

"Rose has a key to the cabin. Will you be all right until she comes?"

"I'll be fine, but I do hate to be so much trouble when I came here to help!"

"You know very well you'd do the same for us," Aunt Jessica said, then her eyes glimmered with amusement. "And in this case—as far as I am concerned—it surely is more blessed to give than to have received your bruising and bumps!"

Betsy had to smile herself, though it pained her chin. "Yes, I expect it is."

"I'll lock the door behind me," Aunt Jessica said. "We shall have to be more careful about that."

Betsy nodded in acceptance. "Why, oh, why must there always be evil about?" she lamented again.

"Proverbs says, 'Fret not thyself because of evil men.'"

As usual, her aunt had Scripture to suit every occasion, Betsy thought. "I do not intend to," she replied. "I intend to get well and return to school." That in mind, she began to eat her eggs and porridge, determined to consume all of them in the hope that it would hasten her recovery. She must be well and teaching by Monday.

By mid-morning, she had already slept several more hours and only awakened when Rose let herself in with the children. After much hushing and whispering in the parlor, Rose tiptoed into the bedroom with a glass of buttermilk. Seeing Betsy, she halted in shock. "I'm so sorry—"

"Do I look that frightful?" she asked weakly.

"I—have seen worse," Rose equivocated. "I'm so sorry such a thing would happen to you, or to anyone else. It seems especially terrible because we had so hoped you'd like it in Oak Hill. I do hope you won't want to leave us."

"I'll survive," Betsy declared, "and I expect I'll still like it in Oak Hill." She accepted the glass of cool buttermilk and slowly drank it down, and, as soon as Rose left, fell asleep again.

At midday Louisa brought a bowl of chicken soup and, while Betsy ate, her cousin told how Aunt Jessica's idea of a church supply of extra household goods for sharing with newcomers had already been helpful for emigrants who'd arrived by covered wagon last week.

"Aunt Jessica is just the kind of helpful person we need in our church," Louisa said. "She's a walking example of what we should all strive to be, and she doesn't even have any idea of it."

Betsy nodded. "She does put her trust in God. And He gives her His love for people . . . often enormous love. She has a good many ideas of how we can help people here."

When Betsy finished the chicken soup she said, "I intend to teach this afternoon." She swung her feet out of bed. When she stood up on her swollen foot, however, pain shot through it.

"Adam Buchanan says you must stay in bed all day, and most of Saturday and Sunday," Louisa said. "By then your face should be . . . better, as well."

Betsy lay back again. "Could you please bring me the mirror, Louisa?"

Her beautiful auburn-haired cousin shook her head. "Time enough for mirrors later," she said, then her blue eyes brightened. "Or are you expecting an important caller?"

"Only Dr. Buchanan late this afternoon."

"Good," Louisa said, then added, "I do wish he'd bring his family to church. I think Selena would see there how Christ can fill the hole in our hearts. And Mellie could begin to make friends with children her age."

"I thought I might offer to bring Mellie if the opportunity arises," Betsy said. "Perhaps Selena, too."

Louisa beamed. "Wouldn't that be wonderful! Not that it would surprise me too much with all of the amazing things that have happened thus far in the church here. And now, my dear cousin, time for your medicine and more rest."

Betsy sat up long enough to take another spoonful of the bitter mixture, then lay back on her pillow again.

"I'm on my way to school now," Louisa said. "I baked little honey cakes for the students. I thought a bit of honey might sweeten them for Aunt Jessica this afternoon."

"I'm sure it will help," Betsy replied, "but perhaps you had better not go there alone."

"Jonathan is accompanying me. He's taking the children to Rose now. In fact, he's going to visit at the school this afternoon."

"To watch for Hollis?"

Louisa nodded. "The men think he's fled, but they're taking turns watching the schoolhouse for several days. Rufus spent the morning on watch, and Jonathan is taking a turn now. Did you know the land behind the church and the school run down to the river?"

"I've assumed that—"

"There's a path behind the graveyard to a lower level, a flat area in the woods, and the men found evidence of it being used as a hideout or a meeting place. The stagecoach robbers, or at least a gang of them, always disappear so quickly that the authorities suspect they have prearranged hideouts. Our men think this may be one of them."

"Then Hollis and others might have been there before I even came to Oak Hill?"

"Yes."

"That puts an entirely different light on the matter," Betsy decided. "Still, what if . . . what if Hollis has a gun or a knife? I hadn't even considered that."

"The men worked out precautions at the meeting at our cabin last night," Louisa assured her. "And Adam is going to speak with the federal authorities."

Betsy's spirits wavered. "I do feel it's all because of me."

"No, Betsy—because of Hollis. He's not just a threat to you, but to all of the girls and women here," Louisa replied. "They've asked all of us to be careful, to lock our doors and windows until we're certain he's left the area."

"I'm so sorry to think of Jonathan taking time from his church work to sit there this afternoon—"

"He doesn't mind in the least, nor will his time be wasted. Aunt Jessica asked him to teach on what Israel was like when the Lord grew up there, so the children will have history and geography right from the Bible."

"A fine idea," Betsy responded, lying back against her pillows, "but then Aunt Jessica's usually are."

"You know, 'all things come together for good to them that love God, to them who are the called according to His purpose,'" Louisa said. "In the midst of tribulations, it doesn't seem possible, but when I think of my own life—of fleeing from my horrid situation in Virginia—I see that the verse is surely true. To this day, I can hardly believe I survived a shipwreck and the jungles of Panama. Yet, if that had not taken place, I might never have married Jonathan, and he—and this life—are worth everything I endured."

"Thank you for reminding me," Betsy replied, growing sleepier as the medicine took effect. "Thank you, my dear cousin." As she drifted off into sleep, she murmured, "You're a wonderful pastor's wife."

"Not nearly as good as I should be . . . but I know you're a wonderful teacher."

Late in the afternoon, Adam Buchanan brought Aunt Jessica home. "I'm pleased to see you're feeling better," he said to Betsy with that compassionate look in his eyes. "Continued rest is important."

Still groggy with sleep and medicine, she replied, "You can be a most personable man when you're not being so—difficult."

"Is that so?" he asked, his dimples deepening.

She had to smile herself, though she still wished he were not on the school board.

Saturday morning Mr. Wilmington came to wish her well. He was as pleasant and encouraging as the rest of her visitors, but Betsy continued to feel a niggling sense of blame for the problem. If only she had locked the schoolroom door . . . if only she had handled her assailant differently. Likely Mr. Wilmington was also wishing they'd hired a man.

She disliked missing church on Sunday morning and dinner afterwards at Louisa's and Jonathan's. On Sunday afternoon, however, Betsy was on her feet again, and Rose brought brown face lotion from the Mercantile. The swelling had gone down, and the two of them laughingly attempted to cover what remained of the bruises on Betsy's face.

"What if the children ask questions?" she asked.

"Few people in Oak Hill know exactly what happened or to whom," Rose said, "and children are often so full of their own selves they might not even think to ask. Aunt Jessica only told them you were ill, so they would have little reason to inquire further."

"I hope so," Betsy said. "If not, I can always rely on Aunt Jessica's solution to steering a classroom discussion away from a subject: ask a question!"

In the midst of their experimentation with the brown face lotion, her aunt brought a letter into the bedroom. "For you, Betsy. Dilsey delivered it, and she insists on waiting outside for your reply."

Perplexed, Betsy opened the letter and read the beautifully formed handwriting.

> *Sunday*
>
> *Dear Miss Talbot,*
>
> *Mellie and I would be delighted if you would take tea with us tomorrow afternoon. If you can honor us with your presence, I shall send my brother, Fayette, or Rufus for you when school lets out.*
>
> *Sincerely,*
>
> *Selena Williams Buchanan*

"Selena Buchanan has invited me to have tea with her and Mellie!" she told her aunt and Rose in amazement.

"Perhaps this is your opportunity to befriend them," Rose suggested.

"Yes . . . perhaps it is."

Aunt Jessica said, "If you could delay your visit until next week when your strength has returned, it might be better."

"In Selena's state of mind, she might feel slighted," Betsy replied. "I think I should accept the invitation now, and I do feel much better. Let me send my reply with Dilsey."

After her reply had been dispatched, Betsy said, "I didn't know that Selena had a brother living with them."

"Only visiting again, I expect," Rose said. "He's her twin, and he comes and goes. I must warn you, Fayette Williams is quite possibly the most handsome man out at the diggings, if not in the entire state of California."

"Why, Rose Anne Talbot!" Betsy exclaimed. "What about my brother, your dear husband?"

The circles of color on Rose's cheeks deepened. "Joshua is wonderfully handsome to me, but I know it's partly because I love him. Fayette, however, is another matter. Whether one loved him or not, he has staggering good looks. Be careful, Betsy. He'd be easy to fall in love with, even if he did bring a dozen slaves with him to work the goldfields."

"He brought slaves?"

"He and several other Southerners did. The miners were outraged, of course, and didn't allow them to work the diggings. That's where the mining law started, 'One man, one claim.' The truth is, the white men thought themselves too good to labor alongside slaves. To make a short story of it, Fayette's slaves ran off, all except Dilsey and Rufus, doubtless because they're too old."

"I'm glad to hear it, that the others ran off." She glanced at Aunt Jessica with a wry smile. "I'm just waiting for you to say it: 'Handsome is as handsome does.'"

Her aunt laughed. "I can save my breath then, since you've spared me the trouble!"

Betsy's return to school on Monday morning was not in the least uncomfortable, since Aunt Jessica accompanied her. On the way, however, they did keep a sharp eye on the church graveyard and the woods beyond.

Betsy wore the new pale green lawn frock her aunt had sewn for her, and it lifted her spirits. The dress had a high lace collar and lace cuffs, and the fabric was so soft and lovely that no one would guess it had been made from a length of fabric left over from their new curtains and bed coverlets.

"Two teachers!" the children exclaimed as they trooped into the log schoolhouse.

"No, today I am only visiting," Aunt Jessica told them.

"We been havin' lots o' visitors," one of the children replied. "Old Rufus is sittin' outside on the steps, and Pastor Chambers, and now Mrs. Alcott."

"A good many people are interested in whether or not you are learning everything you should," Betsy said, determined to keep her response as honest as possible. "Your education is not only important to you, but to the welfare of the community and ultimately to the entire nation. Can anyone explain why that is so?"

Aunt Jessica tightened her lips to conceal her amusement, and Betsy had to fight a smile herself, for her question did seem a masterful change of direction.

The only other reference to visitors was Garnett Jurgen's, "Can my new mama visit the classroom someday?"

"Of course. We like to have visitors," Betsy replied. She recalled that Lucius Alden had volunteered his guarding services for tomorrow afternoon, and she added, "Tomorrow Mr. Alden will visit. He's the new stagecoach agent, and he helps at the Mercantile, too. Perhaps he'll tell us about his years of driving on the National Road, which goes from Maryland to Illinois now. Learning is often much more interesting when people share such aspects of their lives with us."

Garnett said, "Our new mama came from San Francisco. Remember you saw her come in on the stagecoach?"

"Indeed I do," Betsy replied. "It was such a pleasure to see all of you there."

George Jurgen said, half in anger, "Garnett don't know anything. Our stepmother came from New Orleans. San Francisco was just another one of her stopping places."

Suspecting that George did not quite approve of his new stepmother, Betsy said, "It would be interesting to learn something of New Orleans. Many of us will never have the opportunity to see it or to see the Mississippi River, which runs through it."

Farrell Williamson offered, "We saw the Mississippi River when we come by covered wagon. She's so wide, we had to cross 'er on a ferry."

"When we *came,*" Betsy corrected and decided not to tamper with the rest of his speech for the time being. She headed for the map. "Here's the Mississippi River. Where did you cross, Farrell?"

"By St. Louis."

"Here's St. Louis," Betsy showed them on the map. "And here is New Orleans. Perhaps some day soon we could all discuss how we came to California. Just now, let's do it briefly with a show of hands. How many of you came here by covered wagon through the Rockies and the Sierra Nevadas?"

Most of the children raised their hands.

"That's how I came in 1846. And how many of you came by ship around the Horn?" she asked, pointing out Cape Horn at the southerly tip of South America.

Two hands went up.

"How many through Panama or Nicaragua?" She pointed out both routes and looked over the classroom. "No one. Perhaps you know that a railroad is being built across Panama now, which means you may have fellow classmates by next year who have crossed the Isthmus. You already know two grown-ups who did—the Reverend and Mrs. Chambers, although they came through the jungle long before a railroad was even considered."

As the children contemplated that, she added, "How many of you were born here?"

Only Tilda Stoddard's hand went up.

"Then your family must have come before the gold rush," Betsy said to Tilda.

Tilda nodded. "My folks came in a covered wagon 'fore I was born."

"Tilda is one of the few Californians born in our state," Betsy said. "And now, let us have our psalm for this morning."

The remainder of the day went well, and it was only at lunchtime and during the afternoon recess that Betsy remembered Hollis again. When they were outdoors, she and Aunt Jessica kept a sharp eye out on the graveyard area on one side of the grounds and on the woods by the Buchanans' house, but there was no sign of him or anyone else, not even of Mellie Buchanan at the edge of the woods or at the schoolhouse window. The children, who played a rousing game of fox and geese during the recesses, seemed oblivious to their concern. Nor did they seem to take notice of the brown lotion on Betsy's face.

Finally the afternoon ended. When all of the children had left, Aunt Jessica said, "Are you feeling well enough to go to Selena's for tea?"

Tired, Betsy shook her head. "I shall go nonetheless. I do wish you'd been invited, as well. I must confess I'm a bit uneasy about visiting her."

"The Lord will direct you," her aunt assured her. She gave Betsy a wry smile. "I am half sorry to miss it myself, since Fayette's looks were described so glowingly by Rose!"

"Oh, Aunt Jessica!"

"How could I resist?" her aunt laughed as she began to close up the room. "You had better put more brown lotion on your face and rearrange your hair."

"I suppose I should." She took the brown lotion and small mirror from her desk and covered the yellowing bruises with the lotion, then tucked the stray wisps of hair into her chignon. "I hear a buggy now."

They quickly finished closing up the classroom and let themselves out the door.

"That must be Fayette," Betsy said as they hurried down the schoolhouse path to the hitching post where the horses and buggy had pulled up. The dark-haired man, perhaps thirty, wore a fine brown frock coat and matching trousers. He stepped down lazily from the buggy and, nodding, gave them a languid smile as they approached.

"Miss Talbot," he said. His voice was low and his accent southern. As he looked at her she realized that he possessed the most compelling brown eyes she had ever seen.

"Ah'm Fayette Williams," he said, "Selena's brother."

Betsy nodded. "I am pleased to meet you. This is my aunt—" She stopped, realizing that Fayette intended to kiss her hand, a courtesy now rarely kept.

His lips, full and sensual, grazed her fingertips, silencing her introduction entirely. Looking up at her, he was the very picture of manly comeliness: straight nose, strong chin, thick dark brows, and wavy dark hair. His individual features, however, were only a part of it, for there was an aura of masculine magnetism about him, from his well-polished brown boots up to his tousled hair. He was indeed handsome, slaver or not!

His drowsy brown eyes filled with admiration. "Ah must say, the reports of your loveliness were not sufficiently eloquent, Miss Talbot."

"Thank you, Mr. Williams," she replied, wondering who might have spoken about her. "This is my aunt, Mrs. Alcott, who lives with me."

"It is a rare pleasure to meet you," he said, bending to kiss Aunt Jessica's hand as well. He studied her face carefully. "Ah see quite a familial resemblance, Mrs. Alcott. Yes, a clear resemblance."

"Do you?" Aunt Jessica asked, pleased.

"I do indeed," he replied. "In a backward place such as this, where we so seldom see handsome women, this is a memorable moment for me, though Ah daresay it would be if Ah had met you anywhere else in our country. Ah fervently hope you will afford me the honor of driving you home, Mrs. Alcott."

"Thank you," Betsy began, "I had hoped you might—"

"Thank you, Mr. Williams," Aunt Jessica interjected firmly, "but I am certain that I can manage by myself."

"Now, Ah shall not hear of it," he said. "If you were my aunt, Ah would hope that a kindhearted gentleman would escort you safely home. Ah am reminded of doing unto others as we would have them do unto us."

Aunt Jessica softened at that and returned his smile. "Thank you. Since you put it like that, I shall accept your offer with gratefulness."

He helped Aunt Jessica into the buggy with utmost courtesy and insisted that she sit beside him in the middle of the seat. "And, Miss Talbot, if Ah may assist you?"

His hand was warm and sure, and he seated her as though she were a treasure, then asked both of them most solicitously, "Are you certain y'all are comfortable?"

Betsy might have smiled at his elaborate concern, if it did not also seem quite genuine. Never having met anyone from farther south than Virginia, she decided to enjoy his courtliness, a quality seldom evident in California men.

He started the horses forward with a sure hand, and it occurred to Betsy that he was the kind of man who would be especially good with horses—and perhaps with women.

After they'd delivered Aunt Jessica to the cabin and Fayette had seen her safely in, he climbed up into the buggy with a slow smile at Betsy. "Ah encountered several men at the northern goldfields who could not say enough about the lovely new schoolmistress at Oak Hill," he said. "They met you and members of your family on a Sacramento riverboat."

"Sven Lindborg and Ralston Stone?"

"Yes, Sven and Ralston. They are singing your praises throughout the country. You will have an endless procession of admirers now that your whereabouts are known."

She gave a wry laugh. "That confirms the scarcity of women in California!"

"Not at all," he protested as he flicked the reins over the horses. "You would be remarkable even in Savannah. And now it remains for me truly to make your acquaintance, Miss Betsy Talbot."

Father often called her an innocent, and to prove she wasn't, at least to herself, she taunted, "And what, pray tell, does a southern gentleman mean by that expression . . . 'truly to make your acquaintance?' "

He laughed softly. "Why, Ah expect what any other gentleman hopes for . . . coming to know your interests and your hopes and your heart's desires."

"I already have my heart's desire," she said softly.

"Which is?"

"Teaching school here at Oak Hill."

He darted a sidelong glance at her. "Ah thought a lovely young woman like you would have other desires as well."

"I am quite content."

He smiled rather knowingly. "Are you now?"

She was on the verge of retorting a bit too sharply at his probing, for it minded her of Adam Buchanan's suspicion that she was seeking a husband, but she restrained herself. "Indeed, I am content."

He had an amused look about his face even in repose, she realized. "Are you content, Mr. Williams?" she asked.

He gave a laugh. "Touché! In truth, Miss Talbot, Ah would be far more content if Ah hit a good solid vein of pure gold, one that never gave out."

She had to smile, for everyone seemed to have that same wish. "You mentioned Sven and Ralston. You must be working in the northern goldfields."

"Yes, indeed."

She was dubious about his being a miner since he possessed neither a leathery, sun-browned complexion, nor work-toughened hands. "What did you do before that, if I may inquire?"

"Of course, you may. Nothing is more important than knowing a person's family background to learn more quickly about him," he said. "Our family owned a house in Savannah and a plantation out in the country. My dear sister, Selena, and I come from a long line of landholders."

He slowed the horses so as not to raise dust near the Buchanan house. "Well, here we are now. Poor Selena . . . Ah don't know how she manages out here in the wilderness."

As they drove up to the two-story brown clapboard house, Betsy said, "But this is one of the least rustic dwellings I've seen since leaving San Francisco. It's quite a nice house by California standards."

"That may be," he replied, "but in my mind's eye, Ah still see Selena in the parlor of our Savannah house or the veranda of the plantation house . . . or being received by nobility in Paris or Vienna. You may know that she gave several private violin concerts in Europe."

"I heard she is a fine violinist."

"Yes. Unfortunately, we were not reared for the wilderness," he said. "It's difficult to change one's way of life."

"I've never met Selena, but I can imagine you riding out on a fine horse from a great plantation stable."

He smiled as he reined in the horses. "Can you now?"

"Indeed, I can, Mr. Williams."

"You are a most percipient young lady. Ah wonder if it would be amiss for me to ask you to call me Fayette. Mr. Williams reminds me all too sadly of my dear departed father, and then of my departed mother, as well."

"Yes, of course," Betsy replied, knowing how bereft she would be if both of her parents were no longer living. It was bad enough not to have a mother alive, particularly one who was always described as so kindly and beloved.

His thick, dark brows rose hopefully, and with a hint of a smile, he asked, "And dare Ah call you Betsy in private without risking your wrath?"

"Certainly. I have always been Betsy to everyone, except to the schoolchildren, of course."

He helped her down from the buggy, his strong hand cupped under her elbow. As their eyes met, a surge of attraction passed between them that jolted her to the soles of her feet. She quickly put her skirt to rights, and when she dared look up, he proferred his arm most politely.

"Ah do believe Ah shall always remember this day of making your acquaintance, Miss Betsy Talbot," he murmured.

Had he experienced the same sensation, she wondered, both encouraged and dismayed.

"And now, before Ah speak out of turn, allow me to escort you in to meet my dear sister, who is all too much in need of an intelligent lady friend. Ah do wish to advise you that she has an artistic temperament."

"Yes, I am sure that she must," Betsy replied with mixed emotions.

They crossed a spacious veranda made of gray river slate, whereupon stood white benches for enjoying the wooded scenery and the sound of the river below.

Inside, the formal entry held mahogany Eastern Seaboard furnishings, but lovelier yet was Mellie, wearing a pink dress and with her hair tied back in a great pink ribbon, peeking around the corner at them.

"Mellie," Fayette said, "come here and let me introduce Miss Talbot, the schoolmistress."

As he made the introductions, Mellie stepped out shyly, caught up her frilly dress, and bobbed a curtsy. "How do you do, Miss Tal-bot," she pronounced tremulously, then glanced up at her uncle for approval.

"It's a pleasure to meet you, Mellie," Betsy said, deciding to make no mention of their earlier encounters.

"How do you do, Miss Tal-bot," Mellie repeated with more enthusiasm and bobbed another curtsy, her eyes suddenly dancing with their secret.

Betsy bit back a laugh.

"That was very nicely done, Mellie," her uncle said in dismissal, then to Betsy. "Won't you please come into the parlor?"

As Betsy stepped forward, still curbing her mirth over Mellie, she saw that the entire parlor was furnished in shades of rose. Selena had been watching the proceedings from the

At length Dilsey brought in a black violin case and took out the highly polished instrument. Handing it to Selena, Dilsey asked, "You sho' you want to play now, Miss Selena?"

Selena glanced at Fayette, then she nodded. "Ah am sure, Dilsey." With that, she stood up from the settee and took the violin and bow. "Ah shall play by the windows."

"A nice, quiet piece," Fayette suggested. "Perhaps the one you wrote about the sun's circuit of the earth."

Selena smiled at him, then moved with perfect grace across the room to the windows overlooking the woods, her ivory lace frock trailing elegantly behind her. At the window, she tucked the violin under her chin, raised the bow to the strings, and touched them tentatively, then quickly adjusted the wooden pegs.

Silhouetted against the light and the woods, she raised the bow in earnest. She touched it to the strings and began to play softly, like the twitter of birds at dawn. As the music grew in strength and filled the parlor, it seemed that she and the violin were one, joined at her shoulder and chin, an earthling who made the air quiver with ethereal beauty.

Although Betsy had never heard such music before, she knew it spoke of far more than the sun's daily circuit of the earth, but of life and its joys and sorrows. From sunrise, the music moved on to waterfalls tumbling joyously, then to shadows and light, finally, to dark clouds blotting out the brilliant rays of sunset and ending with eternal darkness.

When it was over, Selena shook her head slightly as though perplexed as to her whereabouts. Clearly, the music took her out of herself and far away, perhaps back to the courts of Europe or to the veranda of her plantation home.

Mellie said, "Oh, Mama, it was so pretty!"

Fayette added, "It was superb as always, Selena. As excellent as when you played in Paris. You are the true instru-

settee upon which she sat in an exquisite ivory lace frock. Seeing her, Betsy felt all too aware that her own dress matched her cabin's green curtains and bed coverlets.

Selena made not the slightest effort to rise in greeting, though she smiled quite charmingly. She was an even more beautiful woman than the one who had run wildly through the woods in her nightdress. Her dark wavy hair was done up in a chignon, with tendrils curling artfully on either side of her perfect oval face. Her brown eyes were enormous, like Fayette's, and her rosy lips were equally full and sensuous.

As her brother made the introductions, Selena said, "Ah am delighted to meet you, Miss Talbot. Forgive me for not coming to greet you, but Ah am not as well as one might hope."

"I am sorry to hear that, Mrs. Buchanan."

Smiling graciously, Selena turned to her daughter. "Mellie, dear, please ask Dilsey to bring in the tea things."

Mellie's hazel eyes widened with excited understanding. "Yes, ma'am," she answered and hurried out.

"Miss Talbot," Fayette said with a smile at addressing her formally again, "would you care to sit here?" He indicated a rose parlor chair opposite the low tea table and the settee.

"Yes, thank you."

As she took her seat, Mellie shouted from somewhere in the house, "Dil-sey, bring the tea things now!"

Selena smiled indulgently. "Ah fear that my daughter is not as well versed as she should be in the social amenities. If we still lived in the South or even Maryland, where my husband was born and reared. . . . ." Her voice trailed off, but it was clear she held a low opinion of California social life.

"She seems a very lovely child, more mannerly than most," Betsy said. "I can scarcely recall seeing a child curtsy nowadays."

Fayette sat down on the settee beside his sister and replied rather proudly, "Ah expect that we Southerners hold fast to our customs as long as we are able."

Betsy wondered if that included slavery, but this was no time to ask. Instead, she said, "It is so kind for you to have invited me to your lovely home."

Selena glanced at her brother rather fetchingly, and he quickly put in, "You are our schoolmistress, and the Williams family has always promoted education, whether it be reading or writing or arithmetic . . . or the arts, of course."

"I am glad to hear of it," Betsy said, turning to Selena. "I understand, Mrs. Buchanan, that you are a fine violinist."

Selena shrugged her elegant shoulders. "Ah'm unsure that Ah can still play well enough to be worthy of the name."

"Of course, you can, my dear sister." Fayette patted her arm encouragingly. "Ah hoped you would entertain us this afternoon. Surely Miss Talbot misses the cultured life, too."

"Fayette, you know Ah don't wish to—"

"Ah know only that you have had little opportunity to practice lately, Selena," he said, placing his hand over hers, "but your playing, even without practice, has always been far superior to that of many who practice most assiduously."

Betsy felt certain that Selena would object, but Fayette raised a warning brow. An interplay of unspoken messages flowed between them, such as one often heard took place between twins. She had never witnessed anything like it, and she looked away in embarrassment.

At length Selena said with a rather vague smile, "Fayette has always been most persuasive, Miss Talbot. Perhaps Ah shall play one piece after we've had our refreshments, but only if you like."

Betsy forced a smile in return. "Of course. I would enjoy it very much."

Dilsey carried in the tea tray and set it on the low tab between them, and Mellie distributed the small rose-color tea napkins.

"Thank you, Mellie," Betsy said.

"You're welcome, Miss Tal-bot," the small girl responded as pleased as though she had been taught such social grace just recently.

Selena's elegant hands trembled slightly as she served the tea and small sugared cakes. It appeared that Fayette's pres ence and graceful assistance were of great importance and consolation to her.

The scene reminded Betsy of a play. They were pretend ing that Mellie hadn't called them to come to her rescue last week . . . that Selena hadn't run wildly through the woods in her nightgown . . . that a tea here in the woods was quite the usual social function. As they ate the small cakes and drank their tea with perfect politeness, she was uncertain what else in the charming scene might be pretense.

When Dilsey returned to clear the dishes away, Fayette said, "Dilsey, Miss Selena is going to honor this occasion by playing her violin for us."

The black woman shot him a worried glance. "She gonna play her violin?"

"Would you bring it here, please, Dilsey?"

"Yas, suh, Mr. Fayette," Dilsey replied and scuttled off unhappily.

Betsy inquired, "Have you known Dilsey long?"

Fayette gave her an amused look. "Since we were babes, Miss Talbot. She was our mammy in Savannah, and Rufus was the butler, first at the plantation, then at the Savannah house. They know us well, don't they, Selena?"

"Very well, Fayette," Selena replied with a secretive smile at him.

ment, and we are only the poor peons enthralled in your spell."

"I have never heard such beautiful music," Betsy said quite truthfully. "Thank you, Mrs. Buchanan. If only you might play at church, or at school for the children. Everyone would enjoy it so very much."

"Yes," Fayette said, "people would enjoy it, Selena. And you know how your teachers spoke of sharing your talent."

Selena's brown eyes shone with pleasure and it appeared she might accept their suggestion. Suddenly she looked toward the back of the room.

From behind Betsy, Adam Buchanan said in a most even tone, "Your playing was magnificent as usual, Selena. Perhaps you should excuse yourself now, though, and take your afternoon rest. I'm sure that Miss Talbot would understand."

"Yes, Selena," Fayette added softly, "perhaps you should rest after such a brilliant exhibition."

8

As Fayette drove Betsy home in the buggy, she remembered Adam's words to his wife: *Perhaps you should excuse yourself now and take your afternoon rest.*

How dared he speak to Selena as though she were a child? Betsy wondered. True, Selena had run wildly from him in her nightclothes that first morning, but there might be a reasonable explanation for that.

She asked Fayette, "Does Selena usually take an afternoon rest?"

Fayette shot her a sidelong glance. "You don't mean to say an afternoon nap isn't common to all women?"

"Not to me, nor to anyone else I know, unless they are ill." She closed her mouth belatedly, realizing her words might be construed to mean Selena was not well.

He kept his eyes on the horses, a matched pair of grays who trotted in perfect unison along the wooded trail. "We've always had such sultry weather in Savannah that an afternoon rest is a custom. Ah hadn't considered it might not be as commonplace elsewhere."

"I see," she replied, not quite believing him.

"I expect southern women might be different," he said.

"I wonder," she replied. "The only ones I know are from

Virginia, my cousin Louisa and her friend, Tess Fairfax. Until Tess sold her restaurant, I'm told she worked just as hard here as she did at the tent restaurant she once managed in San Francisco. She even continued to work when Hugh's bank became a success. And Louisa works hard as a pastor's wife. Neither of them has household help."

Fayette replied amicably, "The state of Virginia, of course, is not in the Deep South. I suppose our customs are as much a state of mind as anything else. We do treasure our women."

"I see," she said again, suspecting that their entire conversation had been a cover-up for Selena's mental condition. When he glanced at her again and smiled, however, Betsy did feel treasured. She quickly looked forward at the matched pair of grays. "What is it like to be a twin to such a beautiful and talented woman?"

Fayette smiled, his eyes fixed on a distant point in the woods. "Ah do take great pleasure in seeing her and in hearing her play the violin," he allowed, "but likely the only difference between being fraternal twins, as we are, and ordinary siblings, is that we share our birth date. We grew up together and played together, of course, until we were sent off to our respective boarding schools."

"Nothing else?" Betsy persevered.

He shook his head. "Ah do feel very close to Selena, and Ah expect she feels close to me, but isn't that the way a loving relationship between a sister and brother should be?"

Betsy recalled the unspoken messages that had passed between them. *Close* scarcely seemed the word for their relationship.

Fayette broke into her thoughts. "Ah was so sorry to hear of your ordeal at the schoolhouse last week, and glad to see that you have weathered it so well."

He wished to change the subject, she decided, but she

did not care much for this one. The mere thought of Hollis flooded her body with weakness.

"Ah hope you don't condemn all of us men for the action of one," he said.

"No, of course not."

"Are you certain?"

She shrugged. "Perhaps not entirely. Such an . . . onslaught makes one suspicious."

"A normal reaction after an ordeal. Ah can't help wondering, did he wear a mask, or did you see him clearly?"

"He may have considered his beard mask enough, but I saw him clearly, and I heartily wish I had not. If you don't mind . . . I would prefer not to discuss it anymore."

"Of course. It was thoughtless of me to bring it up, and Ah ask your forgiveness." He halted the horses and buggy in front of her cabin, and said with regret, "And Ah was just marshaling my courage to ask to escort you to church on Sunday. For your reassurance, Ah would be most pleased to take your aunt with us to serve as a chaperone."

Surprised, it took Betsy a moment before she said, "Why, yes—thank you, Fayette, I'd be happy to attend with you, and I am sure that Aunt Jessica would, too, but she has a gentleman friend who has been attending services with her. In any case, we would not need her to accompany us to church, though I do appreciate your thoughtfulness."

He beamed. "And Ah am pleased that you've accepted my invitation. Thank you for your trust." Still smiling, he leapt lightly from the buggy and hurried around to her side.

This time she was not quite as unnerved by his touch as he helped her down. "I hope you'll invite Selena and her family to attend church, too," she said. "It's a fine place to make friends . . . and I'd like to know her better."

"Perhaps Ah shall. Selena needs friends." He added, "Ah

would like to call on you sooner, but Ah must go up north for a few days."

"I see," she replied, wishing for the second time that he were not quite so handsome.

He walked her to the cabin door and, as she thanked him for driving, he kissed her fingertips again.

"My privilege," he assured her, his immense brown eyes gazing at her intently. "If you were one of our southern belles, you would expect a gentleman to pay homage whether he wished to or not."

"But I am not a southern belle, nor even a northern belle," she returned with a small laugh.

"Oh, come now, Miss Betsy Talbot, you would be a belle in my eyes anywhere you were, and you know it quite well already."

As he smiled at her, a languid sweetness swept through her veins, and it occurred to her that, foolhardy or not, she liked Fayette Williams more than might be sensible.

Benjamin Talbot sat down at the desk in the white-washed adobe parlor and took up his quill thoughtfully. He must write to his family again about the threat Emile Martene had made on his life—and on theirs—without frightening them unduly. Somehow he must warn them anew to take heed. He had not yet received a response to his first letter on the matter. Likely they attributed his suggestions for caution to those of an overly protective father. This time he must speak more strongly about their safety.

Dear Betsy and Jessica,

How heartening it is to know that you approve of my activities here in San Francisco. It is one thing to tell others of Christ's redeeming love and of doing good in the community, but quite another to stand up publicly against specific evils. Yet tolerance of evil is a dangerous error, for no one in the world is free to behave in any way he pleases, which is what I say in the churches I am asked to visit. I am sure you must realize there are those who would like to silence me through any means. I ask you again to be cautious, for you are my family and our enemy is vicious.

I often think of you two in your cozy cabin nestled among the trees. You must feel quite safe and protected, but we must remember that evil is always on the march, ofttimes in advance of the banners of morality. I cannot ask you strongly enough to take heed.

I am gratified to hear that school is going well, Betsy. As for the older boys who are troublesome, you might quote the Proverbs: "He who heeds instruction is on the path to life, but he who rejects reproof goes astray" and "It is like sport to a fool to do wrong, but wise conduct is pleasure to a man of understanding." If they are resistant to Scripture, you might also tell them that boyish mischievousness often leads to real evil.

Benjamin shook his head at himself. He sounded old and tedious. But how else to warn them?

On the other hand, there had been no further threats despite his speaking out in churches against gambling establishments and other unsavory places. Best to finish his letter with a lighter tone.

On a happier note, I attended a brush arbor revival near Stockton last Sunday that puts our camp meetings along the stream to shame. It was not ten to twenty thousand Californians praising God for a week to two weeks, as we heard of last year, but it was nonetheless a most memorable experience. This one began with three hundred people on Saturday morning, and so many souls were awakened to God that the populace doubled by late Sunday afternoon when I arrived with Seth Thompson.

He closed his eyes and remembered as though he were still in attendance, almost smelling the straw that had been strewn to hold down the dust.

In the nearby fields, horses and mules had swished their tails, and their occasional brays and whinnies had sounded between the singing. Overhead, branches and brush had been spread over the makeshift arbor for shade, and beneath it, the worshipers sang out in praise and thanksgiving. Behind them, people still arrived on horseback and in buggies and farm wagons. As he and Seth walked toward the brush arbor in the late afternoon sunshine, the very air seemed to shimmer with joy and expectancy.

The congregation, some seated on rustic benches and some on quilts on the ground, sang with all their might,

> *My faith looks up to Thee,*
> *Thou lamb of Calvary, Savior divine!*
> *Now hear me while I pray,*
> *Take all my guilt away . . .*

Although he was usually too circumspect, Benjamin pronounced to Seth, "I think mighty things are going to happen here. Mighty happenings."

"I sense it myself," Seth replied with excitement, for he was to preach in the evening. "May God give us wisdom."

"And joy and strength!" Benjamin said with a laugh, "though a few in my congregation at home claim that dignity is the foremost ingredient."

Seth smiled. "I wonder if God doesn't see some of man's so-called dignity somewhat differently than we. Perhaps as stiff-necked rather than dignified?"

"It might be. It might be."

By evening, however, few of the worshipers could have been considered stiff-necked. Word had come out that Seth would be preaching, and the crowd had grown to what Benjamin estimated was nearly a thousand. Most of them had visited after the mid-day singing and prayers, then eaten their picnics as they sat on the ground on quilts. Now they gathered again under the brush arbor, with many spilling out around the sides, a sight most unlike his father's staid Boston church.

A soft murmuring filled the air as people prayed, a reassuring sound as the soft breeze stirred the nearby pepper trees and the sun began its evening descent in the west. The murmur of prayer grew louder and louder, and suddenly a man shouted, "Lord, we come in repentance! Revive our spirits . . . revive us . . . revive this craven place where men rush for liquor and debauchery instead of to Thy wondrous embrace!"

"We are unworthy . . . unworthy!" a woman cried out.

The cry was taken up. "Unworthy . . . unworthy . . . unworthy. . . ."

Benjamin folded his hands in prayer and, to his amazement, called out to the very heavens, "We rest in Thy hands, Lord! Thy will be done here this evening! Thy will be done!"

Others joined in until the soft air filled with praying and occasional beseeching cries. At length someone in the crowd began to sing "Fairest Lord Jesus," and the others took up the wondrous words. As Benjamin accompanied Seth to the front of the crowd, another group began a new hymn, then another and another until four or five hymns were being sung at once.

As Seth readied himself to step forward, his eyes filled with joy and fire, and he said to Benjamin, "Pray, my friend. Pray as never before!"

Benjamin fell to his knees in the midst of the throng and silently beseeched God, *Awaken souls, Almighty and gracious Father! . . . awaken us!*

The crowd had quieted and, to Benjamin's astonishment, Seth called out the very same words: "Awaken souls, Almighty and gracious Father . . . awaken us!"

From that moment on, even before Seth began the sermon, the miraculous had begun, for three men ran forward, their souls afire to accept Christ.

Seth spoke with great force. "These three men, who have surrendered their lives to Christ, will find love, joy, and peace, for Christ transforms people by converting their minds and their very lives if they will stay close to Him. Are there others here who wish to make their peace with God now, who wish to receive a mind informed by Christ?"

Men, women, and children rose from everywhere in the crowd and moved forward while the congregation shouted, "Glory to God!" and "Halleluah!" and "Amen!"

Twenty-three of them! Benjamin counted. He'd heard that sometimes an entire community was transformed by a rivival, but he'd never witnessed it with his own eyes. *Thank Thee, Lord! Thank Thee!* he prayed, knowing that it was the Spirit of God who genuinely changed lives. There might be imitators caught up in the emotion of the meeting, but the difference was always clear in the end: true converts gave glory to Christ, not to men.

Once those who'd come forward had received prayer and made their peace with God, Seth preached on repentance and God's mercy, and it seemed to Benjamin that the Spirit of God was so mighty among them that they might all rise skyward.

As the sermon ended, the huge congregation stood as one to sing "Amazing Grace," the words reaching up to the very heavens. Tears welled in Benjamin's eyes, not only for the awakened souls who rushed forward, but for his daughter Rena, who had so often sung those very words and who had been buried in the desert to the singing of that hymn. In his memory, Rena's melodious contralto rose with the others during the second verse,

> 'Twas grace that taught my heart to fear,
> And grace my fears relieved;
> How precious did that grace appear
> The hour I first believed!

The congregation under the brush arbor seemed to gather strength as they sang out,

> When we've been there ten thousand years,
> Bright shining as the sun,
> We've no less days to sing God's praise
> Than when we first begun.

Benjamin pulled out a handkerchief and gave his nose an undignified blast before joining in with joy and exultation,

> Praise God . . . praise God . . .
> Praise God . . . praise God. . . .

God truly inhabited the praise of His people, he reflected. As for the revival, prayer and repentance had made all of the difference. It had all taken place just a week ago, nearly one hundred and fifty souls saved, and there was talk of a week-long brush arbor meeting soon.

Now, back in his adobe parlor, Benjamin looked up from his half-finished letter to Betsy and Jessica. Outside the window, Daniel and Luke were silhouetted against the sunset as they rode in from their evening rounds. Jeremy would be out in the stable tending to the new foals.

As he watched, a volley of shots rang out, and Luke's gray gelding, Soot, dropped from beneath him in a heap. Daniel wheeled his horse, aimed his rifle, and a shot rang out.

Benjamin jumped up, his blood running cold. *God, help us!* he called out as he dashed through the house to them. Outside, he could see Daniel astride his horse looking beyond the oaks by the stream. After a moment, Daniel rode to Luke and helped him up behind him on his horse.

Benjamin ran to the barn for his horse, but by the time he was mounted, Daniel and Luke rode up the lane, dust billowing behind them.

"Luke, are you all right?" Benjamin called out.

Luke waved his reassurance, and Benjamin let out a deep breath, grateful that his son-in-law was well.

"Who was it?" he shouted.

"Don't know," Daniel replied as they rode up. "There were four of them. Looked like a warning party."

Luke dismounted from behind Daniel, his expression grim. "They got old Soot. Shot him right out from under me. I've never seen the like of it!"

"I'm heartsick for you, Luke," Benjamin said, knowing the inelegantly named gelding was one of Luke's favorites. "Truly heartsick. But I'm grateful it wasn't you."

"They could've got me, too, if they'd wanted," Luke said.

Benjamin nodded his agreement. "We'll have to put out guards for now. Either that, or I must stop my speaking out."

Luke shook his head. "I never saw a Talbot retreat when the work of God was involved."

Benjamin nodded. "No, not yet."

"I can take the first watch," Daniel offered.

"Let me get a fresh horse," Luke said. "We need to be sure we're quit of them. Those buzzards won't get the better of us."

Lord, help us, Benjamin thought again.

The last rays of sunshine dimmed to darkness, and he recalled that it was Satan's first concern to keep a believer from his prayers. Well, he, for one, was set on praying so long and hard that he'd drive old slewfoot from mere concern to cross-eyed vexation.

On Sunday morning when Fayette called for her, Betsy found his drowsy morning expression even more appealing. She was pleased to hear him say, "Selena, Adam, and Mellie will meet us at the church."

"I can't think of anything to make me happier," she replied in truth.

"Then Ah'm happy as well," Fayette said, his brown eyes admiring her. "It's a fine summer morning for church. Is your aunt already gone?"

"Yes, she often plays the new church organ and puts up the flowers by the pulpit. Her friend, Lucius Alden, came by to accompany her."

"A true churchwoman," Fayette remarked.

"Yes, that she is." She darted a glance at him to see if he were being facetious, but he looked at her quite openly.

As the two of them made their way up the path toward the church, sunshine slanted through the feathery pines overhead and birds twittered their cheerful greetings. With Fayette Williams at her side, it seemed there had been no finer day in the entire history of the earth. She said, "Aunt Jessica is going to invite you and your family to stay for dinner."

Fayette smiled broadly. "Ah speak only for myself, but if Ah may sit at your side, Ah shall accept her invitation."

She returned his smile.

As they came in sight of the graveyard behind the church, however, Betsy gave an inward shudder.

Fayette offered his arm solicitously. "It can't be easy to see that place every day when you come and go to school."

"No, it is not. I—I try not to think of it, yet we must watch and be careful."

He nodded. "I admire your courage. Not every woman would go on as you have."

"I am not so courageous as you might think," she replied.

The sounds of voices and buggies arriving at the church diverted their attention. Fayette said, "There's Selena and Adam and Mellie now—"

Brightening, Betsy hurried along with Fayette toward them. "Good morning," she said, "I'm so happy to see all of you here this fine morning."

In the midst of their greetings, Mellie's sweet voice piped out with pride, "Mama came to church with us."

"And I am so pleased she did," Betsy said, turning to Selena Buchanan. "I still think of how beautifully you play the violin. I can never thank you enough for playing for me."

The woman's brown eyes probed hers, then she visibly relaxed. She looked beautiful in her pale yellow frock, and, although her yellow parasol was out of place in such a rustic setting, it matched her silk dress. "It was my pleasure, Miss Talbot. Fayette encouraged us to come to your church, though Ah believe it will be quite different than the chuch we attended in Savannah."

"I had never been in a log church before myself," Betsy said, "but it seems quite suitable for this setting, as I am sure yours must have been in Savannah."

"It was very beautiful," Selena said with great regret.

Adam said, "This one, while rustic, was built by the parishioners instead of imported Italian artisans."

"As ours was in Savannah," Selena explained unnecessarily. "We had the finest of workmanship, and the floors were of Italian marble."

"I fear ours are just gray slate from the river," Betsy said.

"Well, Ah do like the river, especially the sound of it rushing out to the ocean," Selena acknowledged. "The river is the very best part of Oak Hill."

Adam cast a peculiar look at his wife.

Lord, help her to like the church, Betsy thought. In the morning's hustle and bustle, she was not what Aunt Jessica called "prayed up" and regretted it mightily.

As they made their way in, she watched Selena eye their rustic surroundings. Inside the sanctuary, Aunt Jessica played the prelude on the new pump organ and, though she played well, she was the first to admit her share of musical talent was no more than modest.

Betsy glanced at Selena, whose closed expression did not bode well. It appeared that she'd already decided against the music and now disapproved of the furnishings, too. *Lord, help her to know the church is not made of mere buildings,* Betsy prayed, seated on a pew between Selena and Fayette. Beside her, Selena smoothed the skirt of her yellow silk dress, then glanced around with an expression of disapproval.

When the music ended, Jonathan Chambers stood before the congregation. "Today we shall sing hymns authored by Isaac Watts, who received a great talent for writing and used it to author the words to the music of over six hundred hymns. Among them are such familiar ones as 'Joy to the World' and 'When I Survey the Wondrous Cross.' Shall we begin with his joyous 'This Is the Day the Lord Hath Made'?"

Aunt Jessica played the introduction, after which they all sang out joyously,

> This is the day the Lord hath made;
> He calls the hours His own;
> Let heaven rejoice, let earth be glad,
> And praise surround the throne. . . .

When the final verses rang out with their joyful hosanna, Betsy glanced sidelong at Selena and was grateful to see that she apparently knew the music and sang, albeit without much conviction.

The sermon was entitled "Employing What God Hath Given," and was about using one's talents for the glory of God. Jonathan read the parable of the talents from Scripture, concluding with, "But from him that hath not, shall be taken away even that which he hath."

Selena apparently understood all too well what taking away her talent would mean for, clutching her hands in her lap, she listened intently as he spoke about using one's talents to God's glory.

The service ended with singing another of Watt's hymns, and Betsy sang out fervently, for it conveyed her heartfelt wish,

> Let children hear the mighty deeds
> Which God performed of old;
> Which in our younger years we saw,
> And which our fathers told.
> He bids us make His glories known,
> His works of power and grace;
> And we'll convey His wonders down
> Through each succeeding race.

After Jonathan pronounced the benediction and Aunt Jessica played the postlude, members of the congregation stopped by to invite Selena and Fayette to visit again.

Betsy noticed that Selena was quietly polite, though apparently touched by their friendliness.

Mr. Wilmington visited for a moment, making them welcome, then added, "I wonder if I might borrow Adam from you for a few minutes to discuss some community concerns."

Selena stiffened visibly and reached for Fayette's arm.

"Of course," Fayette replied. "Ah shall see to Selena and Mellie until your return." Adam nodded his thanks and walked with Rose's father to the side of the log sanctuary.

At the narthex door, Selena shook hands with Jonathan Chambers, who said with his usual kindness, "I understand you have a great musical talent. I hope you will employ it here in our church someday."

Selena replied in a hushed tone, "Ah fear Ah am sorely out of practice."

Fayette put in, "Ah shall urge her to practice for it, Reverend Chambers. Ah assure you, Ah shall."

When they got outside, Selena asked her brother with some irritation, "Why did you say Ah might play for them?"

Fayette patted her arm. "Why, Selena, Ah know you wouldn't want to lose your talent. Didn't you hear that sermon? You know how Mother always told you to take heed of a sermon for your own good."

"Ah heard," Selena conceded unhappily.

"Then you must begin to practice daily again," her brother told her. "Why, Ah wouldn't be in the least bit surprised if Betsy wouldn't welcome you to play for the children at school someday soon."

"I know the children would enjoy it," Betsy said. "They have all too little exposure to the arts. I do hope you will consider it, Mrs. Buchanan."

"See, Selena," Fayette said, "you would be welcome." He glanced back. "And here comes Adam now."

At the sight of her husband hurrying toward them, Selena relinquished her hold on Fayette's arm and put up her yellow parasol as though reminded she must strike a beautiful pose for her husband. She was truly breathtaking, Betsy thought, but judging by Adam's expression, her beauty was not now paramount on his mind.

Fayette half-taunted Adam, "Are your community concerns well in hand?"

"I hope so," his brother-in-law replied, unamused.

Fayette suggested lightly, "Then perhaps you should see to your wife."

Adam blanched, but offered his arm to Selena. "Yes, of course." He added a rather arch, "Thank you, Fayette, for always being so helpful with the ladies."

Fayette laughed. "My pleasure. I can't think of any way I would rather be of service to the community."

Betsy concluded that Fayette and perhaps Selena resented Adam's involvement in community concerns. On the other hand, after witnessing Selena's flight through the woods in her nightgown, it was conceivable that she played a strong role in driving her husband from their house, too.

The small drama ended as Aunt Jessica joined them and introduced Lucius Alden, who grinned at her side. She said to Selena, "I regret that it is such short notice, but I should like to invite your family to have dinner at Betsy's and my cabin."

Betsy noticed an almost imperceptible withdrawal on Selena's part, though she did say most graciously, "We thank you, Mrs. Alcott, but Dilsey has already prepared dinner for us at home. Perhaps we might come another time."

Adam, who still held his wife's arm, added rather stiffly, "Yes, thank you. Another time."

"Next Sunday then?" Aunt Jessica persevered.

"Ah don't know—" Selena began, and it appeared that Adam would also resist, but Fayette said, "Ah shall accept on behalf of all of us. Dilsey is a fine cook, but she could use a Sunday of rest. It would be a most Christian thing to do."

Betsy glanced at the others, as did Aunt Jessica.

Unfortunately, their expressions evinced only reluctant acceptance.

Aunt Jessica said, "What a pleasure it will be then to have all of you come for dinner after church next Sunday."

Selena shot Fayette a peculiar look, which he returned with a smile of confidence. "And Ah shall have the pleasure of tellin' you of the fine food and company you will have missed with Miss Talbot and Mrs. Alcott today."

As they bade each other farewell, Betsy noticed that Adam Buchanan scrutinized her and Fayette with pained interest. Difficult as it was to fathom everything Adam might be thinking, he was obviously concerned for her welfare and not as happy as one might expect the husband of such a beautiful wife to be. Betsy was surprised to find her heart go out to him.

"You surely are one of the loveliest young ladies Ah have ever had the privilege to meet," Fayette said as he escorted Betsy along the wooded path to her cabin.

"Oh, Fayette," she protested. "I suspect that's the way you southern gentlemen always talk."

He gave her a rueful glance. "Aren't you the one who thought there was not such a difference between southern and northern women? If we are to follow your reasonin', then men must be the same everywhere, as well."

"Touché," she replied with a grin.

"Just so you don't practice discrimination against me," he warned with amusement. "All of that notwithstanding, Ah still find you one of the loveliest young ladies Ah have ever met."

His drowsy brown eyes were full of sincerity, and her reluctance to accept such a compliment receded. "Thank you, Fayette."

"May I offer my arm?"

She nodded and took it, amazed at the strength concealed under his genteel brown frock coat. It was not that he seemed stronger than her brothers, who sometimes lent her their arms, but Fayette seemed too much the gentleman to be so strong. All in all, it made him even more attractive.

As they strolled onward toward the cabin, he asked, "Aren't you going to inquire why I find you so lovely?"

"Should I?" Betsy asked.

"Now there's another reason why I find you so. You are entirely ingenuous. Most young women would ask that I compare their eyes with another lady's . . . their hair, their lips, their nose, their chin."

"Their chin?!" Betsy returned incredulously. "I can scarcely believe that!"

"Nonetheless you have a delightfully fragile chin."

Betsy found herself blushing. "All the more so to accent my chipmunk cheeks," she said with a laugh.

"No, I should say they are most kissable cheeks, from a gentleman's perspective." He had been studying her face most intently, and now his voice softened. "And most kissable lips."

"Fayette!" she said indignantly. She pulled her arm from his, then quickly felt a pang of regret.

To her relief, he continued on with her. "Ah am sorry if Ah have shocked you by speaking the truth, Betsy. Ah would be less than a man, however, if Ah did not notice that aspect of your lips from the moment we met."

She swallowed with difficulty. "I do believe you are a flatterer, Fayette."

He caught her by the arm and slowly turned her to him right there in the shaded thicket. "It is said, Miss Betsy Talbot, that the most subtle flattery a woman can receive is conveyed by actions, not by words. To that end, Ah should like to prove what Ah have said."

"Never mind, Fayette Williams!" she said as she might to one of her students, though it took an effort to pull away from him again. "They'll be waiting dinner for us!"

He gave a hearty laugh as he hurried on with her, and she couldn't help smiling herself. They seemed to float happily over the path to her cabin, where Rose, Joshua, and their little ones had already gathered with Aunt Jessica and Lucius, all of them watching her arrival on Fayette's arm with great interest.

At dinner, she sat between Fayette and Joshua, who continued to watch them closely. Her brother's scrutiny, however, did not faze Fayette, who was as solicitous of her as Lucius Alden was of soliciting their laughter with his droll tales. When the older man began again on his illustrious ancestors, Aunt Jessica put in with a wry smile, "We are related to royalty ourselves—God's first children, Adam and Eve. For that matter, we are related by blood to the King of kings."

"Now, Jessica, bless my soul, ye know I weren't talkin' 'bout that," Lucius objected.

"I know it, Lucius," Aunt Jessica replied in her usual kind way, "but I do wish you'd invest more time remembering your godly heritage than your descendancy from English royalty. In the end, it is more important to take the long view of matters . . . to consider our eternal destiny."

Lucius nodded. "Expect ye be right 'bout that, Jessica. Trouble with gettin' older is yer head's been aplayin' the same tunes agin 'n agin."

Aunt Jessica smiled. "But we are never so old that God can't make a new creature of us, that He can't put new and wonderful melodies in our heads."

"Ye think so?" Lucius asked.

"I know so," Aunt Jessica answered, "for I've seen it happen myself time and again. Why, I've even heard of converted miners whose mules would no longer work for them. The mules were so accustomed to being beaten and to blasphemy rolling around their ears that they didn't know what to make of their 'new' owners, who otherwise looked somewhat the same to those confused beasts. Now, do have more roast beef, Lucius."

Betsy glanced at Fayette, who had been following the interchange with quiet amusement.

As their eyes met, he caught her hand under the table and looked as though he was contemplating kissing her again. How could she even consider such a thing after the recent attack on her by Hollis? On the other hand, Fayette was so very appealing. Perhaps when she saw him out the door later—

Quite suddenly she recalled Aunt Jessica's oft-stated warning: "A proper young lady does not allow a man to kiss her until he has declared himself and proposed marriage. There is plenty of time for kisses then."

Betsy blushed, taking pleasure at the thought. Still, if Fayette tried to kiss her again today, she must not give in. She must not, no matter how much she might wish it.

Monday afternoon, as the students trooped out the schoolhouse door, Betsy saw Fayette strolling up the trail with Selena and Mellie. Suddenly all aflutter, she tucked a stray wisp of hair back into her chignon and was glad she had worn her flowered challis frock.

"What a fine surprise," she said as they approached.

Fayette smiled warmly. "Mellie wanted to see the children, and Selena and Ah thought we'd have a walk."

"I like to watch the children myself," Betsy said.

Beside her, Mellie was intrigued by the departing students as their final good-byes sounded along the paths and the river trail. And Selena, though silent, looked interested, too. Fayette, however, kept his compelling brown eyes on Betsy.

She smiled and managed, in what she hoped was a serene voice, "Children are a lively sight in the classroom or out."

"That they are," he conceded, still scrutinizing her.

She forced her gaze away, wondering what he thought of her. Yesterday after the Sunday dinner, when she'd walked outside the cabin to bid him farewell, Joshua had loomed over her like a brotherly sentinel. With such a stalwart brother nearby, there had been no question of her resistance.

"Won't you come in and see the schoolroom?" Betsy suggested. "I daresay Mellie would like to see it, since one of these days she'll be a schoolgirl herself," she added, hoping the child would not give away her secret visits.

Mellie's eyes brightened. "Can we see it, Uncle Fayette? Please, can we see it?"

"*May we*," Fayette corrected, then turned to Betsy. "Ah should like to see it myself. Wouldn't you, Selena?"

Selena smiled and responded softly, "Ah would."

"I'd be pleased to show it to you," Betsy said. When she escorted them into the log schoolroom, however, she felt conflicting emotions. On one hand, she was enormously proud of the frontier room and the children's work that decorated the back wall and windowsills; on the other hand, she suspected Fayette would find her passion for teaching foolish, likely even misplaced.

Beside her, Mellie's eyes widened. She was so taken with actually being in the classroom and inspecting the artwork and other papers on the plank cloakroom wall up close that she beamed with excitement.

Selena remarked, "Ah'm still not accustomed to log

buildin's." She turned to Betsy. "Fayette tells me you live in a log cabin."

"Yes, as do most of us here."

Selena eyed the edges of the room with suspicion. "Don't snakes and spiders come in through the cracks?"

"If the walls are kept chinked, we have no more such invaders than in any other house," Betsy replied. "I grew up in a log house in Missouri, and we never had a snake in the house. I daresay it's more a matter of keeping the doors shut. As for spiders, I've seen no more in our cabin than we had at *Casa Contenta.*"

"Ah see," Selena said, relaxing a trifle. "Don't some of those big boys bring snakes to school?"

"No, I can't say they have."

"Fayette used to at our plantation house, just to scare poor Mother and me," Selena said with an indignant glance at her brother. "When he was little, of course. Now he has other interests."

Fayette gave an indulgent laugh. "Boys will be boys."

"Yes," Betsy agreed. "That I know all too well."

Selena said, "Ah am mortally frightened of Indians, too."

"Most of them have fled far into the mountain wilderness," Betsy assured her. "They're as leery of us as we are of them, and for good reason." Seeing that Selena glanced at the windows with trepidation, Betsy halted her speech. This was no time to dwell on how badly the migratory California Indians had been treated and their acorn crops decimated.

Fayette remarked, "You have river slate floors here, too, just like the verandas at your cabin and Selena's house."

"We have a slate chalkboard, as well," Betsy added, aware that he'd redirected the conversation. "As you can see, we are beginning to plan our part in the town's Fourth of July celebration." She pointed out the class's tentative list on the chalkboard:

—Pilgrims landing the *Mayflower* at Plymouth Rock

—Revolutionary War soldiers singing "Yankee Doodle"

—signing the Constitution

"Don't know that Ah'll be here for the festivities," Fayette said, "but Ah'm certain Selena and Mellie would like to come." He turned an ironic smile on Betsy. "Ah expect that Adam, as a pillar of the community, will have a part in it. He will doubtless deliver the main speech, or, at the very least, be George Washington."

Betsy gave a laugh. "I can't imagine him as Washington unless he powdered his hair and shaved off his beard and moustache. Perhaps we can recruit his black medical bag, however, for one of our students to play the part of a doctor in the Revolutionary War. As for the speech, I do know that my father has been asked to give it."

"Ah see," Fayette replied, then took a new tack. "Your father is said to be a remarkable speaker."

"Have you heard him?" Betsy asked.

Fayette shook his head slightly. "No, only of him."

She was on the verge of inquiring further, but Mellie had quietly inspected the room, and now she asked Betsy, "Please, can I sit at a desk?"

"Yes, of course, you may, Mellie."

Mellie clambered up into one of the little desks in front and, once in place, smiled at them with great satisfaction.

Betsy said, "Mellie Buchanan, don't you look like a schoolgirl?"

Mellie gave a giggle and, swinging her legs, pronounced with dignity, "I'm a big girl now."

"You surely are!" Selena agreed.

Mellie was so delighted that they were all caught up with her in the wonder of the moment.

Fayette observed, "Mellie is going to be a great beauty someday."

Selena said, "Mellie, Ah do believe you are goin' to make your mama cry, lookin' all grown up like that."

They all laughed, except Mellie, who quickly jumped down and ran to embrace her mother reassuringly. "I'm your little girl, Mama! I'm your little girl! I love you, Mama!"

It was a heartwarming sight, albeit too intense. On the other hand, perhaps matters at the Buchanan house were not as bad as they seemed. Perhaps the morning Selena had run through the woods in her nightgown had been a rare exception. Betsy most sincerely hoped so.

Later, as they began to leave the classroom, she said, "It would be such an honor if you would play the violin for the children, Selena. Have you considered it?"

Selena's brown eyes shone with pleasure. "Ah would be most pleased to do so."

"You will?!"

"Ah shall," Selena replied with a fast glance at her brother. "Would tomorrow just after the children's midday meal be a good time?"

"Yes, it would be perfect!"

"Fayette thought I should play something light and happy for the children. Perhaps Mendelssohn's Italian Symphony, parts of the last movement. It's all images of Italy's white towns, blue lakes, gay songs, and exuberant, leapin' dances in the open air. Ah could tell them what it's about beforehand and let them try to identify the images."

"A wonderful idea," Betsy said. "I don't know much about Mendelssohn, only that he restored much of our Christian music to us. It will be an extraordinary opportunity for all of us. And, if it's not asking too much, would you also play the piece you played for me the other day?"

"It would be my pleasure," Selena replied most graciously. "May Mellie and Fayette come with me?"

"Of course. I should like to bring Aunt Jessica myself."

Selena's brown eyes darkened. "No, please. Just Fayette and Mellie . . . and you and the schoolchildren."

"Fine," Betsy quickly agreed. "No one else."

"Then it's all arranged," Fayette said. "We shall be here just after the midday recess."

As the four of them stepped out of the schoolhouse, it occurred to Betsy that they had planned the event before their visit. Be that as it may, she hoped that Selena would not back out of her promise, for she seemed the type who might.

To her joy and relief, the next day as the children were finishing their midday recess, Fayette drove up in the buggy. With him were Mellie and Selena, who wore her yellow silk frock and carried her violin in its case. Early in the day Betsy had told the children, "We may have a special visitor this afternoon. If she comes, I expect you to be especially polite."

Now she hurried over to the buggy to welcome them. "What a privilege this is," she told Selena, who looked nervous. "I'm sure some of these children have never even seen a violin."

Selena drew a deep breath. "Then perhaps they'll not be too . . . critical."

Fayette chuckled as he helped her down. "Most likely they will only object if the concert lasts too long."

Inside the classroom, they settled into their places: Selena at Betsy's platform desk, and, nearby, Fayette and Mellie at students' desks.

Betsy went out to ring the school bell. "Time to come in, students!" she called out. "Our special visitor has arrived."

As the children filed in and sat down at their desks, they glanced curiously at their guests, and Betsy wondered whether they had heard of Selena's wild runs through the woods. If so, best not to give them time to discuss it.

"Students, we have with us today a lady who has been a concert violinist," she said, standing in front of them. "She has played the violin not only on our Eastern Seaboard, but in concerts in Europe, so you see how very privileged we are to have her perform for us."

She turned to introduce Selena, who appeared more and more nervous. "This is Mrs. Buchanan, and I believe she is going to tell us a bit about the music so we can better understand and enjoy it."

Selena rose with her violin. "It is a—a rare pleasure for me to be here with y'all today." She glanced at Fayette and seemed to gain strength from him. "Ah'm goin' to play music written by Felix Mendelssohn. He called this his 'jolliest' music, and he wished those who heard it to imagine Italy's shinin' white towns, blue lakes, happy songs, and people dancin' and leapin' with delight. If—if you will close your eyes while Ah play, perhaps you can imagine it."

She tucked the violin under her chin, raised the bow, and, as her gaze drifted far away, brought the bow to the strings with a burst of vigor and exhilaration.

The vivacious music filled the schoolroom gloriously, and the children listened, some wide-eyed, some remembering to close their eyes. As the movement continued, Betsy, despite her limited musical background, knew it was a virtuoso performance, and she sat as though in the sunshine of Italy, in awe of Selena's talent.

When the music ended, Betsy led the applause, and Selena made a slight curtsy in acknowledgment. After the room had quieted, Selena said, "Miss Talbot has asked that Ah play a piece Ah composed about the sun circlin' the earth."

She raised the bow again, then touched it to the strings and began to play, softly at first: the awakening of birds at morning light, the sun moving over the earth. The music grew in strength and filled the schoolroom, and again, it seemed that Selena and the violin were one, a being of light and lengthening shadows.

When the piece ended, Selena curtsied more deeply to their applause. Then Fayette was at her side, accepting the violin from her and smiling at Selena. As though instructed, Mellie was immediately behind them, and they made their way quickly through the seated schoolchildren to the back of the room.

"Thank you so much, Mrs. Buchanan," Betsy said, following in their wake. She'd thought the children might discuss the musical images with Selena, but Fayette seemed intent upon hurrying them out of the room. "What a special treat this was for us," she called after her. "I do hope you will play at church some Sunday."

"Our pleasure," Fayette called back, "and Selena will play in church on Sunday. Ah shall arrange it with Chambers this afternoon before I leave for the northern mines. And we shall all be pleased to accept your aunt's gracious dinner invitation after the church service."

Selena spoke in a strangled voice, something Betsy did not quite catch. It seemed one moment they were there and the next they were gone. All in all, it was a most surprising and dramatic exit.

9

On Sunday morning, Selena did indeed play her violin at church, and the congregation was enthralled to hear her powerful rendition of "A Mighty Fortress Is Our God." She must believe in Him, Betsy thought, for the young woman's playing conveyed an overwhelming passion. Or was the passion for the music itself?

As her performance ended, there was only awed silence and the rush of the river far below, a sound most fitting after the powerful anthem. Selena quickly sat down in the front pew between Adam and Fayette.

When the equally inspired church service let out, members of the congregation thanked Selena most heartily for playing, and there was many a "We hope you will play for us again soon."

"She shall," Fayette assured them, as Selena's brown eyes grew wider with agitation. "She shall indeed."

It was evident that Fayette had talked Selena into playing both at school and at church, and Betsy hoped he was not pressing his sister too onerously. She would mention it if he walked her home from church, Betsy decided. But Fayette drove Selena home with her violin and, to Betsy's amazement, it was Adam Buchanan, dressed in his fine black suit, who walked along the wooded path to the cabin with her and Mellie.

Betsy felt oddly pleased that she'd worn her light green dress with the lace around the neck and collar, though it compared rather poorly with Selena's ivory silk.

"What a pleasure to have Selena play for us today," Betsy said as they set off. "You must be very proud of her."

"Yes," Adam replied, "she is extremely talented."

Betsy darted a glance at him and guessed he had mixed emotions about his wife's success.

"Didn't Mama play beautiful?" Mellie asked. She wore her frilly pink frock and a flowing pink ribbon in her hair, and had no idea of how adorable she looked.

Smiling at his small daughter, Adam patted the top of her head fondly. "Yes, Mellie, your mama played beautifully."

"Was your wife already an accomplished violinist when you met her?" Betsy asked.

"Yes. She was a child prodigy and had already performed in Paris when she was seventeen."

"You must have had an unusual courtship."

"Indeed we did," he said reflectively. They walked at a slow pace to accommodate Mellie. After a moment he added, "I was called in to see Selena as a doctor, a very new and young doctor. And she was very young and talented and beautiful."

Betsy prompted, "And you were impressed?"

He stared fixedly ahead. "Any man would have been impressed. I surely was. And she was gravely ill." He cast a glance at Mellie, who was chasing a butterfly. "Selena sometimes suffers from deep melancholy, as is often common to those with an artistic temperament. 'Walking in the shadows,' she calls it. The shadows are real to her, as distinguished from light. Perhaps you gathered that from her piece about the sun's circuit of the earth. To her, the shadows are always lengthening."

"I . . . see."

"I only tell you because it seems she would like to be your friend."

"Selena wishes to be my friend?"

He nodded. "Fayette has been encouraging her as well. I hope you are willing."

"Yes, of course," Betsy replied. "I—I'll not tell anyone of her . . . illness."

"Thank you," he said. "I only ask if she ever seems overly distressed that you let me know."

"I shall," Betsy replied, marveling at this turn of events. "I appreciate your confidence."

They strolled on past the wooded thicket where Fayette had spoken of her kissable lips. Adam must have read her mind, for he said, "It appears that Fayette is rather fond of you."

Betsy felt her face grow hot.

"Take heed," he warned softly.

"Thank you, but I am old enough to look after myself," she replied a bit too heatedly.

Adam looked as though he doubted it. At length he said, "I am pleased to hear about your teaching. Evidently you are very good at it."

"Thank you. I do enjoy it." It was only the second time she recalled his saying anything commendable about her work.

They walked on in silence while Mellie skipped along the path. After a while Adam said, "I don't like to bring this up, but do you think you could identify your assailant if such an opportunity presented itself?"

The thought of a confrontation with Hollis was daunting, but she said, "Yes, I—I believe I could. Do you think he'll be caught sometime soon?"

"At this point, we can only hope that it's possible."

"Yes," she agreed, "it surely is my hope."

When they arrived at the cabin, Rose and Joshua and the children had already arrived with Aunt Jessica and Lucius Alden, and Fayette and Selena were just driving up. Betsy was thinking what a striking couple they made when she noticed that Selena was gazing at her and Adam with suspicion.

Betsy stepped forward to her quickly. "I didn't have an opportunity to tell you how beautifully you played this morning."

Selena nodded and thanked her most courteously, but Betsy could only recall the time she had shrieked: "Don't you evah go neah my husband again!" And here she was with Adam!

Yet why the woman should be jealous of her was beyond imagining. Selena had removed the short matching jacket to her ivory silk dress and now, even with a discreet neckline, looked most voluptuous. Not a woman in Oak Hill could hold a candle to her beauty.

The tables—one in the parlor, the other outside on the veranda under the huge cedar tree—were already set. Betsy served lemonade to all the guests, taking special care to keep her distance from Adam. Perhaps, if he were her husband, she reflected, she would tend to be jealous of other women herself.

Rose and Joshua insisted on sitting outside with the children, leaving the inside table for Jessica, Lucius, Fayette, Selena, Adam, and Betsy. Aunt Jessica and Betsy had done most of the cooking yesterday: fried chicken, potato salad, carrot and cabbage slaws, and strawberry pies—leaving only the green beans and biscuits to be prepared at the last minute.

Joshua said grace for both tables and, as they passed the food, Selena said, "Ah swear Ah don't know how you ladies can manage all of your work without household help."

Aunt Jessica smiled. "The truth is we're accustomed to it. I'm grateful to this day that we have a stove instead of a greasewood fire or worse to cook over outside as we did when we came to California by covered wagon."

"We came by covered wagon, as well," Selena said, as if to point out that the Talbots were not the only ones to have endured hardships.

Fayette chuckled. "But with Dilsey and Rufus to help with the cooking and other work." He turned to the rest of them. "We southerners do spoil our womenfolk."

Selena spoke sharply. "Ah don't know about that. Ah'm the one who lost my baby!"

Adam's eyes narrowed unhappily, but before he could speak Aunt Jessica put in, "I am sorry to hear that, my dear."

"What a blessing that you have Mellie," Betsy said. "She is one of the loveliest little girls I have ever met."

"Yes, Ah suppose she is," Selena replied absentmindedly.

"It's a pleasure to come here for dinner," Fayette said with alacrity. "You have made a charming home of this cabin."

"Aunt Jessica's doing, for the most part," Betsy explained. "She can work miracles. She's lived in so many places that she's made an art of it. I expect she could make an Indian tepee seem like home."

"Now, now—" Aunt Jessica objected. "You know what Daniel would quote about flattery."

Lucius Alden beamed at her from the head of the table. "If ye were a bit older, Jessica, 'n if I a wee bit younger, I'd ask yer hand in matrimony so fast yer head would spin."

Aunt Jessica's mouth opened with astonishment. "Now, Lucius, why ever would you do that?"

"Why, I'd do it fer yer fried chicken, if nothin' else."

They all laughed at his outrageousness, and Aunt Jessica, her eyes still shining, finally said, "You are most gallant to reverse our ages, too, Lucius. In any case, I would be honored by your offer, but as it is, I am more than content to be your friend and to invite you for Sunday dinners for as long as we both do live."

They all laughed again, and then, to their amazement, Selena said, "Ah do hope, Betsy, that you will be my friend."

"Of course, Selena—" Astonished by the childlike offer, Betsy reached across the table and patted Selena's hand. "I am truly honored."

Beside her, his brown eyes more compelling than ever, Fayette chuckled. "Ah do hope, Miss Talbot," he said quite formally, "that you will also consent to be my friend."

Reminded of last Sunday's flirtation, and aware that the others watched with interest, Betsy patted the top of his hand lightly, too. "Of course, Mr. Williams. We might just say that we have a table full of fine friends."

Across from her, Adam Buchanan raised a brow and continued to eat with utmost politeness. It seemed that as compassionate as he was with his patients, he was most uncomfortable around his wife and Fayette.

Boom!

Benjamin Talbot sat up in bed, jerked from his sleep. The bedroom was dark gray, the curtains pulled shut.

Boom! Boom! Boom! The air around him seemed to shake.

The Fourth of July! he thought and remembered he was at Wilmington's house at Oak Hill.

From the bedroom next to his Wilmington asked, "You awake, Benjamin?"

"Indeed, I am!"

202

"Sounds like the British must be coming over at the blacksmith's shop. I expect he's exploded gunpowder under the anvil like last year. Go back to sleep."

"No, it's a good day to be up early," Benjamin replied. "Think I'll go visit Jessica before breakfast. Don't forget you're invited, though I'd just as soon have our mutual grandchildren to myself!"

"And allow you to spoil them?" Wilmington answered in jest.

Benjamin chuckled. He had arrived on the stagecoach from Sacramento City the day before, followed by a fine reunion with his Oak Hill family and a visit to town with Joshua. Last night, he and Wilmington had discussed their land title troubles and the fact that California was losing a quarter of a million settlers because of the insecurity of land titles. Today the festivities for the Fourth would begin at midmorning in front of the schoolhouse. He hoped festivities like these would encourage newcomers to stay in the state.

Boom! His bedroom window was open, and the sound startled him again as he dressed. After the final boom passed, there was only the sound of the river rushing far below and the morning cheeping of the birds in the oak, pine, and cedar trees.

Ten minutes later, when he arrived at Jessica and Betsy's cabin, Jessica was already out back picking strawberries in what was otherwise a vegetable garden.

"Well, look at this garden!" he said, impressed. "Did you and Betsy put it in by yourselves?"

His sister straightened up slowly with her bowl of strawberries, her brown eyes shining with pleasure at him and then at the garden. "We paid Moses to work it up, but the rest we managed ourselves. It's just a small one since we arrived here so late, but you know how I enjoy a garden."

"I do. And it shows."

At the far end of the garden, the corn grew lustily, its long green leaves moving softly in the morning breeze. Nearby, cucumber vines reached out, their tips uncurling beyond their patch of spreading leaves. Next came rows of peas, green beans, greens, radishes, and green onions.

"Looks as though you've turned the cabin into a home, too. Not that I should be surprised."

"It does feel like home now," Jessica said, glancing fondly at the log cabin with him, then turning back to the garden. "Betsy enjoys the garden, too. She's already eaten breakfast and has gone over to the school. They're finishing the children's costumes for their part of the celebration."

"Good."

She eyed him carefully. "She's a fine teacher, Benjamin."

He nodded. "I thought she'd be. She's a lot like you."

Jessica laughed. "One of her gentlemen callers said she favors me in appearance, as well."

Benjamin didn't quite see it, but his sister looked so pleased that he said, "Familial similarities. I expect we all share them. Who is this gentleman caller, if I may ask?"

"Fayette Williams, a southerner. He's Adam Buchanan's brother-in-law, and likely the most handsome man you've ever seen."

Benjamin asked as steadily as he could, "Is it serious?"

Jessica shrugged. "I have no idea."

"That, at least, is encouraging."

"She gets plenty of attention from men here . . . a novelty for her, though she scarcely seems to notice and gives them no encouragement. Sven Lindborg and Ralston Stone, the young men we met on the Sacramento riverboat, came last week and were quite taken with her again. Joshua tells me that when he drives Betsy into town on Saturday mornings there's not a single man in town who doesn't strain his neck. You'd laugh to see Joshua watch over her, though. He's more protective of her than you've ever been!"

"Joshua?!" Benjamin said, then chuckled. "It's hard to envision. When I think of him just six years ago—"

"He's matured. He's turned into a fine husband, father, brother, and nephew."

"And son," Benjamin put in.

Jessica nodded, and started toward the cabin. "Now about you, Benjamin . . . What is transpiring with all of your speeches in San Francisco? One can't go about rallying churches against gambling and drinking establishments without raising some ire. Have you had any reactions?"

"Not many," he replied, following her up the garden path.

"Some then," she deduced. "What happened?"

"Emile Martene, one of their spokesmen, threatened me, and we had a warning attack. As a matter of fact, Luke's horse was shot out from under him—"

"Shot out from under him!"

Benjamin nodded. "Soot. I'm afraid he was."

"You didn't write a word about it! I assume, at least, that Luke was uninjured."

"Amazingly so. As for my not telling you, you know very well that worry will not add one cubit to your stature."

"No need to quote Scripture at me," she objected good-naturedly.

"For that matter, you didn't mention Betsy being courted by this . . . Fayette."

"Yes, well—" she prevaricated, allowing her brother to open the cabin door. "I knew you were coming, and Fayette is not always at Oak Hill. In fact, he has just returned from a lengthy absence, so you can meet him. His twin sister, Selena, is a brilliant violinist, and she and Betsy have become friends. But that's surely nothing like having Luke's horse shot out from under him!"

"I did try to warn you to be careful here. One never knows where such people might strike."

"Indeed!" she agreed, then turned reflective.

"Jessica, are you withholding something?"

"Nothing that will add one cubit to your stature, either," she returned puckishly. "Come along, Benjamin, I've already set the table. Let me see now . . . ham, eggs, corn bread, fruit compote with the strawberries. . . . Do sit at the table so I can think. Let me give you some coffee."

She'd tell him in her own good time, he decided, and her judgment was usually good.

He sat down and had scarcely sipped his steaming coffee when Joshua and Rose arrived with baby Rosie, who gave a happy chirrup to see him, and Charlie, who called out, "Grandfather Talbot!" and headed straight for his arms. They had scant time to get to know each other again before Wilmington arrived, and Benjamin tried not to be jealous as their mutual grandchildren greeted him joyously, too. After all, he told himself sternly, Wilmington had no other grandchildren, while he himself had a growing army of them at *Rancho Verde*.

Time disappeared as quickly as their breakfast, and before long they were rushing down the wooded path to the schoolhouse for the Independence Day festivities. Others were arriving from all directions: ladies in colorful summer frocks, men in shirtsleeves, and students in historical attire that transformed them into everyone from Revolutionary War soldiers to Pilgrims. In front of the schoolhouse, a crowd had gathered near the new platform made of raw yellow wood and the equally new flagpole from which the Stars and

Stripes fluttered in the mid-morning breeze. Boys raced along the paths, laughing and holding their ears as firecrackers crackled like corn popping. From time to time another *boom!* rent the air from the blacksmith's anvil in town.

At ten-thirty, Jonathan Wilmington strode through the crowd toward the platform, a young man following behind him. Mounting the steps, Wilmington stood under the new flag and waited for the crowd to quiet. "Ladies and gentlemen, girls and boys," he said as he surveyed them, "it is the school board's privilege to sponsor today's program. Today we stand in the new state of California under the flag of the United States to celebrate our glorious Fourth of July, and it wouldn't be right to celebrate without telling what it's all about. One of our students will recite the Declaration of Independence from memory, and we hope you will consider it well. May I present Spencer Tucker."

Benjamin watched the youth, who was perhaps sixteen, as he stood nervously before them. He was a freckle-faced young man with sandy hair and an intelligent mien, likely the student Betsy thought held such promise.

Spencer drew a deep breath and began the familiar words. "When in the course of human events it becomes necessary for one people to dissolve the political bonds which have connected them with another, and to assume among the powers of the earth the separate and equal station to which the laws of Nature and of Nature's God entitle them, a decent respect to the opinions of mankind requires that they should declare the causes which impel them to the separation.

"We hold these truths to be self-evident, that all men are created equal, that they are endowed by their Creator with certain inalienable rights, that among these are Life, Liberty, and the pursuit of Happiness. . . ."

Benjamin listened with pleasure to young Spencer Tucker, but with renewed dismay to the list of the crimes of the King, which most people had forgotten as quickly as they forgot their history.

"He has endeavored to prevent the population of these States.

"He has obstructed the administration of Justice.

"He has made Judges dependent on his will alone.

"He has erected a multitude of new offices, and sent hither swarms of officers to harass our people and to eat out their substance.

"He has plundered our seas, ravaged our coasts, burnt our towns, and destroyed the lives of our people. . . .

When Spencer ended his lengthy recitation, the mood was so solemn that Wilmington stepped up behind him, raised an arm and shouted, "Three cheers for the brave men who wrote that fine document!"

"*Hip, hip, hooray!*" the crowd called out with him.

"Three cheers for the brave men who beat the British in 1776 and again in 1812!"

"*Hip, hip, hooray!*"

Wilmington raised his arm powerfully again. "Three cheers for America!"

"*Hip, hip, hooray!*"everyone yelled. "*Hip, hip, hooray! Hip, hip, hooray!*"

A slim arm slipped into Benjamin's, and he found Betsy beaming up at him. "It's the first time Spencer has ever spoken publicly. He did a fine job, didn't he?"

"He did well indeed! He must have a fine teacher."

Betsy laughed. "I promised to pray for him. And to see if you knew of any college scholarships. He's a most deserving young man."

Benjamin grinned. "A fine idea. I expect there are others

in the state who are deserving of scholarships as well. I shall talk to some of my friends in town and see what we can accomplish."

"And I shall see to it that you meet Spencer later."

The crowd quieted and Benjamin tensed as Wilmington said, "It gives me great pleasure to introduce a man who came to California in 1846, before gold was found . . . a man who worked for California statehood from the beginning . . . a man who to this day works for law and order . . . a father, uncle, and brother to some of our residents . . . a grandfather to my grandchildren . . . a friend, who instead of cursing the darkness, tries to light a candle . . . Benjamin Talbot."

Betsy patted his arm proudly, then Benjamin hurried to the platform, buoyed even more by the cheers of his family and friends and by Wilmington's clap on the shoulder as he ascended the platform's raw wooden steps.

Once atop the platform, Benjamin surveyed the crowd with quiet satisfaction. "I thank you for your encouragement. It is a mighty undertaking to speak after the Declaration of Independence has been so movingly delivered.

"Nonetheless, 1776 was only the beginning. We have come a long way in the seventy-eight years since then, not all of it commendable. But before we go forward, let us go backward in time again. What happened after the Declaration of Independence and the Revolutionary War ended?"

"The Constitution!" several of the students shouted.

"Right! The Constitution of the United States was written. In the summer of 1787 representatives met in Philadelphia for that purpose. They struggled over it for weeks and had made little progress until eighty-one-year-old Benjamin Franklin rose and addressed a convention that was about to adjourn in anger and confusion. Here is what Franklin, once an avowed agnostic, said.

" 'In the beginning of the contest with Britain, when we were sensible of danger, we had daily prayers in this room for Divine protection. Our prayers, Sir, were heard and they were graciously answered. All of us who were engaged in the struggle must have observed frequent instances of a superintending Providence in our favor. . . . Have we now forgotten this powerful Friend? Or do we imagine we no longer need His assistance?' "

Benjamin spoke on, emphasizing Franklin's arguments. " 'God governs in the affairs of man. And if a sparrow cannot fall to the ground without His notice, is it probable that an empire can rise without His aid? We have been assured, Sir, in the Sacred Writings that except the Lord build the house, they labor in vain that build it. I firmly believe this. . . .

" 'I therefore beg leave to move that, henceforth, prayers imploring the assistance of heaven and its blessing on our deliberation be held in this assembly every morning.'

"And thus," Benjamin Talbot said, "our Constitution was written with prayer. Even earlier, in 1620, the very purpose of the Pilgrims coming here was to establish a government based on the Bible. The New England Charter, signed by King James I, confirmed their goal of advancing the enlargement of Christian religion, to the glory of God Almighty.

"Governor Bradford, in writing of the Pilgrim's landing, describes their first act: 'being thus arrived in a good harbor and brought safe to land, they fell upon their knees and blessed the God of heaven . . .'

"The goal of government based on Holy Scripture was further reaffirmed by individual colonies. The Rhode Island Charter of 1683 begins: 'We submit our persons, lives, and estates unto our Lord Jesus Christ, the King of kings and Lord of lords and to all those perfect and most absolute laws of His given us in His Holy Word.'

"Those 'absolute laws' became the very basis for our Declaration of Independence. George Washington put it well when he said that it would be impossible to govern this nation without God and the Ten Commandments. It is from those roots that our federal Constitution grew. If we here in California or anywhere else sever those roots, it shall be impossible to rule this great land.

"President John Adams said, 'Our Constitution was made only for a moral and religious people. It is wholly inadequate for the government of any other.'

"President John Quincy Adams said, 'The highest glory of the American Revolution was this: it connected in one indissoluble bond, the principles of civil government with the principles of Christianity.'

Benjamin told of de Tocqueville, the noted French political philosopher who visited America in 1831 to find the secret of her greatness. "He examined our young national government, our schools and centers of commerce, but could not discover our strength in them. It was not until he visited the churches of America and witnessed the pulpits of this land 'aflame with righteousness' that he found the secret of our greatness. When he returned to France, he summarized his findings with this: 'America is great because America is good; and if America ever ceases to be good, America will cease to be great.'

"Today we must look at our community, our state, and our nation in that godly light," Benjamin said. "Will it cease to be godly? Will it cease to be great?"

He gathered his strength and pronounced with all of his heart and might, "God, help us each and every one to shed Thy light in this community . . . God, help us to shed Thy light in this state . . . God, help us to shed Thy light in this great land!"

The cheers were immediate, and Benjamin, nodding, stepped back from the speaker's place. The sound of the applause filling the wooded settlement seemed to make the summer air shimmer with hope and resolve.

Betsy stood on the platform now, beaming at him and still clapping. When at last the applause died down, she spoke. "After our students present our historical pageant, you are all invited to visit our schoolroom exhibit of this term's work. The students have put out compositions, drawings, reports, and graphs on our walls, and our shelves hold fossils, bird nests, shells, samplers, pot holders . . . and much more for your inspection. After that, you are invited to attend a potlock dinner at the church."

She smiled at the crowd and began to sing with all of her heart, "*My country, 'tis of thee. . . .*" Then everyone was singing, and tears filled Benjamin's eyes as he joined in.

> *. . . sweet land of liberty,*
> *Of thee I sing. . . .*
> *Long may our land be bright*
> *With Freedom's holy light.*
> *Protect us by Thy might,*
> *Great God, our King!*

As the song ended, it was if together they had made a holy commitment, and Benjamin waited until the applause rose before he pulled out his handkerchief and gave his nose a mighty blast. *Sentimental old fool,* he thought. On the other hand, how many men had the privilege of living in a land like this and of seeing a daughter lead the town in such fervent singing about it! At the moment, despite his respect for Washington and old Franklin, Betsy's leading the singing beat everything the old patriots had ever accomplished.

Minutes later, her students' historical pageant began in front of the schoolhouse and was equally well done. He looked on proudly with parents and townspeople as the children enacted the landing of the Pilgrims and the Revolutionary War, singing a particularly enthusiastic rendition of "Yankee Doodle." As the pageant ended, Benjamin glanced over the crowd for this Fayette who was attempting to court his daughter.

His eyes roved over the people until they hit on Adam Buchanan and the beauty who was apparently his wife, the violinist. Beside her stood a most handsome young man who resembled her closely, and Benjamin decided uneasily that it must be Fayette. The young man must have felt his glance, for he turned, and their eyes met. They nodded at each other, the young man as wary as Benjamin felt about him.

Finally everyone applauded the pageant, and the crowd gradually moved into the chinked log schoolroom to examine the children's work. Benjamin noticed that Betsy had earned the students' confidence as she went about the room with them and their parents.

He remarked to Wilmington, "I suppose I did the right thing in allowing her to teach here."

"And we did the right thing in hiring her," Wilmington said. "Come along, we're not too old to help set up the tables and benches outside the church for the potluck dinner, if they need help."

Benjamin fell into step with his friend. "Tell me about Fayette Williams."

Wilmington shrugged. "Not a lot to tell. He's Selena Buchanan's twin and comes to visit now and then. Only derogatory thing I know is that he brought a dozen or so slaves from Savannah. Most of them ran off. Only two household blacks are left, and Adam, being a 'northerner' from Baltimore, gave them their freedom and pays them wages to run the house."

Benjamin drew a thoughtful breath. "Guess I had better suspend judgment. Williams looks somehow familiar, but I can't put a finger on it."

By the time they arrived with the cheerful crowd under the churchyard trees, the tables and benches were all set out and lines had formed for the food. Rose, Tess Fairfax, and Louisa Chambers were already there to serve the smaller children, who sat at a table with Jessica. And there came Jonathan Chambers, the familiar crease in his chin deepening as he saw Benjamin, and there was Hugh Fairfax.

Benjamin and Jonathan joined the line approaching the tempting dishes: roasted chicken, beef and pork, potato and vegetable salads, black-eyed peas, hams, corn bread, and an all too alluring table of cakes and pies. They found a table in the shade of an oak tree, and it was a most pleasant dinner, with the sounds of conversation, excited children, and an occasional cry of a babe or a blue jay filling the warm July air.

It wasn't until they were drinking their last cup of coffee that Betsy brought the Buchanans and Fayette around. "I'm sure you must remember Dr. Buchanan, who saved our necks when we came in on the stagecoach—"

"Of course," Benjamin said, rising from the bench and shaking hands heartily with the young doctor. "We are eternally grateful to you."

"A pleasure to see you again, sir," Adam said.

Betsy continued, "And this is his wife—my new friend, Selena—and their daughter, Mellie." She turned and gave the young man a brilliant smile. "And, Father, this is Selena's brother, Fayette Williams."

Benjamin shook hands and spoke cordially, all the time thinking his daughter's suitor looked like the type who first swept a woman off her feet and then under the carpet. As the polite conversation flowed around them, he noted the curious glances that passed between Fayette and his equally handsome sister, who was easily the best dressed woman in the crowd in her artfully simple lavender frock and matching parasol.

"How long will you be staying with us, Mr. Talbot?" Fayette asked with a deep southern accent.

"Unfortunately I leave on the morning stage."

"Ah am truly sorry to heah that," the young man said, though he looked less than regretful.

Betsy asked most charmingly, "Fayette, could you help carry the larger pageant props back into the school before they are damaged?"

"My pleasure. Ah'll get the buggy, Miss Talbot. If you will excuse us—"

"Ah'll go with you, Fayette," Selena said. "Perhaps you could drop me off at the house. All of this warm sun has made me so very drowsy."

Fayette turned to her solicitously. "Yes, of course, Selena."

Selena nodded at Benjamin. "It was such a pleasure to meet you, Mr. Talbot. Ah am so fond of your daughter, but Ah do get so very tired. Ah look forward to meetin' you again."

Mellie reached for her father's hand frantically, though she did keep her voice down. "I'm not tired, Papa! I don't want a nap!"

"You may stay up a bit longer. It's not every day that we celebrate our country's freedom," Adam Buchanan replied. He looked oddly agitated, not at all like the man who had rescued their stagecoach from a gang of highwaymen.

An indecipherable glance passed between him and his wife, then she smiled beatifically at Benjamin, scooped up the skirt of her lavender frock with decorum, and made a most charming departure with her brother.

There was something not quite right about the situation, Benjamin thought. Why couldn't Betsy find someone not quite so handsome and not quite so attached to his sister . . . someone more solid? Why not someone more like Adam Buchanan?

Astonished at the thought, he glanced at Buchanan. He looked more at ease now that his wife and her brother had departed, and Benjamin realized he felt more at ease himself.

Betsy said, "Father, I would like you to meet the student who recited the Declaration of Independence, Spencer Tucker—"

"A pleasure to meet you, young man," Benjamin said, rising to give him a hearty handshake.

They spoke at length, and Benjamin found the young man to be a fine godly scholar indeed. He and some of the others in San Francisco might be able to come up with a scholarship. Yes, he was sure they could manage it.

Unfortunately, there was no time alone with Betsy until he walked her to school the next morning, and it was difficult for him to discuss a situation he did not understand himself. He remembered that Betsy and Jessica would be at *Casa Contenta* most of August, but he still felt compelled to speak. They discussed the school program and everything else until it was almost too late. Finally, as the school came into sight, he asked too stiffly, "Are Selena and Fayette believers?"

She shook her head. "I don't think so, but I am praying with all of my heart for them. They are attending church now—"

"A beginning," he said, "though not an end in itself. I hope they'll turn their lives over to Christ, but so often when people are too mutually dependent, they worship each other and refuse to surrender to Him."

Betsy replied thoughtfully, "I suppose Selena is overly dependent on Fayette, but I don't think he is on her. He's only concerned because she's an artist and rather high-strung. He is very proud of her."

"Yes, I expect he is," Benjamin replied. "I expect he is."

Some of the students were already playing outside in the school yard, and one of the girls called out, "Miss Talbot! Wasn't yesterday's program good?"

"It surely was. You all did a fine job."

Smiling, she turned to her father. "Can you come in for a while to see the schoolroom in action?"

"I would like to, but I still have to pack up, and I promised Chambers I'd stop at the church for a few minutes. He thinks I can give him good advice. It's the one commodity I have so much of, and which so few people want."

She smiled again. "Then . . . oh, Father, I don't like to say good-bye so soon to you. We've scarcely had time to talk."

He nodded. "I'll keep you in my prayers, Betsy. And you'll be at *Casa Contenta* most of next month."

"Yes," she replied. "I love it here, but how good it will be to come home and to see everyone there."

She reached up to kiss his cheek, and Benjamin bent a trifle to receive it most willingly. "We shall see you next month."

"Yes, Father," she replied. "In the meantime, give everyone at home my love."

It wasn't until he rode out of Oak Hill on the jolting stagecoach that he realized why her daughter's suitor had looked vaguely familiar. Benjamin gripped the seat in shock.

It was in San Francisco that he had seen Fayette Williams. *He had been with Emile Martene, and they'd just stepped from the door of a gambling establishment!*

All week the students spoke proudly of their parts in the Fourth of July celebration. And every day after school Selena, Fayette, and Mellie came by to visit Betsy in the log schoolhouse. She could not quite understand Fayette, for though he seemed thoroughly intrigued by her, he always had pressing affairs in the evening, usually down in the raucous mining settlement of Oak Flats.

On Thursday, Selena said with petulance, "Fayette is leavin' us again for Sacramento City and San Francisco. Ah don't believe he loves us at all."

Fayette patted his sister's arm. "You know how much it grieves me to leave my family, Selena." He turned to Betsy with a small but meaningful smile. "And my friends, as well."

Betsy returned his smile with some hesitation, and Mellie demanded, "Uncle Fayette, you stay home with us!"

"If only Ah could, Mellie . . . if only Ah could," he said wearily. "A man's got his work in this world. Ah have mining partners and contracts to see to. As it is, Ah take off far too much time to be with you and your mama."

Betsy said to Selena, "I hope you and Mellie will continue your visits here after school."

"Ah don't know—" Selena answered. "Ah don't like walkin' through the woods without a man's protection."

"Now, Selena, it is not far at all," Fayette protested.

"What about th—that person who assaulted Betsy?" Selena asked, her brown eyes widening with fear.

"Ah'm certain it must be safe now," Fayette said.

It was reassuring to hear him say so, but how could one be certain? Betsy wondered. Usually Rufus or Jonathan Chambers or one of the other men still saw her home after school.

Fayette added, "Ask Rufus to accompany you."

Selena blinked with hurt. "Ah don't know. . . ."

"Let me help you lock up the school today, Betsy," said Fayette. "Here, Ah'll get the windows."

When they had finished he said to Selena and Mellie, "If you will please wait for a minute on the front steps for us, Ah have a private word to say to Betsy."

Selena gave Betsy a small smile as she steered Mellie out the schoolhouse door. "Now, don't you be too long, Fayette."

He closed the door behind them, then turned to Betsy, who had just gotten her dinner pail from the cloakroom. "Ah especially don't like to leave you, Betsy. Ah saw those men eyeing you when you led the Fourth of July singing." He reached for her hand.

She couldn't imagine what harm it might do for him to kiss her hand . . . not until he did, and her blood raced wildly through her veins.

"Come heah, Betsy Talbot," he murmured. "Ah wish to show you how much Ah care for you."

Overcome, she allowed him to hold her shoulders and saw his mouth angle toward hers before she recalled her vow: no kisses until he had declared himself.

"No, Fayette," she whispered. "Please, no. . . ."

"Ah can't take no for an answer from you, sweet Betsy—"

"No!" she cried out. "No!"

"Don't you care for me?" he implored.

"That is not the question."

He looked amazed that she would resist him. She wondered if she were the first woman who had.

On Friday after school, Betsy was surprised to see Selena coming up the schoolhouse path alone, leaving Rufus to sit on a stump at the edge of the woods near her property. "Ah needed to get out," Selena explained as she greeted Betsy.

"I'm glad to see you," Betsy replied, inviting her into the

schoolroom. "I wish you'd play the violin for the children again. They often speak of the time you performed for us."

"Maybe Ah shall when Fayette returns."

"But you could play without him."

Selena shook her lovely head. "Not likely. Ah just don't even feel like playin' when he's gone."

"Let's sit down at the desks," Betsy suggested, taking one of the student's desks near the back of the room.

Selena sat down across the aisle from her and smiled. "Why, Ah feel like a schoolgirl again," she said, though she did not look like one in her low-cut yellow dimity dress.

Betsy smoothed the skirt of her sedate green calico frock. "You must have spent many hours of your childhood practicing the violin."

"And the piano," Selena added. "Yes, Ah did have hours and hours of lessons. But let's not talk about me. Ah wanted to talk about you and Fayette."

"About me and Fayette?"

Selena smiled. "He is very fond of you, Betsy. And Ah am fond of you, too. Ah do hope you'll set your cap for him."

"Fayette said that—he's fond of me?" Betsy inquired.

Selena nodded. "He did. Fayette and Ah . . . well, we tell each other most everythin'. Why, he even told me he thought you might be as passionate as we southerners are."

Blood rushed to Betsy's face.

"Well, just look at you blush!" Selena laughed. "You know what Ah told him?"

Betsy shook her head, unwilling to hazard a guess.

Selena's lovely face filled with satisfaction. "Ah told him he should marry you so he could settle down here. Why, Ah believe maybe even Adam wants him to, so we can all be together and live in contentment. I do believe Fayette took to the idea."

The whole notion struck Betsy as sheer fantasy. "I don't know—"

"Now Ah realize it's a surprise to you, Betsy, but Fayette is so handsome and charmin', and he's such a good catch. Why, girls have always been wild about him . . . maybe a little too much. Ah suppose it's scandalous to say, but Ah do wish Ah had a husband like him instead of a doctor who's always out patchin' up the sick."

"Adam is very compassionate, Selena. It is easy to see that he truly cares about people."

"Well, Ah don't like sharin' a husband with strangers. Ah'd just rather have someone excitin' like Fayette."

Surprising as Selena's admission was, it struck Betsy that the woman was far better off with a man like Adam who spent all of his nights at home than with a man who was so often gone like Fayette.

On Sunday, she was pleased to see Selena in church with Adam and Mellie, and even more pleased to hear people tell Selena they hoped she'd play her violin in church again soon. Betsy renewed her prayers for all three of them.

On Monday after school, Selena appeared at the schoolhouse again, and Rufus sat out on the stump. Her visits began to be a pleasant part of every day, for if nothing else, Selena was interesting. As the week passed, however, she confided more and more of her marriage troubles to Betsy.

At length Betsy said, "Adam seems such a good person to most of us, and Mellie is such a lovely child. You'll be happier if you just think of all the blessings God has given you."

Selena sat up in the school desk in bitterness. "What God has given me! This uncivilized country to live in, a husband who doesn't love me enough, and a dead baby?"

"A dead baby?" Betsy asked, remembering Selena had once before mentioned it.

Selena nodded. "On the covered wagon trip west! It was Adam's fault . . . all his fault."

"It must hurt him, too, Selena—"

"Not like it hurt me!"

"Perhaps he just didn't want to show it. Some men are like that."

"He doesn't care one whit about me . . . or my talent . . or my, well . . . my beauty. Ah was sought after all of my life, Betsy, and now Ah have a husband who scarcely looks at me."

"I can't believe that—"

"You've never had men chasing after you from the time you were little like Ah have. You've no idea what it's like to be sought after everywhere you turn, men ever so eager to help you into a carriage and steal a kiss. Why, Daddy always wanted Fayette around to hold them off, but he . . . well, Fayette's always had his own interests." She let out a discouraged breath. "If you had men after you, you'd understand. And you can be angry with me if you like!"

"I'm not angry, Selena," Betsy responded. Instead, she felt a growing sense of pity for a woman whose life revolved around her appearance, her talent, her interest in men . . . in herself.

"Ah'm glad you're not angry," Selena said. "Ah do hope you still want me for a friend."

"Yes," Betsy replied. "I do want to be your friend."

Selena looked perplexed. "Why? Why would you?"

"Because I want to tell you how much the Lord loves you. He can change your life, Selena. He can fill your heart with joy and take away your loneliness."

"Ah have never been a religious person," Selena declared, then added most emphatically, "and Ah surely do not care to become one! I was baptized as a child."

"That's not enough, Selena. One has to make an adult decision and ask forgiveness through Christ—"

"Ah don't care to heah one more word about it!"

The next day after school, Betsy feared Selena wouldn't come, but she was there with Mellie. Once the child was occupied watching ants scurry back and forth to an anthill outside the schoolhouse door, Selena asked, "Have you given more thought to marryin' Fayette?"

Betsy laughed. "He hasn't even asked me, Selena!"

"Well, if he did, would you?"

"Believe it or not, I have been too busy to think of it much. I've been trying to get in all of the teaching I can before this summer term ends. Several of the children will be leaving, and I don't know if they'll ever see the inside of a schoolhouse or even a book again."

"Phooey on school!" Selena returned. "Ah do wish you'd give marryin' Fayette serious thought."

Betsy replied as kindly as possible, "I would like to explain myself, Selena. I truly believe that God has the perfect husband chosen for me, if I am to have one, and I don't wish to spend my teaching time chasing after one."

"You sound like my old maiden aunt," Selena returned scornfully. "She believed like that, too, but 'her Lord,' as she called Him, didn't see fit to send her a husband."

"So be it then," Betsy said softly. "I must admit that I would like a husband and a family someday, but if the Lord has other plans, I believe that His love is sufficient."

Selena shot her a skeptical glance. "Ah don't care to talk anymore about religious matters, so Ah'll go on home now."

The weeks passed with no sign of Fayette. Betsy found that she missed him, but his absence gave her more time to concentrate on teaching. Nearly every afternoon Selena met her after school, sometimes with Mellie and sometimes alone, and always with Rufus on guard in the distance. Mellie no longer peeked in the school window, likely because she could actually come into the schoolhouse now. Betsy might have dreaded the visits if it weren't for the child, for Selena seemed increasingly distraught. She must mention the woman's dejection to Adam the next time she saw him.

On Sunday at church, however, Selena clung to Adam's side, and Betsy thought there might be hope for their marriage.

On the last Saturday morning of July, she encountered Adam in front of the Mercantile. This was her opportunity to speak of his wife's growing despair, she decided, but they'd barely exchanged greetings when the Jurgen family joined them.

Still, Adam had said with appreciation, "Selena values your friendship."

"And I value hers," Betsy replied with what she realized was more than mere courtesy.

Two days before school let out, Selena joined her, looking unhappier than ever. Mellie was not with her, nor was Rufus in sight.

"Where's Rufus this afternoon?" Betsy asked as she locked the schoolhouse door behind them.

"Ah told him to stay home," Selena replied.

"But you were the one who was scared to walk here—"

"Ah am sick and tired of that man trailin' after me every single afternoon," Selena answered. "Ah believe he reports on me to my husband like a spy. Ah truly do believe that!"

Betsy glanced about the school yard and the woods uneasily. If Rufus weren't on watch, there was to be another man guarding when school let out. She saw no one. Even worse, here was Selena dressed in her low-cut yellow dimity frock, just asking for trouble!

Taking up her arm load of books from the schoolhouse step, Betsy decided that a discussion of the matter with Selena was less than useless, and her mind went to the alternative plan. "Let's walk to the Chamberses' house on the other side of the church. Jonathan Chambers or one of the other men will see us home, since Rufus isn't here."

"Ah have no wish to speak with that preacher," Selena pouted. "All he ever talks about is Christ and God . . . Christ and God. You'd think it was the all-out answer to everythin' on earth!"

Betsy hesitated, then decided to be entirely clear about her own faith. "I expect it's because Jonathan has found it to be true. I know it's true myself. Christ is the way to God . . . the only way to Him."

"Ah don't want any of your preachin'," Selena objected. "Ah am no worse than other people, and that is sufficient."

She was so adamant that Betsy decided not to pursue the subject any further just then. "Something seems to be distressing you especially today, Selena. What is it?"

"Ah had a letter from Fayette," Selena answered morosely.

"And—? Is it bad news?"

Selena nodded. "He says he's goin' back to Savannah."

"To Savannah?"

"He's gettin' together money to buy back our house there, but he says Ah can't come! Can you imagine? Ah can't come!"

"But Adam and Mellie are here in Oak Hill!"

Suddenly Selena implored her, "Oh, Betsy, please try to keep Fayette here! You know how hard this month has been with him in Sacramento City and San Francisco. But now that he plans to go home to Savannah . . . Ah shall die without him."

"But how can I keep him here?"

Selena studied her for a long moment, then her eyes began to glimmer with hope. "When he comes around again, and you're alone with him, you look at him the way a woman should." She smiled languidly, as if at a man. "Then you sidle up close to him . . . and maybe run your fingers through his hair."

Betsy backed away a step. "Selena, that is pretense . . . an—an artifice . . . ."

"Ah assure you, with a man like Fayette, it won't be pretense for long. Ah can teach you everythin' you need to know, Betsy. I can teach you. And it's not as though Fayette is hard to love. He is ever so wonderful."

Betsy blurted, "I believe you love him more than you do your husband!"

"And what if Ah do!"

"Adam is a fine man—"

"Ah don't care two beans about him! Ah almost never did! Ah was sick, and Mama and Daddy thought he would be good for me. That's all it ever was, and he is no good for me at all! He doesn't have any idea about how to treat a southern woman, and he doesn't in the least understand my artistic temperament!"

"Oh, Selena!" Betsy objected, shifting her arm load of books.

"Well, that's the bald truth! As for Fayette, Ah love him so much Ah am willin' to show you just how to get him."

Betsy shook her head. "Don't you see that acting like that isn't right for me? That I'm different from you?"

"Different?" Selena repeated, lifting her chin. Her brown eyes darkened with anger. "*Different's* not what you mean, Miss Betsy Talbot! You think you're all-fired *better* than Ah am just because you don't know how to get a man!"

"Not better," Betsy protested as kindly as possible. "Different. If there is a special man who is meant to be my husband, I shall not have to . . . trick him."

"Trick him!"

"I'm sorry, Selena. I shouldn't have said—"

Selena grabbed Betsy's shoulder and shook her. "Ah could shake you to pieces, you goody-good nothin'!"

Encumbered by her arm load of books, Betsy tried to push away, but Selena shook her even more wildly. "Heah Ah offer you Fayette on a platter, and you aren't in the least grateful!"

Enraged, the woman grabbed her throat.

She's demented! Betsy thought. *Demented and full of frightening strength.* "Selena! Selena!"

"Ah'll kill you!" Selena cried out, her fingers tightening around Betsy's neck.

Dropping her books, Betsy struggled to push away. Finally, she tore loose, but Selena rushed at her again. Betsy dodged wildly and ran down the path toward the church. If Jonathan wasn't there, she'd head for Rose's cabin.

"You come heah!" Selena shrieked as she followed. "Pretendin' to be my friend!"

A horse pounded up the path, and Adam shouted from the distance, "Selena! Selena, stop!" Glancing back, Betsy saw Selena veer wildly toward the graveyard path to avoid him.

She shrieked at Betsy, "Now Ah shall have to do it, and it's your fault!"

Betsy cried, "Selena! Come back!"

But Selena raced through the graveyard, angling toward the river embankment, where the woods were thicker and she might escape Adam on horseback.

Holding up her skirts, Betsy rushed after her through the gravestones. "Selena, let me talk to you!" she shouted out over the muffled sound of the river.

227

Selena ran on through the trees and underbrush, finally stumbling down the upper riverbank to where the wooded slope leveled out.

Following through the dense trees and brush, Betsy thought it must be the place Rose had described, a hideout with greenery so thick it nearly blotted out the sun . . . the hideout where Hollis must have been.

Behind her, Adam yelled again, "Selena, stop!"

"Ah hate you!" Selena shot back as she ran. "Ah hate both of you, and Ah hate Oak Hill!"

Betsy stumbled out of the woods and to the edge of the gray slate ledge. "Selena! Please, please let me help you!"

"You stay away!" Selena called back, her eyes glittering.

A thick bush separated them, and Betsy feared if she moved forward, Selena might jump off the ledge. "You have Adam and Mellie to live for, Selena."

The woman made no answer; nor did she respond to Adam, who was now on foot, calling out as he approached. Instead, she stared at the steep slope that led to the rushing river far below.

Betsy darted a glance down the slope. Only a stunted pine growing from the broken slate could save Selena from destruction if she jumped, and the pine was five or six feet away. As she glanced back at Selena, the woman made as if to throw herself over the ledge.

Betsy hurled herself over the slope toward the stunted pine, praying a silent and fervent, *Help me, Lord!*

She skidded upright down the broken gray slate and grabbed for the twisted tree trunk, then held on desperately and turned to grab Selena. To her amazement, the woman had not jumped.

Instead, she was staring transfixed at something just behind her feet. Quite suddenly a fearsome rattle filled the air.

Rattlesnake!

Selena screamed and jumped, and Betsy braced her back against the pine's trunk so she might break Selena's fall.

But Selena was rolling hopelessly to the right down the slate in her yellow frock, tumbling at an angle impossible for Betsy to reach. Just above her, Adam, looking stricken, skidded upright down the embankment on an avalanche of broken slate.

Betsy held onto the twisted pine as the disastrous scene played itself out on the steep hillside. It seemed forever until Selena's body reached the bottom of the slope by the river, but only a few moments until Adam was bending over her, carefully turning her onto her back and feeling for a pulse in her neck, then listening to her heart.

At length, his shoulders shook with sobs.

Betsy's eyes filled with tears, and she heard only the river rushing on relentlessly below them, mercifully muffling the sounds of the man's agony.

10

Benjamin Talbot stood at the bustling San Francisco dock.
As soon as he beheld Betsy and Jessica walking down
the gangplank of their Sacramento riverboat, he knew something was amiss. Despite their obvious pleasure as they embraced him, their faces seemed tired and pinched, as though
they had drunk deeply from the cup of sorrow.

"What is it? What has happened?" he asked while a por-
ter brought their valises around to the carriage.

Betsy's green eyes closed with dismay, and Jessica said,
"Selena Buchanan is dead."

"How on earth did she die?" Benjamin asked. "She
looked in fine health—"

"She—" Betsy's eyes filled with tears, and she fumbled in
the pocket of her gray frock for a handkerchief.

"She fell down the riverbank in the woods behind the
graveyard," Jessica answered for her. "At least, from what I
understand, she fell. The sad part is Betsy feels Selena meant
to kill herself, then seemed to change her mind when she
looked over the ledge. There was a rattler at her feet, though,
and, apparently in evading it, she fell."

Benjamin glanced at Betsy, bringing new tears to her eyes.

"Betsy blames herself, but I can't see that it was in any

wise her fault," Jessica said. "Selena was demented, though she seemed somewhat better of late. Betsy and Adam did their best to save the poor woman from the fall—and from herself."

"And Fayette?" Benjamin inquired.

"He was gone. Adam was unable even to reach him in time for the burial," Jessica replied. "Fayette and Selena were so close, one can only wonder how he will take it."

Slowly the story unfolded as they rode away from San Francisco's waterfront in the carriage. When it was all told, Benjamin said, "I see no reason you should feel at fault, Betsy. No reason at all."

She shook her head. "Perhaps if I'd prayed more . . . if I'd said something else—"

"Yes . . . there we all lie at fault. I doubt there's a person alive who couldn't have changed matters for the better by having prayed more or said something else."

"I'd hoped to lead her to the Lord, but she . . . she refused to hear about Him," Betsy told him, still pained. "I tried, Father . . . I truly tried. . . . "

"If you were meant to, God would have provided the opportunity," Benjamin assured her. "She did attend the church at Oak Hill, and Chambers is very clear in presenting Christ as the one way to God."

"Yes," Betsy agreed. "Jonathan is always clear about it."

"Apparently Selena was not receptive there either."

"No, she was not," Betsy said with deep regret.

Benjamin understood perfectly, having encountered the same situation himself more than once. "Then we leave the problem to God," he told her. "We do not berate ourselves unnecessarily. We pray for forgiveness if we were somehow lax, we pray for constant awareness of His wishes, and we leave the rest of the matter to Him."

He was certain that Jessica had told Betsy the same thing, but such assurances ofttimes bore repetition. As they jolted up a steep hill in the carriage, he said, "Let's have a prayer now."

Betsy still looked troubled, but she replied with gratefulness, "Yes, please, Father, do pray."

Benjamin closed his eyes and composed himself. "Almighty Father, we praise Thy name for the grace that has come to us through our Lord, Jesus Christ. We rejoice in being Thy children and thank Thee for bringing Betsy and Jessica home safely to us. We come, too, in repentance for not praying more, for not turning to Thee more often, for not always being as open to Thy leading as we might be. Merciful Father, heal Betsy of all pain in this matter, whether it is needful pain or not, and heal Adam Buchanan and his little daughter of their pain and loss. We pray this in Christ's powerful name. Amen."

When he opened his eyes, Betsy appeared somewhat relieved, and later, when they arrived at *Casa Contenta*, he said, "It's Daniel's birthday, so let's keep the sad news from them today. In any case, none of them know the Buchanans."

"A good idea," Jessica said.

Brightening, Benjamin added, "You're home now, Betsy, and all will be better soon. You know you do not have to return to Oak Hill to teach—"

She replied softly, "But I do, Father. I have agreed to teach the fall term. At the very least, I shall be there until Christmas. You—were so pleased when you visited for the Fourth that I thought you would approve. Everything happened so suddenly . . . Selena's death and the burial, the summer term ending, and their offering me the fall term. Aunt Jessica and I prayed about it, and she wishes to stay on longer, too."

He turned to Jessica, who nodded, then gazed again at

his youngest child, this young woman with the lovely, pert face. Best not to vent his disappointment when she had suffered more than enough of late. "I must admit I am proud of your work, Betsy. But now you must turn your mind to matters here at home." He cast about for a new subject. "Wait until you see the church we have built this summer . . . and how the children have all grown during your absence! They can scarcely wait to see you!"

In retrospect, he wished he had never given in to her teaching at Oak Hill, but he could not protect her forever from heartache. He glanced at his sister and noticed for the first time that her face had a slight grayish tinge. "Are you feeling well, Jessica?"

She smiled. "As well as can be expected for a woman of nearly threescore and ten."

"Ah, Jessica, you are younger in mind and more joyous in spirit than most women of fifty."

She gave a laugh of protest, but it occurred to him that Betsy could not stay at Oak Hill if Jessica was unable to return with her. Sometime during their stay, he must make that fact entirely clear to Betsy.

Suddenly he felt a sudden pang of fear for both of them. *Lord, keep them in Thy loving watchcare,* he prayed. *I beseech Thee, protect them from evil.*

Three heartwarming weeks later, when Betsy returned to Oak Hill, both she and Aunt Jessica felt renewed and rested. In addition, they were relieved not to have encountered "desperadoes," as Aunt Jessica called them. Betsy, however, recognized the exact thicket where the holdup men had halted their stagecoach five months earlier and remembered the incident all too well.

Disembarking from the stagecoach at Oak Hill just before

midday, they inhaled deeply of the piney air. The late August weather was warm, and the log settlement in the woods was a welcome sight. Rose and Louisa and their children hurried out and embraced them, and neighbors called out greetings.

As they started down the forested path to their cabin, Rose called after them, "We shall expect you for dinner! Wait until you see your garden!"

The river was quieter now at the end of summer, but its murmur underscored the drum of a woodpecker, the midday chirpings of birds, and the soft breeze rustling the oaks, cedars, and pines overhead. When Betsy looked up, she caught a glimpse of the eagle that nested in the lightning-struck pine as the great bird circled over the settlement.

"The fall term will be upon you in just five days," Aunt Jessica remarked.

"Yes. I am eager for it." Strange, she reflected, none of the discipline problems she'd imagined with the older school-children had arisen during the summer term. Instead, all of her problems had come from other quarters.

"We'll need some provisions," her aunt said.

"Tomorrow I can get them in town, but I need to prepare the schoolhouse Friday. I hope we can visit Tess and her babe Saturday afternoon."

"I think I shall wait until next week. I wonder if you might take Mellie Buchanan with you," her aunt suggested.

"What a fine idea! I've been trying to think how we might make her life more cheerful."

They had learned of Tess Fairfax's baby from Rose's letter to them at *Casa Contenta*. Rose had also written that she and Joshua would have another child in March, and that Louisa and Jonathan Chambers were expecting a child as well.

Babies, babies, babies! Betsy thought, for at *Casa Contenta*, Abby and Jennie would have theirs just before Christmas.

Perhaps someday she might marry and have children, though at nineteen years of age people likely considered her a hopeless spinster.

"I wish we could help Adam Buchanan, too," Aunt Jessica said.

"If he is willing," Betsy replied. She recalled how he'd shaken with sobs alongside the river, then had remained stony-faced at his wife's solemn burial. She added, "Despite his compassion as a doctor, he's an extremely private person. I've given thought to how to help him myself, but he's apt to consider any attempt as interference."

"You may be right, but I do hope he'll allow us to spend time with Mellie."

"I hope so, too. She was so white with shock at Selena's burial," Betsy remembered. "I feared she might die right there in the graveyard."

"God has His reasons for preserving Mellie," Aunt Jessica said. "And for preserving you and me."

Betsy nodded, and they walked on in silence. The women unlocked the door to their log cabin and went in. "Isn't this a welcome sight!" Aunt Jessica remarked as they looked about at their furniture and green curtains in the chinked log parlor. "I'm so glad we made it comfortable."

"It does seem like home now, doesn't it?" Betsy replied.

"Indeed, it does. At my age, I'm beginning to think the smaller it is, the better." Aunt Jessica opened the kitchen window. "Just look how well Rose and Louisa cared for our garden—and look at the size of those cucumbers! I'd best salt them down tomorrow, and we might begin to dry peas, corn, and beans." She chuckled at herself. "I can't wait to set to it."

"Are you certain you feel well enough?"

"Oh, Betsy, you know how I enjoy it, even if my back does tend to stiffen in place for a while afterwards."

Betsy shook her head. "I suppose I'm just as bad in my own way. I can't wait to get to my classroom. But, please, don't strain yourself, Aunt Jessica. Don't overdo."

As for now, there were valises to unpack and the list of provisions to write, since they'd depleted their stocks before leaving. It would be good to see Joshua, Jonathan Chambers, her students, and the neighbors again. As for Adam and Mellie, the first encounter with them might be difficult.

The next morning, Joshua stopped by for her in his buggy, and they set out for town. "How are Adam and Mellie Buchanan?" she asked her brother.

He rubbed his upper lip through his luxuriant auburn moustache. "When he's not doctoring at the diggings, Adam stays close to his office, and no one sees Mellie. Rufus comes by the Mercantile for provisions, but he never says much."

"Perhaps I'll go to Adam's office this morning. Aunt Jessica and I hope to cheer up Mellie."

"A worthy plan," Joshua replied, though he looked doubtful.

As their buggy rattled past the livery and the smithy, Betsy saw two of her students, Lucinda and Susanna Webster, sitting outside snapping green beans, and they waved.

The horses turned onto Main Street, and Betsy found the buildings behind the hitching posts much as she remembered: the stagecoach and express office, the Oak Hill Hotel, Hugh Fairfax's bank, Tess's old restaurant, the butcher shop, barbershop, law office, and Joshua's Mercantile, where another student, Farrell Williamson, was already sweeping the boardwalk. There were people on foot on the dusty street and boardwalks, other buggies and wagons, and miners astride their horses and mules. Except when the stagecoach arrived, life in Oak Hill moved along at a fine steady pace.

Betsy smiled. "Unfashionable as it might be to admit it, I

much prefer Oak Hill to booming cities like Sacramento City and San Francisco."

He chuckled. "As do I. And to think that ten years ago, I aspired to building a magnificent mansion near Boston and to being one of the Eastern Seaboard's social lions."

"Instead, you're a cultural lion . . . on the school board at Oak Hill!" she replied with a smile.

"As Father would say, 'Indeed!' " Joshua replied with a hearty laugh.

At his Mercantile, she ordered provisions, then stopped at the stagecoach office to invite Lucius Alden to Sunday dinner. At length, she completed her errands and set out on the boardwalk toward Adam's office with growing trepidation. What if he had misunderstood her motives that terrible afternoon when she'd chased Selena through the woods? What if he held her responsible for his wife's death?

The heels of her shoes clicked against the boardwalk with more certainty than she felt as she passed the new dry goods store, assay office, and restaurant. She swallowed hard as she made her way to the small white house that bore the doctor's shingle: *Adam Buchanan, Physician.* Perhaps there would not be too many patients on such a fine day, she hoped. The door was slightly ajar, but she raised her hand to knock.

"Miss Talbot . . ." Adam said, opening the door wide before her knuckles hit the wood. His hazel eyes met hers steadily, but his expression was strained as he stood before her in his black suit. "What may I do for you?"

"I—came to see if there isn't some way that Aunt Jessica and I can help you with Mellie. We thought she might enjoy the other children's company, or at least ours. . . ."

"Thank you," he replied stiffly, "but I don't think so."

She retreated a step. "Dilsey and Rufus are getting so old, we thought—"

"We can manage our affairs quite well," he interrupted. There were no dimples between his short dark beard and moustache now, only the sternness of a set jaw.

"I'm sure you can manage everything well, Dr. Buchanan. We don't wish to intrude, only to help with Mellie. We are women who love children."

"It's very kind, but no thank you. Is there anything else?"

"No, that was all. We only wished to help. . . ."

He nodded, beginning to close the door. "Good day."

Betsy drew a deep breath and turned away. The sun was still shining, but its light seemed somehow diminished, and even the town seemed ramshackle and dusty, its luster faded.

Never mind, she told herself; she would feel better with Tess Fairfax and her new babe. She would "walk and not faint." What's more, she would continue to pray for Adam and Mellie. God had not finished with any of them yet.

Early Friday morning, on the way to the schoolhouse, everything seemed new: the play of sunshine and shadows through the trees, the rustle and scent of leaves on the ground under her feet, the sound of birds singing joyously.

She remembered to glance at the graveyard and all around for Hollis, but there were only the headstones and the sunlit beauty of the forest. Still, in the midst of the beauty, she felt a surge of grief, for she was reminded of Adam and Mellie at Selena's burial. She must pay her respects at Selena's grave on the way home at midday, no matter how sad it made her feel just to contemplate it.

She hurried on, the sight of the log schoolhouse lifting her spirits again. Moments later, she stood on a thin layer of pine needles on the schoolhouse step and unlocked the door while a squirrel peered at her from the path. He would soon have lots of students to peer at, she thought.

Inside, the chinked log room smelled of ashes, but otherwise it was as she'd left it nearly a month ago: empty windowsills, blank cloakroom wall, the blackboard pristine. *Lord, I ask for a good fall term,* she prayed. *I dedicate it to Thee.* She latched the door, but the room was so musty she decided to open the side windows facing the Buchanans' woods.

After taking inventory of the books on the shelves under the front blackboard, she sat down at her desk to plan the next four months. Engrossed in her work, she was surprised to hear Mellie pipe from the window, "Hello, Miss Tal-bot!"

Betsy rose to her feet. "Why, Mellie—I'm so pleased to see you."

Mellie smiled, then her little face grew serious. "I thought you were dead, too."

Betsy hurried to the window, her heart rising to her throat. "I was at my family's house near San Francisco. I'm going to be here now again. I shall be teaching school here until at least Christmas . . . a long time."

Mellie's small face filled with relief. "Oh."

"I shall be here at school every weekday as I was before."

"Then are you getting dead, too?"

Betsy swallowed. "No, I don't expect so."

"Are you scared to be dead?" Mellie asked.

"No, I don't think I will be," Betsy replied. "When you have Jesus as your friend, you go to heaven to be with Him, and it will be wonderful. We'll be with God, who loves us very much."

After a long moment the child asked, "Is God real?"

Betsy swallowed in amazement, then said, "Yes, indeed! He's the one who puts love and joy and peace in our hearts. That's why He sent Jesus." She felt frustrated at not knowing how to explain Him more clearly to the child, and she wished she felt perfect peace herself instead of those occasional bouts of restlessness. "Have you been going to church while I was away?"

Mellie nodded. "Sometimes. Mama got dead, and they put her in a box in the dirt by the church."

"Oh, Mellie . . . I am so sorry about it. I know you must miss her. I wish you could spend tomorrow with me and Aunt Jessica."

"Me, too," the little girl said.

Engrossed in their conversation, they were both surprised when Adam Buchanan approached the window from behind his daughter. "Young lady," he said, "you know you are not to come here anymore!"

Tears sprang to Mellie's eyes. "But I love Miss Tal-bot, Papa. And I love school."

Betsy's heart melted, and Adam seemed taken aback himself.

"Do let her come in, Dr. Buchanan. I'll bring her home at noon. She can sit at a desk and look at books with pictures and draw a bit. I would enjoy her company."

He glanced from Betsy to Mellie, then slowly relented. "Very well, but you shouldn't be here alone with the windows open, Miss Talbot, for obvious reasons. The school board has voted to place Rufus on afternoon watch as soon as school begins. In the meantime, you must be careful about the windows."

"I shall close them immediately," Betsy promised with embarrassment.

At their words, Mellie's eyes widened in alarm. Just as quickly, her face filled with determination, and she clambered wildly over the windowsill.

"Why, Mellie—" Betsy gasped as the child just barely tumbled into her arms.

"Mellie!" Adam cried out in astonishment.

The child clung desperately to Betsy's skirts. "I want to stay with Miss Tal-bot!" she said, apparently worried that she couldn't come into the schoolhouse once the windows were closed.

"It's all right," Betsy assured Adam with a laugh. "I'm a schoolteacher, remember? I love children."

He tried unsuccessfully to hide a smile. "It does look as though she doesn't mean to lose this opportunity, doesn't it? I'll send Dilsey in an hour so you're not taken advantage of." He nodded and told his daughter, "You be good to Miss Talbot now, Mellie. She has important work to do."

"I'll be good, Papa," the child promised. "I'll be good!"

"Thank you, Miss Talbot," he said. "I regret my abruptness yesterday. You took me by surprise."

"I understand, Dr. Buchanan."

He added, "I almost forgot, Fayette sends his regards."

"Fayette was here?"

"Two weeks ago."

"When . . . when will he return?" she asked.

"One never knows with Fayette. With—Selena gone, I assume that his visits will not be as frequent."

"I see," Betsy responded uneasily. Doubtless Adam thought she had succumbed to his brother-in-law's charm.

"I'll send Dilsey in an hour," he repeated and made his departure.

Betsy settled Mellie at a small desk with picture books and paper, then set to work herself. Glancing up occasionally, she saw Mellie quietly looking at the books or scrawling "pictures." Once Betsy caught the child gazing at her, and she recalled her sweet words: "But I love Miss Tal-bot, Papa. And I love school." It was well worth returning to Oak Hill merely to hear that.

On Saturday morning, there was endless work to do in

the garden and, in the afternoon, to prepare for Sunday dinner. Aunt Jessica asked, "Do you think Adam Buchanan would accept an invitation to dinner tomorrow? Louisa tells me he's attended church the past two weeks."

"I don't know," Betsy said with more uncertainty than she wished. "He strikes me as a man torn in different directions."

The next morning, though, she was pleased to see that he had come to church with Mellie again. When Aunt Jessica invited them to dinner, however, he replied with a polite but firm, "No, but we do thank you for your kindness."

Mellie broke the strained atmosphere. "Oh, Miss Tal-bot, you look so pretty!" she exclaimed, admiring Betsy's green frock.

"Thank you, Mellie. You do, too." Indeed, Mellie looked more enchanting than any small girl had a right to look. How Betsy would have liked to hold the child in her arms.

On Monday, the chinked log schoolroom once again came to life, this term with twenty-five students, most of whom were eager and well-scrubbed. The three Stoddard children had moved to Stockton, and Philip Pierson's family had gone north, but they were replaced with five new students: fifteen-year-old Otis Turner and his younger sisters, Orpha and Olivia, and Elias Young and his sister, Martha. With 12,000 covered-wagon emigrants expected in California this year, it seemed likely that the class would continue to grow.

After the Pledge of Allegiance, Betsy asked, "What did those of you who were here last term like best?"

"The Fourth of July pageant!" someone replied immediately, and everyone agreed.

"It was a great success, wasn't it?" she responded. "Perhaps because the community was involved and saw what you were learning."

They nodded.

"I thought we might have a Christmas pageant this term," she added to their delight.

As the day passed, she glanced from time to time at "Mellie's window," but there was no one there. The school day went so well that Betsy could scarcely believe how quickly it was over. As the children left, she noticed that Rufus sat on his usual stump watching over the schoolhouse.

Minutes after the children's departure, however, Lucinda Webster rushed back, out of breath. "Miss Talbot, Miss Talbot . . . Susanna hurt her foot real bad and can't walk!"

"Is it bleeding?" Betsy asked, hurrying out with the girl to find her twelve-year-old sister.

Fortunately, Susanna was not far down the road to town, and it took only a moment to see that the girl's foot was either badly strained or broken. She was ordinarily a strong and restrained child, but now she cried, "It hurts . . . it really hurts bad!"

"We'd better get Dr. Buchanan," Betsy decided. "Lucinda, please tell Rufus to fetch him, and I'll stay here with your sister."

"I don't like to be trouble," Susanna protested as her sister ran off to tell Rufus.

"I know you don't, Susanna," Betsy assured her and held the girl's hand. "Most of us don't wish to inconvenience others, but when things go wrong we sometimes have to accept help. I remember one time when I was your age and nearly broke my neck. You know what helped me most?"

Susanna shook her head, her eyes full of pain.

"Prayer," Betsy said. "If you like, I'll pray for healing of your foot and for peace in your soul."

"Thank you, Miss Talbot," Susanna said with tears in her eyes.

By the time Adam Buchanan rode up on his big bay gelding, Susanna's foot was swollen and throbbing, but the child seemed calmer. Adam checked her foot carefully while Betsy looked on.

"It's not as bad as it may seem," he said, "but you must stay off it for at least a week. You can't walk home, Susanna."

To Rufus he said, "If you'll get the buggy, and then close up the school, perhaps Miss Talbot will help me see these young ladies home."

He turned to Betsy with a reluctant look. "Is that agreeable with you?"

"Yes, of course. I am free to help in any way."

At last Rufus arrived with the horses and buggy and helped Adam lift Susanna up on it, her leg stretched out onto the front seat.

Betsy said, "I'll sit in back with Susanna, and, Lucinda, you can sit in front with Susanna's foot and Dr. Buchanan."

Lucinda and Susanna exchanged concerned looks, likely about what their parents might say about causing such trouble. Their father, Abe Webster, was the smithy, a strong man known for his temper, even if he did enjoy exploding gunpowder on his anvil on the Fourth of July.

They set out down the road for town, the horses at a fast walk to avoid jostling Susanna any more than was necessary.

"Just listen to the rushing sound of the river," Betsy said soothingly. "I often think its sound is like time rushing along. Before long, maybe when this water we hear running past isn't even halfway to the ocean, you'll be fine, and it will seem as though this day's trouble is far away."

Adam Buchanan cast an odd backward glance at them, but she cared little what he thought. Something as simple as a hurt ankle could be a turning point in a child's life, and she meant to be as kind to her as the Lord would wish.

When they arrived at the Webster house behind the smithy, Lucinda ran in to fetch her father. The girls' parents hurried out, and their mother thanked the doctor and Betsy. Abe Webster even managed a gruff "Appreciate it."

Driving away up the river road, Betsy sat on the front seat of the buggy with Adam. "You're a kindhearted man, Dr. Buchanan."

He turned an amused look on her. "And you're a kind-hearted teacher, Miss Talbot. A good one, too. I must admit I was mistaken in opposing you. I even suspected you might not return for this term."

"When I make a commitment, I make it wholeheart-edly," she assured him.

"I see that now. I regret that I misjudged you."

"Thank you," she replied, gripping the buggy seat as they bumped over the hardened ruts.

He was rather subdued as he sat beside her, reins in hand, looking out over the horses as they trotted along, and it occurred to her that she had seen him as a hero, saving the stagecoach from robbers . . . as a compassionate doctor . . . as a harried husband chasing his distraught wife through the woods . . . as a school board member objecting to a woman teacher. He was also the father who'd brought his daughter to church and the man who'd tried to save his wife's life. But the role she remembered most vividly was that of the sob-bing husband down by the river. Despite all of their prob-lems, he had loved his wife a great deal.

A woodpecker's *rat-a-tat-tat* on a nearby tree broke into her reverie. Judging by the slant of the sun's rays through the trees, it must be nearing six o'clock, she guessed. Late in the day. Just as it was late for not having mentioned Selena since her burial.

She mustered her courage. "I am still heartsick about

Selena," she said. "I had so hoped we could be friends. If I can help you or Mellie in any way, please tell me."

"Thank you," Adam replied, then hesitated. "I haven't made a decision yet on what to do about the house, or even whether we shall stay here or move back to Baltimore, but I have given thought to your offer to spend time with Mellie. She needs . . . someone besides Dilsey to care for her. Louisa Chambers helped a bit while you were gone, but she's busy with the church and. . . ."

And with a new child coming now, Betsy finished for him in silence. "Perhaps Aunt Jessica and I could care for Mellie on Saturdays. Joshua drives me to town in the morning, and I could take Mellie with me. I could arrange special outings in the afternoons . . . perhaps a party with the neighorhood children—"

"It's her fourth birthday next month," Adam said with some reluctance.

"Might we have the birthday celebration for her?" Betsy asked. "Aunt Jessica would enjoy it, too. She likes nothing better than occasions that bring joy to others. I know you're in mourning, so it would just be a small, quiet celebration. . . . Mellie's still a child. . . ."

His brow furrowed. "I couldn't impose— I shouldn't have mentioned it."

"But it wouldn't be an imposition! I love Mellie . . . but then, she is easy to love."

His expression softened. "If you're certain . . . if you're truly certain you wish to do so. But I insist you charge all of the expenses to my account at the Mercantile."

"If you insist—"

"I do." His expression grew stern as he looked out over the horses again.

Stern or not, it was a nice face, even in profile. What

would he look like without his dark moustache and short beard? she wondered. Likely he'd grown them to look older and more professional . . . and possibly in an unsuccessful attempt to hide his dimples. He must have been aware of her glance, for he darted a curious look at her. "Is there something amiss?"

"Not at all. Joshua and I can pick Mellie up on the way to town Saturday morning," she put in quickly. "And . . . yes, I am *certain* that I wish to do this, Dr. Buchanan. Joshua will be ever so pleased, too. I can scarcely wait until Saturday!"

Little by little, they would ease Mellie toward happiness, whether she and Adam stayed here or returned to Baltimore, Betsy decided. Little by little, they would make a difference.

When they drove into the clearing by the school and church, an enormous wedge of ducks and geese passed overhead, migrating south for winter.

"Autumn," he remarked.

"Yes. I can feel it in the air. The children will settle into their schoolwork now."

The first week of school passed without further difficulties, though Susanna Webster had to be brought to school in her father's wagon and had to remain off her feet all day. As for Mellie, all week Betsy watched for her on the wooded path from their house, but she was not to be seen.

On Saturday morning, Betsy and Joshua drove up in the buggy to the Buchanan house. "I hope you know what you're doing, little sister," Joshua warned.

"I am doing what I'd hope another woman might do for my daughter if I died," she replied firmly.

"And what if you fall in love with her father?"

"Joshua! What an idea! Adam Buchanan is a new widower!"

"Nonetheless, such things happen," her brother said. "And the way you care for Mellie, he's just as apt to be attracted to you."

"I am going to pretend that this discussion has not taken place," Betsy returned. She was glad to see they'd arrived at the Buchanan house.

As they stopped at the front door, Mellie hurried out, her eyes shining, and Betsy realized how very much she loved the child . . . but that was all.

Dilsey followed, calling out, "Now you be good, chile, heah? You 'member what Dilsey done taught you!"

"I will, Dilsey! I will!" Mellie promised, rushing down the steps. She wore her dress with the tiny flowers and, as usual, her long, light brown hair was brushed back off her face. The dress was a bit tight, but Dilsey was probably too grieved to consider such matters, and Adam too preoccupied to notice. As for Adam falling in love with her or she with him, Betsy wished Joshua had never mentioned such an unlikely notion. She must put it out of her head this very moment.

She climbed down from the buggy and gave the child a hug. "I'm so glad you could come today, Mellie. I could hardly wait all week for today."

Mellie shyly admitted, "Me, too, Miss Tal-bot."

"Wouldn't you like to call me Miss Betsy? That would sound much friendlier for us."

"Miss Betsy?"

"Yes."

Mellie nodded, pleased.

Betsy helped her up into the wagon. "You remember my brother—"

"Yes, Mr. Tal-bot with the big red moustache," Mellie said, prompting a laugh from him and Betsy as they settled down on the buggy seat.

Betsy turned to the elderly black woman who stood by watching. "She'll be fine, Dilsey. We'll bring her home after supper."

"Dat late, ma'am? Doctah Talbot, he expect her home fer supper. He say he want to be home to eat wid her now."

"Then I'll bring her home in time for it," Betsy promised. "Don't worry, Dilsey. I'm accustomed to children." She recalled the time last spring when she'd encountered the old black woman in town, and Dilsey had said, "Ah cain't see why you's teachin' all them chillin when you could git yo'self a husband 'n hab babies o' yer own, Miss Talbot."

Now Dilsey looked half-worried and half-pleased as the buggy started off. She called after them, "You hab a good time, chile, heah? You be good to Miss Talbot."

"I will, Dilsey, I promise!" Mellie returned. She waved to the black woman until they bumped out of sight on the trail through the woods.

"I expect Dilsey will miss you today," Betsy ventured.

Mellie nodded. "Rufus says it's good for Dilsey. Good for Dilsey and for me."

Betsy laughed. "We're going to have a lovely day," she promised, her arm around Mellie's small back as they rode along. "After we buy our provisions, we're going to Mrs. Fairfax's house to see her new baby. She is ever so sweet, with tiny fingers and toes and a dear little smile."

"Will she be my friend?"

Betsy's heart went out to her. "She's a bit young to be friends yet, but we shall see about finding an older friend for you later. Today we'll have dinner with Aunt Jessica, and then have some surprises this afternoon."

Mellie smiled up at her trustingly.

Betsy returned her smile, then looked out at the lovely September morning. Overhead, the golden eagle circled higher and higher over the river and the settlement. "Look at the eagle!" she exclaimed and pointed it out to Mellie. "Oh, isn't our day off to a fine start!"

Mellie nodded, and Betsy squeezed her shoulder joyously.

Their excursion into town and to Tess's pleasant white clapboard house to admire the baby were such a success that Mellie awaited the rest of the day with unconcealed delight. On the way back to the settlement in the buggy, Mellie asked, "Now are we going to see Aunt Jessica?"

Betsy smiled. "Yes, next we see Aunt Jessica. She was once a teacher like me. Did you know that?"

Mellie shook her head. "Does she know God, too?"

"Why, yes . . . as a matter of fact, she does."

At the cabin, Aunt Jessica had a fine beef stew bubbling on the stove, little honey cakes cooling for dessert, and, in the middle of the parlor table, a smiling rag doll who held a card inscribed, *For Miss Mellie Buchanan.*

"For Miss Mellie Buchanan," Betsy read to the child.

"For me?" Mellie asked, incredulous.

"Yes, I made that doll just for you," Aunt Jessica assured her, placing the soft cloth doll in Mellie's small hands.

Entranced, Mellie examined the doll and said to Betsy, "She's wearing a frock like your nice green one!"

Betsy had to laugh, for the doll was indeed dressed in a pale green frock with lace around the neck and sleeves. "You'll find that it also matches our tablecloth, curtains, and bed coverlets!" she told Mellie. "What do you say to Aunt Jessica?"

"Thank you!" Mellie said, and, looking at the parlor's green curtains, was all the more impressed.

Aunt Jessica asked, "What would you like to name her?"

Mellie turned a shy glance on them. "My Aunt-Jessica-Miss-Betsy doll?"

Betsy and Aunt Jessica laughed and, seeing they were pleased, Mellie joined them, hugging her new doll happily.

After dinner, Aunt Jessica said, "I have a storybook waiting. Betsy could read to you or, if she's too tired, I can."

"Why doesn't Aunt Jessica read before your nap?" Betsy suggested, seeing that her aunt was equally taken with the child. "She's been a story reader for many years more than I."

"Can both of you read stories?" Mellie inquired hopefully. "Two stories?"

Aunt Jessica laughed. "A girl after my heart! Let's take off your dress so you don't muss it while you nap. You can sleep in your chemise."

Later, while they read at Mellie's bedside, the child listened blissfully, clutching her doll. When she drifted into sleep, they crept out of the room, Aunt Jessica carrying Mellie's dress.

In the parlor Betsy asked, "Why did you bring out her dress?"

Her aunt's face crinkled with delight. "I thought we could make her a pale green frock to match yours and her Aunt-Jessica-Miss-Betsy doll's. I can approximate the size from this."

"I shouldn't be surprised!" Betsy laughed.

"You did say her birthday is next month."

"Yes." She shook her head at her aunt and then at herself. "Well . . maybe I'll make her a flowered pinafore to go with it . . . and one for the doll while I'm at it."

After Mellie's nap, they took her out to see the garden and then to Maddy and Moses' cabin. The old black couple, who had traveled to California with Rose and her father, helped in their houses and kept the animals near the outbuildings. There were not only cows and horses for Mellie to admire, but calves and colts and chickens that clucked and scratched about the oak-shaded yard.

"Doan you have animals at home, chile?" Maddy asked.

Mellie furrowed her brow. "Only one mean old cat and one dog and one milk cow . . . and six chickens."

"Well, chile, dat's somethin'," Maddy allowed. "Dere's folks heah who'd call havin' animals 'n a house riches better 'n gold!"

"Papa says it's plenty animals for us," Mellie explained earnestly, "but I'd like a little kitty, too."

Rose came out to join them with Charlie and little Rosie who, to Mellie's delight, toddled everywhere behind her and Charlie in admiration. They were having a fine time when Adam Buchanan drove up in his buggy, but Mellie beamed with pure joy to see him. In a moment, he was down from the buggy and she was up in his arms. "Oh, Papa, look at my Aunt-Jessica-Miss-Betsy doll . . . and look at Charlie and little Rosie . . . and look at all of my friends here!"

Adam held her tightly. "It appears that you've been having a fine day. Maybe I shouldn't have come for you early, but I thought it might be long enough."

"It was just right," Betsy assured him, heartened to see how much he cared for his daughter. "This way we'll have more things to look forward to next week."

"Yes," he said. "I expect that's right." He prompted Mellie, "Are you going to thank Miss Talbot and everyone else?"

"She says I should call her Miss Betsy now," she informed her father, then turned to the rest of them. "Thank you, Miss Betsy, and thank you, Aunt Jessica . . . and thank you, everyone else!"

"It was our pleasure. You gave us a happy day," Betsy said. "We can't wait for next Saturday."

As they rode off, Rose shook her head at Betsy. "As if you don't see enough children all week at school!"

"Mellie is different."

Rose heaved a sigh. "I guess she must be."

As is her father, Betsy mused, then quickly pushed the thought aside.

The next day Mellie and Adam came to church, after which he once again turned down Aunt Jessica's invitation for dinner.

As the month of September wore on, Betsy and Mellie grew more and more accustomed to each other on Saturdays, but familiarity did not lessen their enjoyment or love.

In mid-October, Adam Buchanan did come to dinner one Saturday for Mellie's birthday celebration. For the occasion, Betsy wore her pale green dress with lace around the neck and armbands to match the Aunt-Jessica-Miss-Betsy doll's frock. After dinner, when Mellie opened the package with the matching dress for herself, she exclaimed, "Now I'll look like Miss Betsy and my Aunt-Jessica-Miss-Betsy doll!"

Betsy's gift, the flowered pinafores for Mellie and the doll, evoked still more joy. And miracle of miracles, at Aunt Jessica's suggestion Adam had found a small cat—not quite a kitten, but a cuddly cat—to make the day complete.

As the party ended, Adam asked Betsy and Aunt Jessica to step outside for a moment. Once the door was closed, he said, "I'm loathe to bring up such an unhappy subject now, but the authorities at Sacramento City have Hollis in detention, and they would like you to accompany me there next Saturday to identify him." He looked at Betsy hopefully, then turned to Aunt Jessica. "And I would hope for your company as well, for the sake of propriety."

Betsy asked him, "Why would you go?"

"I believe I can identify him as one of the men who tried to hold up the stagecoach for the gold, too."

"Hollis?" Betsy asked.

"Yes."

"But the holdup men wore masks."

"Not over their foreheads," Adam replied. "Doctors take special notice of scars. From your description, particularly of the scar on the forehead, it could be the same man."

Betsy looked at her aunt with dismay. "I'd rather not face it, but we must. Father has always said it's our duty to fight evil, to uproot it in the fields we know, so future generations might have cleaner soil to till."

"Yes," Aunt Jessica replied unhappily, "like it or not, we must go."

The next day in church it seemed most appropriate to sing "A Mighty Fortress Is Our God," the very hymn Selena had performed. The words confirmed their decision, and Betsy understood their meaning as never before as she sang,

> *A mighty fortress is our God,*
> *A bulwark never failing;*
> *Our helper He, amid the flood*
> *Of mortal ills prevailing.*
> *For still our ancient foe*
> *Doth seek to work us woe,*
> *His craft and power are great,*
> *And, armed with cruel hate,*
> *On earth is not his equal.*

Somehow Selena had opened herself up to that ancient foe so full of craft and power, Betsy thought. Somehow Satan—likely in his guise as an angel of beauty and light—had filled Selena's heart with cruel hatred for her husband.

Betsy sang the next verses, knowing full well that her own strength was insufficient for the fight with evil. Without Christ, man could not win the spiritual battle. In man's eyes, it might seem a strange arrangement, but God's ways were very different. *Lord,* Betsy prayed, *I ask for Thy strength and protection in Sacramento City.*

Saturday morning dawned as dull as tarnished silver, and a chill November rain began to fall as Betsy, Aunt Jessica, and Adam Buchanan set out by stagecoach for Sacramento City. The weather was dreary enough as they rode through the raucous settlement of Oak Flats below, but it was even more disheartening to see some of the bedraggled miners already drunk and staggering toward the sodden gambling tents.

At the Oak Flats stop, the stagecoach picked up three unkempt miners who sat opposite them, smelling as foul as they looked. Sitting between her aunt and Adam on the backseat, it took some effort for Betsy to avoid meeting the miners' all too eager eyes as they all bumped and jolted along.

"Ye the schoolmarm?" one of them asked over the rattle of the stagecoach. His eyes were as bloodshot as his skin was leathery, and he already smelled of spirits.

"Yes, I am," she replied.

"Expect them young'uns don't 'preciate lookin' at a purty thing like ye the way I do."

Betsy felt an angry blush creeping up her neck, and, beside her, Adam Buchanan cleared his throat loudly and fixed the man with a warning glance.

"Ye the doc?" the man asked, undaunted.

"I am."

"We got lots o' bilious fever down here ag'in."

Adam said, "I shall come by on Tuesday, as usual."

The miner added, "I need to talk to ye, but I ain't sure it's suitable 'fore womenfolk."

"Then I suggest you keep it to yourself for now," Adam replied. "Please be so kind as to realize these are ladies, and they are under my protection."

Betsy was grateful for his firmness, and even more so that the miners gave up trying to make conversation, closed their eyes, and slept.

She braced her feet against the trunk at their feet and closed her own eyes. She hadn't slept well last night, for the scene of Hollis's assault in the schoolroom had returned to her for the first time in months, and she dreaded facing him again. Perhaps she should have told Father what had happened, but what benefit could there be in worrying him? She had also dreamed about Adam Buchanan, though she could not recall any of it.

The wet roads delayed their arrival in Sacramento City, and there was no time to change from their damp clothing in the hotel. Leaving their valises in the lobby with the clerk, they hired a carriage to take them to the dreaded meeting. At length, they sat in the dreary jail waiting room in their damp clothing while the guard went for the official in charge.

If Hollis is ever freed, he knows where I teach, Betsy reflected nervously, *perhaps even where I live.*

"Are you frightened?" Adam asked, looking at her with concern.

"A bit," she admitted, "but I know I must do this."

Aunt Jessica said, "I thought of it last Sunday in church when we sang 'A Mighty Fortress Is Our God.' I hope you'll always remember that Satan yields no ground to emotion or to mere sincerity. He retreats only from a believer's authority through Christ."

Adam said, "My family's pastor once said that Satan tries to do as much damage as possible before he's consigned to the lake of fire."

"And did you believe him?" Aunt Jessica inquired.

"At that time I did."

"And now?" Betsy asked, for she had never before heard him mention spiritual matters.

That moment, however, the waiting room door opened, and the guard accompanied a federal agent into the room.

257

The agent nodded unhappily as he approached them. "I must offer my regrets that you've come this long way for naught. Our suspect escaped in a jailbreak last night."

"He's escaped!" Betsy repeated, as appalled as her aunt and Adam.

"We had no way of lettin' you know in time to halt your trip here," the agent said with regret. "You'll feel more at ease, though, to know he was seen ridin' out of town."

There was more about accomplices and that Hollis was the only escapee, but Betsy scarcely heard. Instead, Hollis's last words flew to her mind again: "I'll get ye yet!"

The cold rain continued as they returned to their hotel, and in the hotel lobby, Betsy noticed her aunt's attempt to conceal a shiver. "Oh, Aunt Jessica, you've become chilled—"

Adam reached for her aunt's forehead. "You're not overly warm, but I suggest you get out of those damp clothes and into bed."

"My thoughts precisely," Aunt Jessica said. "I'll have hot tea and soup sent up to the room."

"I will then, too," Betsy decided, concerned because her aunt was so seldom ill. As if matters weren't bad enough with Hollis escaping! If that man caused her aunt harm, even indirectly, she didn't see how she could ever forgive him.

Adam turned to her. "If your aunt thinks it suitable, I would like to take you to dinner. It's been a disappointing enough day without your having to eat in a dreary hotel room."

Betsy began to protest, but Aunt Jessica pronounced, "It's a fine idea. I shall sleep all the better if the room is quiet."

"I insist, Miss Talbot," Adam said. "You've been so good to Mellie that I would like to reciprocate in a small way. I had hoped to take both of you to dinner in the hotel dining room. In any event, you ate very little of that foul fare at our midday stage stop."

The tough beef and rancid beans to which he referred had almost turned Betsy's stomach, but she was hungry now. "Then, thank you, I accept your invitation." She smiled. "You may be sorry, though. I'm dreadfully hungry."

He gave a laugh. "As am I. Let's hope they have enough food in the hotel kitchen for the two of us."

The bellboy arrived to carry their valises and, their humor restored, they followed him up the staircase.

In the hallway Adam told Aunt Jessica, "My bedchamber is across from yours if you should need me."

Aunt Jessica laughed. "For the first time in my life, I am traveling with a personal physician. Either I am growing old or I am moving up in the world."

"It must be the latter," Betsy returned.

At dinnertime, when Aunt Jessica was well settled in bed and Betsy went down to the dining room with Adam Buchanan, he said, "I don't like to see anyone come down with chills, but at your aunt's age, we must be especially cautious. If she has chills or a fever tomorrow, we should remain here longer."

"She would not care for that," Betsy said, "and as much as I love her, I must admit she does have a mind of her own."

"For good or for ill, most of us do," he returned.

The hotel dining room, wood-paneled and hung with brass chandeliers and green draperies, glowed with a mellow warmth. As the black-suited maitre d'hotel led them through the crowded tables, Betsy was all too aware of the men glancing at her. She had worn her new fawn-colored frock with black jet buttons and black satin trim, and she felt more attractive than usual. As for Adam, he looked most handsome in a fine russet frock coat and trousers.

As she was seated at a window table on the "women's side" of the dining room, she saw lanterns bobbing along in the darkness outside. What if Hollis passed by and saw them in the lighted room? she worried. Reminding herself that he'd been seen leaving town, she settled back in her chair to find Adam gazing at her with apparent admiration.

In the flickering candlelight, he was a most appealing man, particularly when he smiled at her like that, his dimples deepening and his hazel eyes shining.

Distracted, she was grateful that the waiter came to present their menus. Opening hers, she stared at the blurred words. Surely Adam meant nothing special when he looked at her like that; surely it was only the candlelight and her imagination . . . and maybe Joshua's suggestion that first Saturday morning when they'd picked up Mellie.

When she looked over her menu at him moments later, however, their eyes met again.

"Do you see something you like?" he asked, appearing perturbed himself, and then doubly so at his own question.

"I'm—not sure," she managed, quickly glancing at her menu again.

"They have venison," he remarked. "The deer must be coming down from the mountains already."

"Yes. Several of the schoolchildren saw some last week, and one recess we saw a bobcat in the graveyard . . . and one day two skunks walked right by the schoolhouse door." She caught her breath, knowing agitation had caused her mouth to run on. Still, by mentioning the children and school, she'd put matters back where they belonged: she was the schoolteacher and he was a member of the school board!

Once they had placed their orders, Adam said, "I didn't expect you to turn out to be such a fine teacher. You truly love your work, don't you?"

She nodded. "I do. And I must tell you that Father has collected scholarship funds for Spencer Tucker. I'm delighted. He's a scholar if ever I've met one. I wonder, too, about George Jurgen. He has such an inventive mind and a mechanical bent, but he's forever getting into mischief. I think he could be a great inventor if he ever takes life seriously and applies himself."

"You take the students more seriously than our previous schoolmasters did."

"Thank you," she replied. "I can't help it. I do care for them and their welfare."

He smiled. "Do you intend to teach all of your life?"

"I—I don't know. I leave that in God's hands," Betsy replied with a slight shrug. "I want to do His will."

"A fine attitude."

"May I ask, Dr. Buchanan—"

"Adam," he interrupted. "I should like it very much if you called me Adam. And . . . may I call you Elizabeth?"

"Elizabeth?!" she asked with a tightening in her chest.

His dimples deepened. "I see you more as an Elizabeth than as a Betsy."

"You are the first person who has ever seen me like that . . . or said so."

"Apparently you do not."

"It's—only that it was my mother's name, and from everything I've ever heard, she was a wonderful woman." Betsy hadn't considered it for a long time, but she was suddenly reminded that she'd been the cause of her mother's death. She looked at Adam, who was waiting for her to continue. "I—don't feel worthy of it . . . not of Elizabeth."

"You might be unaware of how you seem to others."

"Perhaps," she finally replied, then added, "Please call me Betsy."

She must have seemed upset, for he said, "I'm sorry. Betsy it is. Moreover, I interrupted your question."

She was glad to have the subject changed from that of her mother's name. "You may find it impertinent, but may I ask—are you a believer?"

"Yes . . . why, yes, I am," he said after some hesitation. Then, as if to make up for it, he added, "I became a believer when I was a boy of ten in Baltimore. My parents were both believers, as are my sisters. Unfortunately, as a student, I began to fall away from my faith and, as a doctor, I began to think the world revolved around me instead of God. The . . . trouble with Selena and then her death brought me back." He paused. "Chambers helped me see that accepting Christ as Savior is only the beginning, that He must be Lord of one's life, and not just called upon in dire circumstances."

"I'm pleased to hear that."

She was reminded of Fayette's belief that one's family background was the most important thing to know about others. She said, "I think knowing about a person's faith—about his philosophy—is the most important matter to know about anyone, don't you?"

Adam's dimples deepened again. "Yes, one's philosphy affects everything. While we are on the subject, I must ask your forgiveness—"

"My forgiveness?"

He nodded gravely. "For the heartache you must have felt over Selena. I know you tried to be her friend. I often think if I had been a better husband. . . ."

"I'm sure you must have done your best."

"I don't know. We were both too young and unrealistic when we married. I thought that, as a doctor, I could help her through her terrible bouts of melancholy, but my trying made her—hate me."

"Did she say so?" Betsy asked with disbelief.

He gave a regretful nod. "Often. Very often."

"Surely it was only said in anger—"

"No, I think not."

He looked down at his plate unhappily. "She was so beautiful, so very beautiful, but there was nothing inside except love for herself, and for Fayette, of course. She wanted to escape her life as a violinist and come west, but when we did, nothing suited her . . . not even Mellie. If it hadn't been for Fayette, Selena would have been even more miserable, yet he was both a help and a curse. Somehow he controlled her emotions . . . I think since their childhood."

"I see," she said. "Yes, I see now."

"Still, I was at fault, too, that we had so little love in our marriage. As matters worsened, I threw myself entirely into my work and community affairs, and there was nothing but heartbreak and hopelessness. Try as I might, I found no solution until it was too late."

"I'm so sorry," Betsy said, remembering him sobbing alongside Selena's body by the river. She reached her hand out to his across the table. "So terribly sorry."

Holding her hand, he gazed at her. "And now I regret having burdened you with this. I had no intention of ever telling anyone." He murmured, "Please forgive me, Betsy."

She returned her hand to her lap. "I see no need for your asking my forgiveness for this or anything else, but if you believe so, I tell you in all sincerity, you are forgiven. I feel led to tell you, too, that you have a new life ahead with a dear little daughter . . . a whole new life ahead."

"I hope so. I truly hope so," he said.

Their eyes held one another's too long, and she was glad to see the waiter coming toward their table with their first course of oysters. She must keep their conversation lighter, she decided. Perhaps she could tell of some of the humorous incidents that took place in the schoolhouse or on her covered-wagon trip west.

As they ate their dinner, the specter of Selena seemed to be laid to rest. They spoke instead of the waterfalls and huge red-wooded trees recently discovered at Yosemite.

"I should like to see them," Adam said.

"As would I," Betsy confessed. At his surprise, she added, "Teachers are usually full of curiosity. Father says I get the trait from Aunt Jessica, but I think it's common to most of the Talbots."

"I have never known any other women teachers," he said.

She smiled. "I should have guessed."

Two pleasant hours later, they returned upstairs, and Adam asked to see Aunt Jessica. Unlocking the bedchamber door, Betsy ushered him into the room and whispered, "It appears she's sleeping."

Adam followed her quietly, then put a hand to Aunt Jessica's forehead. He nodded with approval, then headed quietly for the door.

"Sleep well," he murmured to Betsy at the doorway, his eyes holding hers again. "Sleep well, Betsy."

"And you . . . Adam," she whispered.

It was the first time she had pronounced his name in his presence and it seemed to hang in the air between them.

Quite suddenly his hands went to her shoulders, and she had no wish to move away.

He drew her into the flickering light of the hotel corridor and closed her bedchamber door quietly, and she knew that he meant to kiss her.

His warm lips met hers, tentatively at first, then with growing ardor. His arms gathered her up to him, and she returned the growing pressure with her lips. It wasn't until she was entirely bereft of all reason that he released her.

She caught her breath and stared at him in wonder in the flickering light.

He spoke softly, his voice deep. "Is this—the first time you have been kissed?"

"Yes. . . . Was it . . . that evident?"

"Not precisely," he replied with a smile, then dropped a kiss on her forehead. "I should not be surprised that a woman who is so passionate about teaching should be so—" He stopped, then kissed her soundly again.

When they drew apart, he murmured, "If only I'd met you before—"

"But we have met now—"

"Yes." He stared at her as though he had no resistance.

Suddenly the sound of voices and footsteps came up the hotel stairwell.

"Sleep well," he murmured again. "Sleep well. . . ."

She closed the door between them and sat down weakly on her bed. Fortunately, Aunt Jessica still slept. For a short time Betsy had forgotten about her aunt and her cold—and everything else. A giddiness flooded through her, and suddenly she wanted to spin around the bedchamber like a child. She cared for . . . no, it was stronger. She loved . . . yes, loved Adam Buchanan. Unlikely as it seemed, she loved him!

Fighting the giddiness, she tried to make herself think.

She'd been attracted to his compassion as a physician the first time she saw him, after the attempted stagecoach hold-up. Slowly, despite bouts of pity and skepticism, that attraction had grown since Selena's death. He was a fine man who had made his mistakes like anyone else . . . a fine man!

The giddiness grew, enveloping her entirely. Not only was she in love but, judging by Adam's actions, he returned her sentiments! All of these years she had awaited the man God meant for her, and now the wait seemed well worth it. She loved Adam Buchanan!

The next morning, the sun broke through billows of dark clouds in Sacramento City as the stagecoach came in sight of their hotel. Not only had the rain stopped, but Aunt Jessica, wrapped up warmly against the dampness, felt blessedly better. And Adam, dear wonderful Adam, had been most solicitous at breakfast in the dining room.

True, he did act a trifle distant when she walked out of the hotel at his side just moments ago, but most likely he was not quite awake either. Perhaps she should not have asked, "Did you sleep well?"

"As well as could be expected," he'd replied without looking at her.

Strange . . . with Aunt Jessica and her, he had been solicitous, but alone with her, he had been distant. It must have been a blunder for her, a young woman, to ask him something as indelicate as how he'd slept. Of course, that was the problem, Betsy assured herself. He looked terribly preoccupied now as he saw to their valises. He had probably spent half the night thinking of her, as she had of him.

She was tempted to tell her aunt that she'd fallen in love with him, then almost laughed. Her love for Adam must be as evident to everyone as the loud thumping of her heart was to herself.

As the stagecoach halted before them, Adam said firmly but quietly to her and to Aunt Jessica, "I must tell you that I have made a decision. Mellie and I will be returning next spring to my childhood home in Baltimore."

"*You are returning to Baltimore?!*" Betsy repeated, stunned.

He nodded, his jaw set, his eyes avoiding hers. "It will be

better for Mellie and me to leave here, to begin our live anew. It will be better for—all of us."

But what of me? . . . What of me? her entire being demanded. There was no time for questions as the stagecoach door was opened, and she stepped up into it with eyes so glazed that she scarcely saw the other passengers.

Aunt Jessica filled the silence as she sat down beside Betsy. "We shall miss you, Adam," she said. "Everyone in Oak Hill will miss you and Mellie very much."

Betsy's heart felt so constricted that it hurt in her chest. *How could Thou allow this to happen to me, Lord?* she asked God. *How could Thou allow this to happen? Thou knowest how much I love Adam.*

11

All the way home in the jolting stagecoach Betsy refused to look at Adam. Why had he broken the news as they stepped aboard? Why such a public declaration?

Her only conclusion was that he wished to break off any love between them as quickly as possible and in a place where she could not respond to his decision—all of which she found unfair, ungentlemanly, and thoroughly reprehensible. How could he? How could he?! How could he?! And how could she stop loving him?

As the day passed, she could not forget it, nor Aunt Jessica's oft-stated warning: "A proper young lady does not allow a man to kiss her until he has declared himself and proposed marriage. There is plenty of time for kisses then."

The days after her return dragged on. Hurt and humiliated, Betsy felt as though God had forgotten her entirely. At home and at school, the hours and minutes were filled with gray dreariness. Even the wits of her brightest students seemed dulled.

All dullness ended, however, on the following Saturday, when a miner raced his horse up the river road yelling, "Stagecoach robbery! Git Doc Buchanan quick! They killed Yank Stevens 'n wounded two passengers!"

"Yank Stevens dead!" Betsy repeated. Riding atop the stagecoach like a knight in rustic armor, he had always seemed invincible.

Betsy and Mellie had just returned from town, and as Adam rode by on his big bay, he called out to them and the others gathering alongside the road, "Stay inside your houses 'til this is finished. Stay inside!"

Hollis! Betsy thought with a shudder. *Hollis or other men who were equally violent!*

She held Mellie's hand tightly as they rushed to the cabin, trying to calm her with the first idea that came to mind. "Today let's make a bonnet for your Aunt-Jessica-Miss-Betsy doll. If it turns out well, there's enough of that green fabric left to make matching hats for both of us."

Instead of her usual excitement over such a project, Mellie said, "Papa says stay inside."

"Yes, of course. We'll make the hats in the house. It's quiet work, and Aunt Jessica needs to rest every day now since she caught that cold."

"Where are the bad men?" Mellie asked.

"Not here in the settlement," Betsy replied, hoping against hope that her words were true. "Scripture says we are not to fret ourselves over evildoers, but we must always ask God for protection, and we must always be careful, too."

"Dilsey and I asked God to make Papa happy."

Betsy squeezed the child's small hand. "I have, too, Mellie. I have, too." Beyond that, she prayed that Mellie could continue her Saturdays with her . . . and that Adam would love her. Now she rarely saw him other than at church, and he always kept his distance.

The next morning, Adam and Mellie were not only in attendance at the log church, but brought Fayette with them. Outside after the service, everyone buzzed about the holdup and the shooting of Yank Stevens. She overheard Adam say, "From what the wounded passengers tell us, it sounds like they're the same road agents who made the attempt last May. Same locale, as well."

"Ah do declare, Miss Betsy Talbot," Fayette said, threading his way through the crowd toward her, "as soon as Ah saw you safe from such villainy, the sun came out to light up this side of the earth."

Despite everything, she had to smile, particularly as he kissed her hand. It was a lovely day for mid-November, and Fayette was as handsome as ever, his white smile gleaming, his drowsy brown eyes admiring her, his fine black suit putting the other men's attire to shame.

She could only think to say, "We scarcely see you anymore."

"Ah shall try to spend more time heah. Ah know that my sister would have wished me to keep an eye on Mellie."

Betsy nodded. "I miss Selena," she said in all truth, for she did miss the Selena who for a short time had shown such promise.

"Ah know that you must. You were the only one in the entire state of California who was kind to her."

"Oh, Fayette, I wish I had done more."

"Ah wish Ah had, too," he said with a grieved shake of his head. After a moment, he looked at her with eyes so like Selena's, then gave her a small smile. "She wouldn't want us to be mournful, would she? Ah hope Ah can repay your kindness by takin' you to dinner at the Oak Hill Hotel this afternoon. It is not Parisian food, nor as fashionable as the Astor Hotel, but Selena and I dined there in a small room off the garden. We will not eat with the regular lodgers, but I promise it is quite respectable."

It would be pleasant to go out, she decided, for their own

271

Sunday after-church dinners had been suspended since Aunt Jessica's sickness. "Thank you, Fayette, I would enjoy it, but my aunt is ill—"

"So Ah understand. But Ah know she wouldn't wish you to deny yourself a few hours out." Before she could protest further, he explained, "When Ah saw she wasn't playin' the church organ this mornin', Ah talked to your sister-in-law, Rose. She assured me she would happily take dinner to your aunt if you wished to dine out. If it's agreeable with you, Ah could take you to town now. Ah brought Adam's buggy with that hope."

Her eyes darted across the crowd to Adam, whom she discovered watching them. She turned quickly back to Fayette. "Does Adam know that—you meant to invite me?"

Fayette raised a curious brow. "He knows Ah hoped to entertain a fair young lady and, as you know, there are precious few as fair as you in all of California."

"Now, Fayette, you know there are very few women of any kind in the entire state!" she returned.

She glanced again at Adam, but he was engaged in conversation with several men. Likely he didn't care whether she took dinner with Fayette or not, she thought.

"Thank you, Fayette," she said. "I do accept your kind invitation. Just let me have a word with Rose. . . ."

Minutes later, Betsy settled herself on the front seat of the buggy with Fayette, and they drove past the crowd leaving the churchyard. Fayette slowed the horses and called out to Adam, "Would you and Mellie like a ride home?"

Adam darted an inscrutable glance at them. "No, thank you, we can manage."

Betsy mustered a smile, but he did not return it. He has no right to be angry, she told herself. She had been all too eager to love him, and he was the one who had broken it off.

As they rode away in his buggy, she was certain that he watched them, and she attempted to be as charming as Fayette. What a fetching picture they must make for Adam and everyone else, she thought, glad she had worn her new russet frock, cloak, and bonnet. What did it matter if she'd accepted Fayette's invitation in part to make Adam jealous. She hoped he was suffering, but she doubted it.

The Oak Hill Hotel was likely plain compared to those in San Francisco and Sacramento City, but dining with Fayette at a small table overlooking the hotel garden was pleasant. They were served by the hotel owner's stout daughter, and Betsy suspected that Fayette had paid well and even sweet-talked her into the arrangement. Nonetheless, he was charming, knew everything that transpired in San Francisco and Sacramento City, and made it all sound most interesting.

"Ah can't imagine why you'd want to stay buried out heah in the country, Betsy," he said. "If you married the right man in San Francisco, you'd have the entire city at your feet. Most women in society there are uncultured and uneducated, not to mention lackin' in both charm and taste. Ah repeat, dear Betsy, you'd have the city prostrate at your feet."

Surely he meant nothing by it, she decided; he was only making conversation. She smiled at him across the table. "I have no interest in such a way of life, Fayette. I'm sure you must think it strange, but I actually prefer Oak Hill."

His face fell slightly. "If you ever change your mind, Ah do hope Ah shall become the first man to know. Do you promise to tell me?"

He was only taunting, she thought. "If ever I change my mind, you will be the first person to know."

When they drove home, he whoaed the horses along a stretch of barren maples overlooking the river. As the buggy stopped, she hoped he meant only to admire the forested slope across the river through the leafless trees, but he turned and reached for her gloved hand.

"Now, Fayette—" she protested, drawing away, "I've had such a fine time. You mustn't spoil it."

"Is there someone else?" he inquired, his usually drowsy eyes alert. "Ah understand those minin' engineers, Sven Lindborg and Ralston Stone, came heah to court you."

"They did visit again several weeks ago," she admitted.

"And did one of them steal your heart away?"

"I scarcely know them, Fayette." They had tried to court her, it was true, but it had been ludicrous for two friends to take turns attempting to win her favor . . . not that other California women hadn't experienced far more peculiar courtships. She had been surprised and even a bit pleased in the beginning, but had felt greatly relieved when they departed.

"Someone from your visit to San Francisco in August?"

"Fayette, please—" It was true that Thad Zimmer had been after her again when she was home in August. In one recent letter, he'd threatened to come at Christmas, but she'd tried to convince him as kindly as possible that any further pursuit on his part was hopeless.

"Ah can't imagine who else it'd be unless—" He frowned. "Don't tell me . . . don't tell me you care about that country doctor brother-in-law of mine."

She turned away toward the woods, her heart stripped as bare as the leafless maple trees.

"Surely not," he said.

Fortunately, the horses snorted, and he took up the reins again. "But if it is," Fayette said, "Ah must warn you against him. For all of his fine compassion for his patients, he made a mighty poor husband for my dear sister. But then, she was accustomed to southern men who know how to treat a woman."

Betsy kept her tone level. "Like you?"

"Yes, immodest though it might sound, like me," Fayette agreed as the buggy pulled onto the road again. "I'd make a far better husband than Adam."

The horses clip-clopped along in silence, but Fayette smiled with reassurance when she looked at him again. "Ah hope you know he plans to return to Baltimore. He wouldn't appreciate a young woman like you anyhow, Betsy, but Ah surely would. Ah don't like to boast, but Ah do have good prospects and they are comin' to fruition in a most impressive manner. There are prospects of a fine city mansion in San Francisco and a place for my wife in society."

"But I thought you were returning to Savannah—"

"That doesn't appear necessary now," he replied as they rode along the river road. "Matters have changed."

"I—am sure you will find a lovely young lady, even without such prospects, Fayette."

"There are a number of young ladies," he said, "however, very few are as refined or as cultured as you, Miss Betsy Talbot, and I have no intention of marryin' someone I cannot admire."

"I see."

Taking the reins in his left hand, he reached for her hand again as the buggy jolted along.

"Please, no, Fayette—"

"You surely are a *nice* young lady, aren't you?"

"I—don't know quite what you mean by that."

He smiled gratefully. "No, I don't suppose you do know what I mean, for which I am most pleased."

And with that, they rode home through the woods along the river road. Most of the leaves had fallen, and she felt almost like the last leaf clinging to a barren tree. In March, she would be twenty years old.

The next day, she found a letter on the doorstep of her cabin. It said only,

> *Think about living in a fine mansion, my dear Betsy. Consider it. I hope to see you again soon.*
>
> *Fondly, if I may say so,*
>
> *Fayette*

At first, it struck her as a theatrical touch to accompany his departure. On second thought, she decided he might be serious, at least for the moment. Surely he would soon forget about her, though. When he'd mentioned a "number of young ladies," she'd been certain he meant that he saw more than one. As for marrying him, she had enjoyed his attention only as a harmless diversion from her heartache. She took the note to school with her and burned it in the black stove.

He was no more than gone, however, than her attention was diverted from Fayette. Mr. Wilmington and Moses had found evidence of someone sleeping in the outbuildings behind their cabins, and they were certain it had something to do with the last robbery.

"We'll post Rufus at the school mornings and afternoons, now that the days are becoming shorter," Joshua assured her.

And the nights are becoming longer, Betsy thought.

Fortunately, there were no further signs of interlopers as the days passed. At night, though, the sound of an owl hooting into the surrounding woods kept her on edge, as did the occasional howls of coyotes.

The next week Aunt Jessica was already on her feet and bustling about the kitchen. "I've invited everyone for Thanksgiving dinner," she told Betsy.

"Oh, Aunt Jessica! I do wish you wouldn't tire yourself now."

"Rose and Louisa are in no condition to undertake a big

dinner, but they're cooking some of the food," her aunt replied most reasonably. "Adam and Mellie need to be with other people, so I've invited them, and Joshua has promised to extend an invitation to Lucius—"

"Adam is coming?"

"Yes, dear, he and Mellie," her aunt replied, her brown eyes probing Betsy's for an instant. "I knew you would want them to have a good Thanksgiving. It's been almost four months since Selena's death."

"It was thoughtful of you, Aunt Jessica," Betsy said more stiffly than she wished.

On Thanksgiving, she insisted on serving the entire dinner to avoid sitting at the table with Adam. She half-hoped he might offer to help her carry in the steaming turkey, but Joshua was always at hand to help. Despite Yank Stevens's recent demise, Lucius regaled everyone with tales about stage drivers, whom he called knights, jehus, whips, and the men who held the ribbons. All in all, the dinner appeared to be a success.

It wasn't until she served Adam a slice of pumpkin pie that their eyes fully met.

"Thank you, Miss Talbot," he said, as though they scarcely knew each other.

She replied with as much civility as she could manage. "You are most welcome, Dr. Buchanan."

She hurried back to the kitchen, aware that both Aunt Jessica and Joshua had observed the exchange.

As though that weren't difficult enough, when everyone was making their departures she found herself alone with Adam. She turned to rush off, but he caught her arm.

"Please forgive me," he said. "I should not have taken advantage of your . . . kindness in Sacramento City and then announced my intentions so abruptly."

She tore her arm from his grasp. "It was not at all my kindness, and I am not in the least sorry about it!"

His hazel eyes widened with surprise, and she hurried away, aghast at her admission.

The moment Benjamin Talbot stepped from the snowy Oak Hill scene into Jessica and Betsy's cabin, his arms laden with Christmas packages, he knew something was again amiss. Despite their delight at seeing him, Jessica looked peaked, and Betsy's beautiful green eyes held shadows of sadness.

"Don't tell me I am too late for the Christmas pageant!" he jested.

"It's tonight," Betsy told him as she kissed him. "We couldn't have a pageant without you."

"You're making your presence at Oak Hill pageants a tradition," Jessica returned. "Before long you can write the critic's column about our school pageants for the San Francisco newspapers."

"That would be the day!" he replied with a laugh as he set the Christmas packages down on the entry floor. "Though with twelve daily newspapers in town now, it might be that I could." He took a deep breath. "What smells so good here . . . chicken fricassee?"

His sister nodded. "Your favorite."

"Ah, Jessica, you must be the most thoughtful sister in this world."

"Now, now, no flattery! Tell us the news."

"Well," he replied, waiting just long enough to exasperate them while he pretended to search his brain, "I expect you'd be interested in knowing about births and such."

"Oh, Father, don't keep us waiting!" Betsy exclaimed as she helped him remove his overcoat.

He chuckled. "Abby and Daniel are the proud parents of another son, and Jenny and Jeremy have a new daughter. The mothers are well, the babes are rosey and content, and the fathers are in a state of shocked recovery."

"They aren't," Betsy objected with amusement.

"Indeed, they are. You have no idea what an effect it can have on a father—" He hesitated, for he'd no more than said the words than her smile faded, and he knew she'd mistaken his jovial intent.

Jessica put in with good humor, "I don't see how my Noah could have coped with childbirth. Nor I, for that matter. Now, tell us what else is happening at *Rancho Verde.*"

"Everyone is looking forward to the Christmas service in the new church building," he said as Betsy hung his overcoat on a hallway peg. "They all send their love."

As they stepped into the parlor, a piney smell mingled with the aroma of the chicken fricassee. "My, what a fine yule tree! And look at those decorations."

"Betsy's schoolchildren made most of them," Jessica told him, "and a good job they did of it, too."

"Aunt Jessica strung the popped corn and cranberries," Betsy added, and he was glad to see she had apparently shaken her unhappiness, for she stood admiring the tree with him.

"Jessica, you've strung the popped corn and cranberries for Christmas trees ever since we were children in Boston," he said, giving his sister's frail shoulders a hug.

"I always have, and I expect I always will," she replied with a fond look at him. "Did you have a good trip here?"

"Yes, it was a good trip. And beautiful with snow on the ground as we came up to this elevation. Most important, it was uneventful. Wilmington tells me they still haven't found the road agents who held up the stage most recently."

"Not yet," Betsy responded. "Not yet."

He sat down with them in the parlor. "I don't know, but I do wish the two of you would come home with me after Christmas. Wilmington said he'd offered you the next four-month term, but you hadn't decided. With snow on the ground, it can't be easy for you to get out, Jessica. And, Betsy, the children at home would appreciate your teaching them again, too. Not that the others aren't good teachers, but they don't have your love for the work, and now with the new babes—"

"Father, have you been conniving?" Betsy asked.

"Only a bit," he admitted.

Jessica said firmly, "I like it here in a small settlement. I'm still useful at the church, and I believe that God wishes me to stay here as long as possible."

"That sounds definite."

Jessica's face crinkled with a wry smile. "Being definite is the only way to address any matter with you, Benjamin. I should know that if anyone does."

He grinned, then sat back and perused the room. "I'm glad to see the cabin holds the heat well, not like our log house in Missouri."

Tomorrow was soon enough to take up the matter of Jessica's health, he decided. She didn't look well. As for Betsy, Joshua had written that he suspected she cared for Adam Buchanan and something had gone awry between them.

"Do you see much of Adam Buchanan?" he asked both Jessica and Betsy, as though it were an offhanded inquiry.

Jessica answered, "He brought us a huge load of firewood for taking care of Mellie. And Dilsey, his housekeeper, made us a fine pecan fruitcake for Christmas."

He glanced at Betsy, and she said rather quickly, "Please excuse me, Father. I must finish preparing for the pageant."

It was obviously best not to ask her questions about the doctor, Benjamin decided.

After she'd stepped out of the room, Jessica said, "I am amazed at how many are coming to Christ in the country-side revivals."

"As am I!" he replied. "Amazed and delighted."

"Our ancient foe will not like it."

"How well we know that. He is doing as much damage as possible."

"Have you heard more from the gamblers? . . . from that Emile Martene?"

"A few unsigned warnings, some bullet holes through my office window," Benjamin admitted. "Our efforts have not taken much of a toll until lately."

Jessica stared at him with despair. "You worry about us here, but I'm far more concerned about unsigned warnings and bullet holes through your office window! If the churches' efforts are beginning to take a toll, the others will attack. Evil-doers leave Christians alone when we don't stand in their way, but once we say, 'That's all, we will no longer stand for it!' matters change. Are you still giving your speeches?"

"Not so often before Christmas."

"Mark my words," Jessica said, "when you give them again, and if the churches make great inroads against evil, Martene and his ilk will attack like cornered rattlesnakes."

For the first time in her life, Betsy was grateful when Christmas was over. The pageant had gone well—every role from the littlest angels to Mary and Joseph—and she'd received some lovely Christmas gifts. Father had presented her with a copy of the parlor painting Abby had made of her in her green silk dress. The others had sent tortoise shell combs for her hair, a small but elegant Spanish wall mirror, and lengths of cloth: fawn-colored silk and a forest green challis for a frock and cloak. Her students had given her tokens of affection, and there'd been the load of firewood that Adam had delivered, as well as Dilsey's pecan fruit cake.

The most surprising gift, however, was an expensive gold brooch from Fayette Williams with a note that the promised mansion was in sight and he hoped to visit her soon. Immediately she decided to return the brooch to him when he came to visit. She would give him no reason for hope.

The best gift was Lucius Alden's acceptance of the Lord on Christmas Day. After church when they'd shaken his hand and clapped him on the shoulder, he had said, "I made my decision during Chambers's preaching, but Jessica led the way by her fine example."

Aunt Jessica embraced him with joy. "We are now brother and sister, and the Lord has promised that someday we will be together in Glory, higher even than the angels. Isn't that an amazing thought?"

Betsy had smiled, but tears had welled in her eyes, too. Aunt Jessica so often spoke now of being with the Lord. How reliant she'd become upon her aunt and her elders. She must learn to become fully reliant upon her heavenly Father.

It snowed well into February, and life slowed in town and even at school, for many miners had retreated to Sacramento City and San Francisco with their families.

On St. Valentine's Day, Betsy received a small package and, opening it, was aghast to find gold earrings to match the brooch from Fayette. The enclosed note said,

> All of my work is coming to fruition. I shall soon be there to claim you, my lovely Valentine. Would you like to tour Europe for a honeymoon?
>
> Fondly,
> Fayette

Appalled, Betsy read it again. She had to speak to someone about this. Yes . . . Rose.

When she explained the situation to her sister-in-law the next day, Rose advised, "You must make it absolutely clear that you are not interested in him."

"I thought I did. Perhaps I was too kind, but I'm sure I did not encourage him. I wrote him after Christmas saying I could not accept the brooch. . . ."

Rose asked, "When you last saw him, did he actually propose?"

"Perhaps he did, but I—didn't take him seriously. I supposed he hinted and made half promises like that to all young women."

"Be careful, Betsy. I don't like to say so, but I doubt he'd make a—faithful husband, and that would be terrible. I couldn't bear the thought of it for you."

"What a thing to say, Rose!" Betsy replied, never having considered such a matter. When she did now, she feared that Rose might be right. Fayette was too handsome, too gallant with the ladies. . . .

"You must be plain about your refusal when he comes."

"I will be," Betsy promised both Rose and herself. "Please don't tell Joshua."

"I promise," Rose said, and Betsy knew her sister-in-law's word was good.

Yet the thought of marrying Fayette came to mind occasionally, and Betsy had to press it away. As for a honeymoon in Europe, she'd rather go with . . . yes, with Adam to the wilderness of Yosemite, even if she'd have to walk all the way up the mountains to the top of the waterfalls.

At the end of February, there was still no sign of Fayette, nor of winter's end. The leaden gray days were so depressing Betsy began to feel the same restlessness she'd experienced before coming to Oak Hill. Again it seemed as if she were doing things for the last time, particularly when she taught her schoolchildren. And now that she knew she could teach in a regular school, it no longer seemed quite as important. Not that her bouts of restlessness stopped her from teaching as well as she could.

Fortunately, she was not alone in her distress. The dreary days made everything so desolate that the school board decided to sponsor a Friday night social at the schoolhouse. She was certain Adam would not be in attendance, since he had been so against the idea when she'd suggested it last summer.

Rose and Louisa were great with child and Aunt Jessica was still not well, so on Friday night Betsy rode to the school in the buggy with Joshua.

"What are we to do at the social?" she asked her brother.

"Lucius and the new barber were all for singing, and some thought your students should speak pieces, but most of us are for something everyone can do—a spelling match."

"A first for Oak Hill!" she laughed. She saw the dimly lit schoolhouse through the darkness. "Someone has opened the schoolhouse for us."

"Adam Buchanan offered to open up."

"Oh?" she asked, suddenly tense.

"Is there something amiss between you two?" her brother asked with concern.

"There is nothing between us to go amiss," she answered.

"I thought—" Joshua began.

"There is nothing," she broke in, trying to appear indifferent. "Look at all of the horses, wagons, and buggies! Most of Oak Hill must be coming!"

Lanterns bobbed in the darkness, and as Joshua stopped their horses at the hitching post, people called excitedly to each other from the dim circles of light.

Betsy wished she could share their excitement; instead, she now felt dread. Inside the schoolhouse the desks looked peculiar, illumined by flickering lanterns, and Adam was lighting a large one on her desk. As usual, the sight of him made her heart constrict.

"I—would rather sit in the back since I am not in charge of the evening," she said, and was glad that her brother acquiesced.

Before long, the desks were all filled, and men stood behind them, while Mr. Wilmington called the room to order. "This meeting was called to dispell the end of the winter dreariness," he said in mock seriousness. "We have suggestions for singing, reciting pieces, and a spelling match, and we've decided to take a vote."

The spelling match won by far, and Mr. Wilmington appointed Adam and Joshua as leaders. Everyone joked as they took their places in the front of the room ready to call out names, and Betsy sat waiting anxiously.

Adam's glance passed over her to their pastor who, like Joshua, had been educated at Harvard. "Jonathan Chambers."

Joshua said, "I choose our schoolmistress and my sister, Betsy Talbot, who can outspell everyone in our family except possibly Aunt Jessica."

Betsy hurried forward to take her place in line, glad for the sake of her position that she had not been called later. One by one others were chosen, first the grown-ups and then the students, forming two lines along the sides of the chinked log schoolroom.

At last everyone was chosen, even the smallest students, and the lines stretched from her desk all around the walls to the schoolhouse door. Mr. Wilmington opened the speller.

He began with the primer words, and Betsy received "roe," then the words became longer, and spellers began to go down. First Adam's side was shorter, then Joshua's. Everyone grew warm from laughter and excitement. Betsy might have been in her element, had she not been so conscious of Adam across the room and his frequent glances in her direction.

More and more spellers began to go down until there were only three left on each side: on Adam's, Jonathan Chambers and Spencer Tucker; and on Joshua's, George Jurgen and Betsy.

George Jurgen went down next, and then Spencer Tucker and even Jonathan Chambers. Betsy was so caught up in the excitement and Adam's presence that she suddenly realized she'd been given a word—*Grecophil.*

"Grecophil," she pronounced, and she spelled quickly, "G-r-e-c-o-" Wildly she thought, "Grecophyll," and in a rush she ended, "p-h-y-l-l."

Mr. Wilmington shook his head, and she clapped her hands to the sides of her face, realizing what she had done wrong.

Adam was next, and she saw him glance at her before he faltered and then misspelled *xylophagous.* But Joshua spelled it with great confidence, "x-y-l-o-p-h-a-g-o-u-s."

Mr. Wilmington snapped the speller shut, and thunderous applause greeted Joshua's win.

"Won't Aunt Jessica be proud!" she exclaimed as he joined her, for she had taught all of them the rudiments of spelling. "She's the true winner!"

Still warm and excited over the evening, everyone pulled on their wraps, discussing the possibilities of another meeting in mid-March.

Betsy was buttoning her cloak when Adam arrived at her side and said, "I hoped I might see you home after I close up the schoolhouse."

Her fingers stopped on the button. "I . . . I . . . Yes, thank you," she managed.

Joshua eyed them, and she remembered to finish buttoning her cloak. Her brother asked, "Shall I pick you up to go to town tomorrow morning, Betsy?"

She nodded. "Yes, please."

She felt as though in a dream, for before she knew what had happened, the schoolroom was empty and she stood in a pool of lantern light with Adam at the door. Why had he asked to take her home? From all reports, he was leaving for Baltimore at the beginning of April. *Oh, Lord, I love him,* she thought. *I can't help myself!*

"I wished to speak with you tonight," he said.

She clenched her hands at her sides.

His expression was grave; his voice was deep. "I can't hurt another woman as I did Selena. It is only fair to tell you that."

But I am so different from Selena! she thought. *Don't you see that Selena was the one who damaged your marriage? Don't you know she did it by her own selfishness? By caring more for her brother than for you?*

Adam went on, "I can never thank you and your aunt for how much you have both helped Mellie, and, in turn, me."

Betsy responded, "And I . . . can only reply with what the Lord told us, 'Do unto others as you would have them do unto you.' Moreover . . . I love Mellie."

And you, her heart cried. *And I love you!*

He nodded regretfully and opened the schoolhouse door for her.

Snow fell lightly again, and she wondered whether he meant to walk her home, for he'd doubtless come on his horse. To her surprise, his buggy was at the hitching post—he had planned to take her home! Perhaps there was still hope!

He helped her into the buggy, and they rode through the softly falling snow in a taut silence. *Oh, Lord, show me what to say, what to do,* Betsy prayed.

No answer came in the silent snowfall.

Minutes later, the buggy halted in front of her cabin, and Adam helped her down. She trembled at the door as he held the lantern for her.

"Thank you," she said and looked up at him hopefully. Didn't he see how much she loved him? Didn't he see how much she wished to be in his arms?

"Good night, Betsy," he murmured, and turned away abruptly.

"Good night," she whispered.

She opened the door and hurried in. *Farewell, Adam,* she thought, hot tears streaming down her cheeks. *Farewell.*

Benjamin Talbot sat at his parlor desk and wrote in his precise hand:

March 5, 1855

> *Dear Jessica and Betsy,*
>
> *When I visited you at Christmas, I felt so uneasy about your remaining at Oak Hill. I have constantly berated myself for allowing you to go there in the first place, and then for allowing you to stay. Since you have no summer term there this year, I hope you will come home to please your crochety old brother and father.*
>
> *I see Fayette Williams here in town occasionally and am sorry to write that he keeps company with Emile Martene and the owners of the gambling establishments. Despite my clear and renewed public stand against them, he always inquires about you, Betsy, so there is one blessing about your not being here! I sense*

a deep evil in the man as I did in his unfortunate sister,
and I am certain he is up to no good. Even with him
here, I feel an impending attack of evil on both of you
and have been praying mightily on your behalf.

Benjamin reread his words, then angrily tore the letter to shreds. He could not frighten them with this; he must couch it differently or perhaps not worry them at all. Yet, why was it he so strongly felt the forces of evil had turned their wrath toward Betsy and Jessica?

He drew a deep breath and threw the shredded paper into the fireplace. As the flames ignited the pieces, their edges curled inward until the words became ashes. *I entrust Betsy and Jessica and their safety to Thee, Almighty Father,* he prayed. *I entrust them to Thee for once and all.*

In mid-March the days lengthened, and the river, high from melting snow on the mountains' loftier slopes, hurried out to sea. The river rushed along as quickly as Betsy's twentieth birthday arrived and passed with her pretending happiness, both water and days rushing on, rushing on.

Adam did not attend the next spelling match. Betsy could scarcely bear the minutes and hours and days flying by, for soon he and Mellie would be gone. Not that there wasn't enough to distract her from their leaving. Rose's baby was born—little Elizabeth, a namesake for Betsy and, of course, for her mother. Next into the world came Louisa's son, Oakley, named after Jonathan's brother. Betsy held them in her arms and loved them despite her heartache.

Adam was seeking work for Dilsey and Rufus and had put his house up for sale. She would never be his wife, nor Mellie's mother; she would never again hold him or his child in her arms.

As though that were insufficiently heartbreaking, Aunt

Jessica had been in bed for days. This morning she'd been so tired she was unable to attend church. Still, Betsy reminded herself, she must give thanks in spite of their circumstances.

She sat in her pew and prayed, *Thank Thee, Lord . . . thank Thee, in spite of these trials . . . thank Thee for being my Savior and Lord. Thank Thee in spite of Aunt Jessica being sick . . . thank Thee in spite of Adam and Mellie leaving. . . .* Though she meant every word of it, her soul seemed leaden, her prayers earthbound.

This morning Jonathan Chambers spoke on being salt and light in a raucous community, and she felt as though she were no longer salt and light anywhere.

"Satan wishes to stop your living and working for God," Jonathan said from the pulpit. "We are in a spiritual battle. We wrestle not against flesh and blood, but against principalities, against powers, against the rulers of darkness of this world, against spiritual wickedness in high places."

Betsy knew the words by heart: "Wherefore take unto you the whole armour of God, that ye may be able to withstand in the evil day, and having done all, to stand."

No matter what happened, she did mean to stand.

At length, her mind wandered to another aspect of the battlefield. Before the service, she'd sought out Adam to tell him about her aunt.

"I shall stop by to see her after I take Mellie home," he'd said as though she were a stranger seeking his services.

Tears had burst to her eyes then, and they did again now. At the end of April, the school term would be over. Adam and Mellie would be gone, and she and Aunt Jessica would return to *Casa Contenta*. Last spring they'd set out full of hope and excitement, and now Aunt Jessica was so often ill.

It would be best for them to return to their family, Betsy decided, for her to marry someone like Thad—if she married at all. *Retreat,* she thought, feeling defeated. *Go home.* Perhaps she should marry Fayette. He, at least, would be diverting. The idea, though coming to her in church, was strangely frightening.

From the pulpit, Jonathan said, "If there is anything in your past for which you might be angry at God, anything that prevents you from giving your life entirely over to Him . . . that causes you lack of peace . . . give it to Him now."

Lack of peace was the cause of her restlessness! Betsy realized with sudden insight. As for anything that angered her, there was one such thing. She dug it out of her heart with surprising alacrity: her mother's death.

Quite suddenly she was railing at God: *How couldst Thou allow me to begin life like that, my birth causing Mother's death?* Always before, she'd hidden her anger, but now it rushed on with astonishing force. *How couldst Thou allow me to be the death of such a godly mother . . . to deprive my family of her? How couldst Thou do such a thing to an innocent child? I am so angry . . . so very angry with Thee . . . and even angry with the mother I never knew!*

She closed her eyes in anguish.

Peace, be still. My ways are not your ways. . . . My ways are not yours. . . .

Aunt Jessica had once said, "We may think of death as an ending, but I believe God sees it as a beginning when we step with Him into a glorious new life."

As Betsy released her anger and heartache to Him, a wondrous peace began to displace her restlessness, and with it, a great surge of faith, trust, and love flooded her soul.

As the service ended, she felt strengthened and renewed. Outside in the churchyard, her joy grew as she spoke with neighbors and friends.

When she left for home, she saw great flocks of geese

winging northward, high above the trees, in anticipation of spring. All the way up the wooded path to the cabin, the beauty of the earth and God's goodness filled her heart. The bracken and grasses were sending forth new shoots; bursting buds flourished on the tan oaks. Joy lifted her spirits so wondrously that she knew, even if she never married, she was thoroughly loved by God.

She opened the cabin door with a joyous, "I'm home, Aunt Jessica! Everyone at church sends their love!"

"Aunt Jessica?"

The cabin was quiet. Not stopping to remove her cloak, Betsy hurried through the parlor toward the bedroom where Aunt Jessica was likely reading her Bible. Instead, her aunt lay still in bed, the green coverlet half-covering her face.

"Aunt Jessica!"

As Betsy rushed into the bedroom, a man stepped out from behind the door and grabbed her, clamping a rough hand over her mouth. "I got ye this time, teacher! Shut up or I'll cut yer throat!"

Hollis!

At the sight of his scarred forehead, matted dark beard, yellow teeth, and the knife, her knees nearly buckled from under her. He quickly gagged her with a torn dish towel and, with the other half, wrapped her wrists behind her back.

"Come on, teacher!" he said, dragging her from the bedroom. "If ye got ideas o' runnin', I got this knife in yer back!"

Lord, help me now! Betsy prayed with a last backward glance at her aunt. To her amazement, Aunt Jessica opened her eyes and blinked with all of the assurance she could muster, then quickly closed her eyes again.

Pretending . . . she'd only been pretending! Betsy realized, further relieved as she turned to Hollis and saw he had not witnessed it.

"If ye hold hope from her, she's gagged and trussed like an old turkey," he muttered as he shoved Betsy through the parlor and to the door, his knife pricking the back of her neck.

Betsy bit at the gag. Everyone would be home from church now, and the chill March weather would likely keep people indoors, she realized. Yet something in her spirit continued to trust God.

"Come on, now," he muttered, "to the graveyard, 'n not by the paths."

Behind the graveyard again! Selena had headed there, and now Hollis.

The greening woods were thick and tangled off the main paths, and he shoved her through the underbrush angrily. As they came in sight of the river road, three men rode up and called to someone, "Stage holdup between here 'n Oak Flats! Caught one road agent 'n wounded another, but one o' 'em rode off with the wounded one!"

Hollis pushed her down to a crouch in the bushes and gave a soft laugh. "Got yerself a rich man here, teacher," he whispered roughly. "Expect ye'll give a rich man a kiss?"

She gagged in revulsion, for his red flannel shirt and rough pants were so filthy it looked as though he'd slept in them for months. Even outdoors he gave off a fetid odor.

"Ye'll like my kissin'," he rasped. "I promise thet."

Lord, let those men see us, she prayed.

But her hope in the horsemen faded as they rode steadily onward along the river road toward town. Her only hope now was that Adam would remember to stop in to see Aunt Jessica, and Betsy prayed furiously that he'd come after her—and soon!

Hollis rose and pulled her to her feet. "We cross the road now, teacher! Mind what I say!"

Moments later, he pushed her across the road and, knife

at her neck, forced her to run toward the trees by the grave-yard. Before long, it was too late to hope for the settlers to see them: they were beyond the outer gravestones and in the dense woods along the path by the river embankment—the path down which she'd chased Selena that terrible day.

The sound of the river grew ever louder as he forced Bet-sy along the path through the woods. Finally, she stumbled down the riverbank to where the wooded slope leveled out, and the trees and brush grew denser, blotting out the light.

"Stop here, teacher," he ordered. "Think yer too good fer me, don't ye? Well, I aim to teach ye a lesson!"

She tried to pull away, but he gripped her arm tightly. "We're stoppin' here, 'fore we git to Fayette."

Before we git to Fayette! her mind echoed.

Hollis smiled at the surprise in her eyes. "Don't yell when I take off yer gag or ye'll feel this knife. As fer Fayette, he ain't in no condition fer lovin'. He ain't in no condition at all. Thought he was the brains o' our outfit, but ye'll soon see his brains are 'most shot out."

Her mind flashed beyond Hollis.

Fayette was behind the stagecoach robberies! She recalled his question about Hollis: "Could you recognize him if you saw him again?" And Yank Stevens had said one of the high-waymen was a southerner . . . and last time Fayette had arrived in Oak Hill was just after the stage holdup . . . and the time she'd been assaulted, too. His "prospects" were built on stagecoach robberies and who knew what else!

Knife in hand, Hollis stared at her through angry blood-shot eyes, then sliced the gag from her face. His matted beard parted to reveal his yellow leer. "Thought Fayette was sech a southern gentleman, didn't ye? Well, him 'n Emile Martene aimed to git you good in return fer all the trouble yer old man's caused 'em!"

She countered uneasily, "Fayette wished to marry me."

"Only to git him a Talbot, 'n ye'd 'a been a sorry wife. Now, shet up!"

She shuddered, then knew what she must do, for Christ had already won this battle, whether she lived or died. She prayed with great trust, "Almighty Father, bind Satan, in Christ's name!"

Hollis cursed furiously and reared back to hit her.

Screaming wildly, she tore away from him. She dodged a tree, barely escaping his grasp as he tripped on the tree's roots. Crying out as she ran, she heard shots ring out from the woods above them.

"Come 'ere, teacher!" Hollis shouted.

She ran on and on until she found herself out of the trees and on the gray slate ledge overlooking the river. She turned, breathless. Hollis was right behind her, panting and enraged. Only the all too familiar thick bush separated them—the same bush that had separated her from Selena.

Hollis lunged through it.

Her only escape was down the slate slope, and she jumped over the ledge toward the stunted pine below. Skidding frantically down the broken slate, she barely managed to grab one of the pine's branches, then caught hold of its rough twisted trunk.

"I'll get ye!" Hollis yelled as he crunched down the slope toward her.

Betsy clutched the pine's trunk as step by half-skidding step he made his way down the broken slate, one huge black boot raising dust, then the other.

Lord, help me! she prayed again. *Lord, help me!*

But instead of her prayer stopping Hollis, she saw him with new eyes. In the brightness of midday, he looked like an angry child bent upon having his way, like one of her schoolchildren, and she knew she must tell him, as she had Selena.

"Hollis," she began, and despite everything, forced herself to say, "no matter what you've done, Christ loves you so much that you can have forgiveness through Him."

Hollis swore furiously. In that moment, he began to skid down the bank, cursing her and cursing God, tumbling down the broken slate head over heels as Selena had last summer.

Betsy held onto the tree, closing her eyes and shaking.

"Betsy—hold on!" a voice shouted from up on the ledge. Adam.

Turning, she glanced up at him and breathed a prayer of thankfulness.

"Hold on!" he called out again, then looked behind him. "Here comes Joshua with a rope."

She clung to the stunted tree while Joshua quickly took in the scene and threw the rope down to her. "Tie it around your waist!" he yelled.

She couldn't have made it up the slope alone this time, she thought as she caught the rope. She tied it around her waist and gripped the length between them. Moments later, the men pulled her up through the broken slate to the ledge, and before she knew what had happened, she was weeping in Adam's arms.

Joshua nodded at them, looking more pleased than surprised, despite the circumstances. "I'll go for help to get Fayette's body out . . . and Hollis's."

Betsy held onto Adam with all of her might. Fayette dead, too, somewhere here in the woods, in the darkness. And Adam to be reminded of Selena's death like this.

"I'll stay with Betsy," he said.

She gazed up at him through hot tears. "I—I'm so grateful you came! I prayed you wouldn't forget to call on Aunt Jessica, and I knew she'd send you—"

His lower lip quivered, then he shook his head hopelessly and drew her against his chest. "When I realized Hollis had you, I ran out vowing to your aunt that if God gave me the chance to save you, I would never leave you again."

He grabbed a deep breath. "Even more than that, I realized how much I love you. I love you enough to stay in Oak Hill or to move to San Francisco or anywhere you please, if you'll only be my wife and Mellie's mother."

"Oh, Adam . . . Adam—"

"I know you're different from Selena, and I love you differently. This time I propose with a heart full of God's love."

"As I have for you," she replied. "I accept, Adam . . . I do accept!"

He kissed her again and finally, breathless, they moved away from each other. As she gazed up at him, she caught a glimpse of movement high over their heads.

Above them the golden eagle circled, its wings skimming over the oaks and pines and cedars of Oak Hill. "They that wait upon the Lord shall renew their strength," she quoted, and Adam said with her, "They shall mount up with wings as eagles."

In that moment, her heart overflowed with a joyous paean of thanksgiving to Him who had sent not only the eagle to fly over them but, even more wondrous, had sent them His Son so they might know His love.

ABOUT THE AUTHOR

Elaine Schulte is a wife, mother of two sons, and a writer whose short stories, articles, and novels have been widely published. Her first novel in The California Pioneer Series is *The Journey West*, in which Abby Talbot comes to California with her Uncle Benjamin's covered wagon train in 1846.

The second book is *Golden Dreams*, which brings Abby's best friend, Rose Wilmington, around Cape Horn by clipper ship into the beginnings of California's gold rush.

The third novel is *Eternal Passage*, in which cousin Louisa Talbot Setter flees an abusive past in Virginia in 1849, enduring the dangers of sailing by gold ship and trekking through the jungle of Panama. Finally she sails by coastal steamer to California, only to learn that she cannot outrun her past.

In researching *With Wings as Eagles*, Elaine found that early schoolteachers were usually treated with great respect. In one mining community, when the young schoolteacher was forced to step off the so-called sidewalk by an unsavory character, the miners ran the offender out of town posthaste.

Elaine tells us, "It was heartwarming to learn that gamblers, drunken miners, and dance hall girls weren't the only early inhabitants of California. From the beginning, the decent people started the churches and schools. Camp meetings were held, as there were no buildings suitable for the huge crowds. According to accounts from that day, as many as ten to twenty thousand people camped and worshiped God for periods as long as several weeks! By 1855, San Francisco alone had thirty-two churches with denominations that ranged from African Methodist to Welsh Presbyterian."

In 1856, as a result of people like Benjamin Talbot working for law and order, 25 dangerous criminals were deported from San Francisco and 800 others left voluntarily.